THE CHRISTMAS FAIR KILLER

THE CHRISTMAS FAIR KILLER

Amy Patricia Meade

This first world edition published 2020
in Great Britain and the USA by
SEVERN HOUSE PUBLISHERS LTD of
Eardley House, 4 Uxbridge Street, London W8 7SY.
Trade paperback edition first published
in Great Britain and the USA 2020 by
SEVERN HOUSE PUBLISHERS LTD.

British Library Cataloguing in Publication Data
A CIP catalogue record for this title is available from the British Library.

ISBN-13: 978-0-7278-8989-8 (cased)
ISBN-13: 978-1-78029-708-8 (trade paper)
ISBN-13: 978-1-4483-0429-5 (e-book)

All Severn House titles are printed on acid-free paper.

Severn House Publishers support the Forest Stewardship Council™ [FSC™],
the leading international forest certification organisation.
All our titles that are printed on FSC certified paper carry the FSC logo.

Typeset by Palimpsest Book Production Ltd.,
Falkirk, Stirlingshire, Scotland.
Printed and bound in Great Britain by
TJ International, Padstow, Cornwall.

ONE

'If I could work my will, every idiot who goes about with "Merry Christmas" on his lips should be boiled with his own pudding and buried with a stake of holly through his heart,' boomed the top-hatted figure from the center of the stage.

'Oh, how I love the Williamsburg Theater Group!' Julian Jefferson Davis exclaimed as he took a sip of cocoa. 'I so wanted to see them perform *Cyrano* when they were in Mechanicsville this June, but both dates sold out and then they were off to South Carolina. But *this* – this is better. And talk about being in the stalls! We're so close to the action you can almost make out the edges of Scrooge's prosthetic nose. If these were actual theater seats instead of a concession stand, we'd have paid top dollar.'

Letitia 'Tish' Tarragon, owner of Cookin' the Books Café and Catering, unpacked a stack of recyclable cardboard containers from a corrugated cardboard box and loaded them on to a shelf beneath the front counter of the ten-foot-by-eight-foot canopied food-vendor booth. The wooden edifice had been rented just for the occasion. 'This is only the dress rehearsal. Just imagine the fun when there are children and families in the audience. Personally, I can't wait to see their evening performances of *Twelfth Night*.'

'A matinee of *A Christmas Carol* during the afternoon and a performance of *Twelfth Night* at night, four days in a row,' Jules mused. 'That's a tough schedule.'

'So is ours. Let's not forget we're here to feed people, not just to take in shows.'

The Hobson Glen Holiday Fair was the largest of its kind in the county. Drawing entertainers, food vendors, and crafts-people from Richmond and beyond, the festival stretched far beyond the thirty-foot stage and the horseshoe-shaped array of food stalls encircling the grassy viewing area. In the row just behind Tish's booth there stretched tent after tent of artisans – woodworkers, fabric artists, glass blowers, florists, bakers, candy-makers, and the like – selling their wares. Behind the food booths opposite, there stretched a carnival midway to rival those of the best state fairs, with cotton candy and popcorn carts, rides for children of all ages, and games to match or challenge any skillset.

Jules understood the importance of the event. 'Don't worry, your trusty barkeep is on the alert. I have several canteens of hot tea and coffee already brewed, and my hot cocoa is, as usual, a paean to perfection.' He took another sip. 'By the way, my boss gave me the go-ahead to cover the festivities, so I'll be at your disposal for the entirety of the Holiday Fair.'

Julian's primary occupation was as weatherman and occasional anchor for the local Channel Ten evening news, but that never prevented him from pitching in with Tish's business whenever possible.

Tish's blue eyes danced. 'Oh, that's wonderful. Be sure to thank your station manager for me. I have a feeling I'm going to need all hands on deck for the next few days.'

'You'll be fine. You wouldn't have been given a prime spot at the fair if the committee didn't think you could handle it.'

'My prime spot is due to Augusta May Wilson and the rest of the library board speaking on my behalf,' Tish explained. 'The library had state money that needed to be spent before year's end, and Augusta came up with the excellent idea of purchasing illustrated children's editions of *A Christmas Carol* and *Twelfth Night* to be distributed in themed box meals to accompany the theater performances. Part of the boxed meal proceeds go to the library; the rest is mine. The hope is to promote literacy, the arts, and proper nutrition by making reading, healthy food, and theater fun for kids and parents.'

'That's an awesome idea. And she picked just the right person to help pass along their message.'

'Well, Sam Noble, the owner of the Hobson Glen Bar and Grill, might disagree with you.'

'Noble? Why should he care?'

'Because he thinks he should have had first shot at partnering with the library.'

'Oh, please. Noble doesn't have the chops – pun fully intended – to do what you do. I happened to check out the blackboard outside his tent earlier, and do you know what he's serving? Fried catfish, fried chicken, baked beans, French fries, and coleslaw. The most festive offering he has is a turkey leg, not served with gravy and mashed potatoes, but smoked and drenched in barbecue sauce to be eaten by hand. Why anyone would order such a thing is beyond me, unless they wanted to walk around the fair looking like some hillbilly Henry the Eighth.'

Tish burst into laughter. 'That's awful, Jules.'

'What's awful is his menu. Holiday food should be like a warm hug. His is like the sudden grip of cardiac arrest. So, honey, tell me what sort of boxed meals you're serving.'

'For the matinee performances of *A Christmas Carol*, adults can choose from *The Bob Cratchit* – a sandwich of turkey, apple butter, sage, and English cheddar on potato bread, with a clementine and Mrs Cratchit's Christmas pudding bonbons – or *The Ebenezer Scrooge* – a slice of sourdough bread, moldy cheese (in this case, Stilton), a bitter greens salad with stringent mustard vinaigrette, and lumps of coal.'

Jules raised a well-tweezed eyebrow. 'What are the lumps of coal?'

'Dark chocolate, cinnamon, and chili truffles. They're dangerously good. Children will be given a *Tiny Tim* tin, which isn't a tin, but a recyclable foil container featuring half a grilled cheese sandwich or half a turkey sandwich, a cup of either Peter Cratchit's vegetable alphabet or Jacob Marley's bean and barley soup, a clementine, and a gingerbread cookie. All the lunchtime meals have gluten-free and vegan options.

'Night-time is a bit less structured,' Tish continued. 'No boxed meals, but a hearty menu of either beef or root vegetable stew with exotic spices, savory cheese pies, veggie pies, *Twelfth Night* almond cake, mince pies, and a gluten-free golden fruitcake.'

'My mulled wine, hot cider, and winter ale selection should pair nicely with your evening menu,' Jules stated. 'And, of course, I'll still have the afternoon selection of coffee, cocoa, tea, and soft drinks available.'

'Perfect. As I told you when I asked you to create drinks, *Twelfth Night* feasts were all about warmth and seasonings.'

'*Dost thou think because you are virtuous there shall be no more cakes and ale?*' Jules quoted.

'Did you actually read the play?' Since Tish, Jules, and their best friend, Mary Jo Okensholt, had graduated from University of Virginia, Tish hadn't known Jules to read anything beyond the headline news.

'I perused.' Jules drew out the letter 'u.' 'But I got lost. I may have to order one of your *Tiny Tim* tins to get the children's version.'

'Seeing the play should help clarify things.' She smiled. 'However, I can't help but notice the only line you remember involves cakes and ale.'

'You know me. Food, booze, and clothes, not necessarily in that order.' He ran a hand through his impeccably coiffed head of chestnut hair. 'Speaking of cakes, where's our resident sugar plum fairy?'

'Celestine? She'll be here shortly. Her youngest granddaughter is performing in a Christmas pageant.'

As if on cue, Cookin' the Books' baker, Celestine Rufus, arrived, wheeling a handcart of lidded plastic storage containers across the Hobson Glen Recreation Park main field. Bundled in a dark purple coat that clashed with both her unnaturally bright-red hair and the hot-pink frames of her eyeglasses, Celestine had added some seasonal sparkle to her workday wardrobe with a pair of jingle-bell earrings and red-and-green laces on her trademark white sneakers. 'Ho, ho, ho, darlin's,' she greeted as she drew closer to the booth.

'Ho, ho, ho,' Tish echoed.

'Hey, Celestine. You sound like an elf with those earrings,' Jules teased before giving the woman a warm hug.

'That's all grandmas are this time of year. Great big elves.'

'How was the pageant?' Tish asked.

'Fun. Those kindergarteners sure are cute. Seems like only yesterday my own kids were that little.'

'What part did your granddaughter play?' Jules enquired.

'The angel, if you can believe it. I don't know who came

up with the casting for this little play, but, boy howdy, that person better not have any dreams of Hollywood.' With a loud cackle, Celestine reached a candy-cane-stripe manicured hand into her coat pocket and extracted a handful of homemade dog treats. Leaning down, she proceeded to feed them to Julian's recently adopted Bichon Frise, who was curled up in a heated dog bed. 'My word, what an adorable Santa sweater Biscuit is wearing.'

Much to Celestine's delight, Jules unzipped his fur-lined parka and proudly stuck forth his chest to display the same garishly colored Christmas sweater. 'Lookie there! You're twin-sies. Where on earth did you find matching sweaters?'

'I didn't. My mother knitted them for us and mailed them from West Virginia last week. Aren't they terrific? I have lots of ugly Christmas sweaters—'

'Lots,' Tish emphasized as she stacked hot cups and lids in a cubby adjacent to the beverage dispensers.

'But nothing I had coordinated with the dog Christmas sweaters I saw in the pet stores, so Mama decided to rectify the situation.'

'Sweet. You seein' your mama for Christmas?' Celestine inquired.

'No, she's spending Christmas with my sister in Tennessee. My sister is a born-again Christian with six children who doesn't approve of my "lifestyle choices"' – Jules drew quotation marks in the air – 'so Biscuit and I haven't been invited. But I'll make a trip to see my mama when she gets back home. We'll celebrate New Year's together.'

'Jules, Mary Jo, Schuyler, and I will be celebrating Christmas at the café,' Tish explained to Celestine. 'Mary Jo's folks live out in California, and she and Glen always packed the family up for a holiday visit, but what with the divorce, Mary Jo can barely afford to heat her house, let alone pay for airfares for herself and two kids.'

'What about her folks? Can't they travel out here?' Celestine asked.

'No, her mom hasn't been very well as of late. Not only would the flight exhaust the poor woman, but she and Mary Jo's dad have had to dip into their savings to pay for Medicare deductibles, copays, and the treatments and medications the plan doesn't cover.'

'Getting sick ain't for poor people, that's for sure,' Celestine lamented. 'What about your daddy, Tish? Is he comin' down from New York?'

'No. I offered to pay for a train ticket, so he didn't have to drive, but he still had no interest in traveling all this way.'

'That's a shame.'

'He'll be fine. He's always had lots of . . . friends.'

'Well, y'all are more than welcome to spend Christmas at my house. We have a crowd, what with my four kids, their spouses, and the grandkids, but there's always plenty of food and drink to go around, so long as you don't mind sitting in patio chairs and eatin' off TV trays.'

'That's very generous of you, Celestine. Thank you' – she gave the woman a warm embrace – 'but I think we'll stick with having dinner at the café. I'm not sure Mary Jo is quite up to a big noisy holiday.'

'Of course, honey. I understand. It's Gregory's last Christmas before he heads off to college, ain't it?'

'It is,' Jules confirmed. 'And since Kayla and Gregory are spending the evening with their dad, it's also the first Christmas Eve MJ will be away from the kids. But we have plans to keep her busy. We'll be with y'all at the interfaith center dishing out hot meals for those on hard times. Then, for afterwards, I've picked up a few bottles of Prosecco and pomegranate liqueur for my signature Poinsettia cocktails and, because I did a nice spot welcoming their business to town, the new Thai restaurant gave me a bunch of free meals.'

'Which are in my freezer waiting to be defrosted and warmed in the oven,' Tish interjected.

'Then Christmas Day is gifts under the tree with the kids, classic movies, some board games, and roast turkey.'

'Which I'm cooking, along with the stuffing and giblet gravy.'

'It's dressing, not stuffing,' Jules jokingly corrected. 'You're in the South, girlfriend. But for fun, and to ease Tish's work-load, each of us is bringing a side dish that reminds us of Christmases of our youth. I'm making my memaw's collard greens. Mary Jo's making some California avocado, orange, and shrimp appetizer. Mary Jo's kids are baking up some dinner rolls. Tish is making Brussels sprouts with chestnuts. And Schuyler is . . . what *is* Schuyler bringing?'

Hobson Glen attorney, Schuyler Thompson, was both Tish's landlord and newly established main squeeze. 'Schuyler ordered a Yule log from Sub Rosa Bakery, because the apple pie he once baked for me looked far better than it tasted.'

'Oh, I remember that pie. He brought it to your grand opening party. I thought it was potato or jicama, not apple.' Jules brought a hand to his mouth.

'In other words, Schuyler figures if he doesn't cook, no one can get sick and sue him,' Celestine paraphrased.

'Pretty much,' Tish confirmed.

'Oh, well. He's handsome, successful, likable, and kind.' Jules ticked Schuyler's best traits off an invisible list. 'You can't have everything.'

'I'm certainly not complaining.' She turned to Celestine. 'Since Jules, Schuyler, and Mary Jo will be around to help at the interfaith center next week, I don't necessarily need you to come along, should you want to spend that time with your family.'

'That's mighty thoughtful of you, but nah,' Celestine declined the offer. 'I'm actually looking forward to doing some good this holiday. Every year, my family and I get together and do the same thing. Serving up some of our café food to folks who've got nowhere else to go appeals to me greatly.'

'Are you sure? Not that we don't love having you around, but I know it's Christmas Eve and you may not get home until after eight. I don't want you to miss out on time with the little ones or your Christmas Eve dinner.'

'Eight is plenty early. The grandkids are too excited to go to bed at any reasonable hour, and my daughters are putting up supper that night, so I'm out of the kitchen. It's just sandwiches, salads, devilled eggs, and Christmas cookies, but it's been our tradition since I was a little girl at my grandmama's house, partly because my grandmama couldn't afford to buy the ingredients for more than one big family dinner and partly because we kids were too anxious for Santa to arrive to sit at the table and eat a big meal. But it worked for everyone. Still does. No dishes to do after, so we can sit and watch a Christmas movie together and then go to the late church service before calling it a night.'

'Sounds lovely.'

'Sure is. Now, Christmas Day – well, that's when we go all out. Mr Rufus starts the morning by makin' a breakfast of biscuits and gravy. Then, after everyone opens presents, I start in on the late-afternoon feast. There's the relish tray of olives, carrots, gherkins, celery, pickled okra, and green onion, then the Coca-Cola-glazed ham, macaroni and cheese, corn bread, green beans, rutabagas, and yams topped with pecans. Then, for dessert, there's ambrosia salad, banana pudding for the kids, and my mama's classic coconut cake.'

'Girl, you're making me hungry.' Jules rubbed his stomach.

'You're *always* hungry,' Tish pointed out.

'True.'

'Well, if you're good and get your drinks prepared before our five o'clock opening, I'll let you have a *Twelfth Night* cake,' Celestine promised.

'Bribery. Nice.' Tish gave Celestine a fist bump.

'Gotta do something to get the boy motivated.'

'You two are a regular riot,' Jules deadpanned. 'So, what's a *Twelfth Night* cake?'

'Buttery puff pastry with a rum and almond filling.'

'Mmm, sign me up for one of those.'

'Will do.' As Celestine unloaded the bins of cakes from the handcart, a wintry breeze swept through the booth, prompting Tish to turn up the collar of her black wool coat and pull her leopard-print beret further down on her blonde head. 'Feels like snow.'

'I doubt it. Not only is there no snow in the forecast, but there hasn't been Christmas snow in central Virginia for twenty years. Besides, it's not cold enough for it to snow.' Belying his own words, Jules zipped his coat to his bronzed chin and wrapped his cashmere scarf around his neck.

Both fully aware that Jules's prediction of no snow was tantamount to General George Armstrong Custer proclaiming that there weren't enough Native Americans in the world to destroy the Seventh Cavalry, Tish and Celestine exchanged commiserating glances and set to work stocking the booth with the evening's provisions. Jules, meanwhile, prepared the mulled wine and spicy warm cider for a long, low simmer.

Three hours later, with their work complete and the booth redolent with the aromas of wine, cider, simmering stock, and earthy spices, the trio swapped celebratory high fives and watched as the festival lights were illuminated, the gates to the fair opened, and the Richmond Revolutionary Re-Enactors' fife and drum band marched visitors on to the fairgrounds to the tune of *Joy to the World*.

Leading the crowd through the horseshoe-shaped arrangement of food purveyors, the re-enactors made a sharp left at the stage and assembled on the grassy area that traditionally served as the recreation park's football field. After a rousing rendition of *The Little Drummer Boy*, the infantrymen fired their rifles in unison.

'Gunfire and Christmas carols. What better way to evoke the memory of holidays spent with family?' a familiar voice joked.

They turned around to find a fortyish man with spiky dark hair, deep-set gray eyes, and a few days' worth of stubble standing just a few feet away from the booth. He was dressed in jeans, a heavy black peacoat, and a pair of thick-soled motorcycle boots.

'Ain't that just the truth, Sheriff Reade,' Jules greeted. 'Family holidays are all drama, drama, drama.'

'Mine ain't,' Celestine asserted. 'When anyone whines or complains, I tell 'em to save the drama for their mama. Then I remind them that I don't like it either.'

'Hiya, Miss Celly,' Reade replied with a laugh as he stepped closer to the counter.

'Hey, Clem. Good to see you, darlin'.'

'Hi, Clemson, what brings you here?' Tish asked. 'Getting in the holiday spirit?'

'Yeah, a busman's holiday. I have a team directing traffic for the festival. Knowing you had a booth here, I thought I'd stop by and get them some coffee. It's going to be a long night and a cold one.' Reade rubbed his hands together and turned up the collar of his coat. 'Almost feels like snow.'

'Nope. No snow in the forecast,' Jules maintained. 'What kind of coffee would you like, Sheriff? Gingerbread or caramel?'

'How about just regular coffee? Do you have any of that?'

'Yes, for the timid.'

'Perfect. I *am* timid – about buying other people flavored coffee.'

'I have tea and cocoa too.'

'Hmm, one of my officers loves chocolate. I'll have one cocoa and three regular coffees, please. And, Miss Celly, do you happen to have any of your beautiful baked goods on hand?'

'Of course.' Celestine pointed to the pristine pastries on display in the glass display case on the countertop. 'You want some mince pies, some gluten-free golden fruitcake, or some *Twelfth Night* cakes?'

'I'll take two of everything,' Reade requested. 'What's cooking in those pots back there, Tish?'

'Elizabethan spiced stew.'

'Sounds interesting. I'll take a cup of that as well. Missed my lunch today.'

'Beef or root vegetable?'

'Root vegetable, please.'

Tish was surprised by his choice. 'Really?'

'Yes, really. Just because I carry a gun to work doesn't mean I don't eat my broccoli,' he joked.

'I know, but it's just that whenever you have breakfast at the café, it's always the *Portrait of the Artist as a Young Ham* sandwich.'

'That's not because I dislike vegetables, but because I like to ease into the morning. I never know what I'm going to find at work, but I do know what ham and egg taste like. And I know that I like the way you cook them. As the day wears on, if things go well, I become more optimistic and more likely to take chances.'

'Wow, given that attitude, I'm surprised you tried my sandwich in the first place.'

'It was my day off,' Reade quipped.

'See?' Jules challenged. 'Timid.'

'Where's your car parked, Mr Davis?' Reade asked with more than a hint of a grin upon his lips.

'Back at the café. I hitched a ride here with Tish. Not that it matters. You wouldn't ticket me anyway. You had a chance to fine me for selling sandwiches out of the trunk of my car a few months back, but you didn't, y'old softie, you.'

'Better not let that get around,' the sheriff warned, 'or we'll have a crime spree on our hands. Wait a minute. If Tish is catering an event, we might already be facing a potential crime spree.'

To that comment, Tish wadded up a paper napkin and tossed it at Reade's head, a fake scowl on her face.

'So, what are you up to this Christmas, Clem?' Celestine asked after the laughter had died down. 'Going up north to visit family?'

'Maybe. An aunt of mine invited me to spend Christmas with her, but I'm not sure. All my cousins are married and have kids, so we don't have much in common these days. I'll probably wind up doing what I do every year. Work double shifts Christmas Day, so that my officers with families can have the day off, and spend Christmas Eve at the interfaith center handing out the toys we and the firehouse have collected.'

'Really?' Tish gasped. 'We'll be at the interfaith center too, dishing out food.'

'You're contributing the Christmas meal?'

'Not the entire meal, no. The Rotary Club donated three dozen or so locally raised chickens, which their volunteers will be cooking, along with the gravy. I'm just doing the side dishes: carrots, roasted potatoes, peas, and dinner rolls. And Celestine has been kind enough to donate one of her brilliant desserts.'

'Just a plain ol' giant sheet cake,' Celestine announced, 'with white-chocolate-and-peppermint-candy-cane frosting. It's been a good year for Mr Rufus and me. Thought I'd share my good fortune.'

'That's mighty generous of you both. My band will be joining us at the interfaith center as well. After Santa finishes his bit, we get everyone to sing Christmas carols. It's cheesy,

I know, but it's a good way to extend the evening and make it feel more like a real holiday instead of just a meal and a wrapped toy.'

'That's sweet of you guys. If we're still around when you start playing, we'll definitely sing along,' Tish promised.

'Absolutely,' Jules agreed. 'Hey, Sheriff, if you decide to stay in Hobson Glen for the holidays and find yourself with some extra time on Christmas Day, you should come on down to the café. We're doing a ragtag, "Island of Misfit Toys" sort of gathering this year, but there'll be plenty of food. And wine.'

'Jules is right. You should come by for dinner,' Tish concurred as she packed the sheriff's order into a paper bag and handed it to him. 'We're having turkey with all the trimmings and then we're playing some games afterwards. It will be fun, but low-key and quiet, unless, of course, Jules loses at charades.'

'You're giving Uncle Jules far too much credit, Aunt Tish.' Fifteen-year-old Kayla Okensholt, bundled against the weather in a military-inspired khaki parka and a pink knit beanie that covered the crown of her brunette head, had stepped out from the crowd and leaned across the counter of the booth. 'He makes a lot of noise when he wins too.'

'You're right. He's as much a sore winner as he is a sore loser,' Tish rejoined.

Jules gasped in mock horror. 'I resent that remark.'

'We know you do.' Kayla giggled and planted a kiss on his cheek. 'Hi, Uncle Jules.'

'Hi, Kayla, honey. How are you?'

'Good, now that it's Thursday night and school's out for two and a half weeks.' Kayla went on to greet Celestine and Tish.

'Hey, sugar.' Celestine enveloped the girl in a bear hug.

Tish and her goddaughter exchanged pecks on the cheek. 'Are you here with friends?'

'No, I'm here with Mom. And your boyfriend.' She grinned.

'Schuyler?'

'He stopped by the café as I was helping Mom close up for the night. I don't know how he did it, but he managed to convince her to come here instead of going home and sobbing over Hallmark Christmas movies, like she's been doing all month.'

As if summoned by Kayla's words, Mary Jo and Schuyler appeared at the booth. MJ was zipped into an oversized black puffer coat that she wore over black pants and ankle boots. Her long, dark-brown hair was pinned into a messy bun held in place by a ballpoint pen and, with the exception of some smudged mascara, her face was completely devoid of makeup.

Having traveled directly from his Richmond law office, Schuyler Thompson was overdressed, but dashing, in his double-breasted navy cashmere coat, pinstriped trousers, burgundy scarf, and black leather driving gloves. His fair hair was trimmed into a short style that played up his chiseled jawline, and his blue eyes sparkled in the glow of the festival lights.

'Hey, y'all,' Mary Jo greeted.

'Hey,' the trio of Tish, Jules, and Celestine replied in unison. Schuyler, meanwhile, gave a brief, friendly wave 'hello' and went directly for a smooch with Tish.

'I see you're full of surprises today,' Tish whispered to him as she slid her eyes toward Mary Jo.

'A good surprise, I hope?'

'A miraculous one. So' – she raised her voice to normal volume – 'how was business at the café today?'

'Slow.' Mary Jo frowned. 'I think everyone was saving their appetites for tonight.'

'That means there's a bunch of hungry people heading our way,' Celestine surmised.

'Do you need a hand?'

'Nope. You and Kayla are under orders to enjoy yourselves,' Tish instructed.

'But—'

'No buts. There's lots of cool stuff going on tonight. Virginia Cooperative Extension is hosting a wreath-making booth, the local dance company is running free belly-dance classes, and there's a candy maker from Richmond handing out samples of ridiculously creamy fudge. In a little over an hour, the Williamsburg Theater Group will start a performance of *Twelfth Night*, and as employees of Cookin' the Books, you're both entitled to dinner on the house. So go and enjoy some girl time together.'

Kayla gave a tiny squeal and clapped her hands together. 'Can we do the belly-dance class, Mom? It would be *so* much fun.'

'Umm . . . OK.'

'Yay! Can I eat something first, though? I'm freezing and starving, and Aunt Tish's stew just smells so good.'

'Sure. As long as it's OK with Tish.'

'Of course. Just let me ring up Sheriff Reade's order and—' Tish searched for the sheriff, but he was nowhere to be seen. 'Where did Reade go?'

'He left shortly after Kayla got here,' Jules explained. 'He mumbled something and handed me this.'

Jules plopped a wad of bills on the counter, which Tish immediately counted. 'This is too much money.'

'He's a regular at the café. Perhaps that's his way of saying thanks.'

'Forty dollars is an awful lot of thanks.'

'You've cooked him an awful lot of breakfasts.'

Tish's eyes narrowed. 'It's still strange of him not to say goodbye.'

'People get strange at the holidays.'

Tish agreed with a shrug and set about dishing out a helping of stew for Kayla, but something about the incident still struck her as odd.

TWO

I t was twenty minutes past nine when the Williamsburg Theater Group took their final bow and the stage curtains closed on the first *Twelfth Night* performance of the long weekend. Having experienced a dearth of visitors during the show, Tish, Jules, Celestine, and Schuyler were suddenly met with a rush of theatergoers purchasing a last-minute cake or hot toddy before the fair closed at ten.

Their food and beverage orders fulfilled, the famished theatergoers departed, only to be replaced by several members of the cast of *Twelfth Night* in various stages of the undressing process. First in the queue stood the star of the evening's performance. Jenny Inkpen, twenty-two-year-old ingénue, was tall and slender with the elegance of a young Audrey Hepburn. Her long brown hair had been rolled into a tight bun at the nape of her neck, and although she had traded her doublets and breeches for a heavyweight pink tracksuit, her face still bore the understated makeup required for the role of Cesario/Viola.

'How much for a coffee?' she inquired with the same commanding voice she had used to enrapture the audience just minutes earlier.

'All food and refreshments are complimentary for theater group members,' Tish explained. 'Courtesy of the interim mayor's office.'

'Really? In that case, maybe I'll have some cake. Do you have anything gluten-free?'

Celestine retrieved a slice of golden fruitcake and held it aloft. 'Dried pear, apricot, ginger, and almond.'

'That sounds amazing.'

'We greatly enjoyed your performance,' Tish complimented as she applied the coffee and cake to the mayor's office tab.

'Thanks. I prefer the meatier roles, but these lighthearted plays are fun for the holidays.'

From somewhere in the queue, someone clicked his or her tongue in derision.

'I'll have a coffee and whatever stew that is cooking.' The actor who had played Sebastian, still in costume, jumped in front of the line. With his soft brown eyes and fine features, he was perfectly cast as Viola's twin brother, for he and Jenny could have been siblings in real life. 'Maybe we can have our coffee together, Jenny, and review tonight's performance? I thought it went really well.'

'You'd be better off using that time to go over your lines,' she replied frostily. 'You flubbed two of them in the second act alone.' With that, Jenny Inkpen collected her coffee and cake, said a quiet thank you to Tish, Jules, and Celestine, and marched off behind the stage.

'Bailey Cassels, you fool,' seethed the actress who played Maria. Short, stout, and middle-aged, she had switched her heavy gown and corsets for a pair of jeans, a bright green parka, and suede boots, but her face was still heavily made-up with thick, waxy foundation, bright-red lipstick, and dark, painted eyebrows. 'That girl's never going to give you the time of day. You have nothing to offer her. Just look what she did to poor Justin here.' She motioned to Justin Dange, the actor who had played Malvolio. 'Jenny only dated him to get into the troupe, and once she was in, she dumped him.'

Dange, in his late thirties, had changed out of his gray wig and costume and into a quilted jacket, jeans, and sneakers. He left his spot at the end of the line to retaliate. 'That's not what happened, Fran,' he insisted to the woman's face. 'Jenny and I broke up because . . . well, it's complicated.'

'Perhaps it was complicated for you, but for Jenny I'm sure it was dead simple. She's a user.'

'I've had enough of this nonsense. Jenny's done nothing but improve the quality of our performances.'

The right corner of Fran's mouth curled. 'In your opinion, perhaps,' she sneered.

'Oh, get off it,' Justin shouted before storming off in the same direction Jenny had traveled mere minutes earlier.

'Justin's right,' Bailey Cassels chimed in. 'Just because Jenny's young and good-looking, the older members of the group think it's OK to trash-talk her. Maybe it's time you guys found a new hobby, like bingo or something.'

As Bailey Cassels took his coffee and headed back toward the stage, Fran and the actor who played Sir Toby approached the counter. 'Sorry you folks had to witness that unfortunate scene,' he apologized.

'That's all right,' Tish reassured him. 'We were discussing earlier how all families have their fair share of drama, particularly during the holidays.'

'We used to be a family,' Fran lamented. 'That's all changed now.'

'My wife and I have been with the group since Rolly

Rollinson founded it back in the late eighties. I'm Ted Fenton.' He extended a hand toward Tish. 'This is my wife Frances.'

'Pleased to meet you.' Tish shook his hand and the group exchanged introductions.

'Williamsburg Theater was founded on the belief that every member of the group had a unique talent to share,' Ted explained. 'Those talents would be used to bring great theater to the public at a fraction of the cost of traditional theater. And, as each of us actors brought something special to the group, material would be chosen so that a different actor would be highlighted with each new production, thus avoiding the jealousies that ensue in companies with a "lead" or "primary" actor.'

'It worked quite well, for a time. But now Jenny Inkpen has been in the starring role for five of the past six productions, including the role of Beatrice in *Much Ado About Nothing*, which should have gone to Lucinda LeComte – Olivia in tonight's performance. Jenny is far too young for the part. But all that seems to matter to Rolly now is the troupe's popularity on social media,' Frances Fenton complained.

'According to Rolly, having followers on Twitter and other such places helps to secure advance bookings. To appeal to the Snapchat demographic, Jenny Inkpen is now the "new face" of Williamsburg Theater Group,' Ted expounded. 'She's on the cover of our new brochure, in print ads, and on the homepage of the group website.'

'Even though Lucinda can act circles around her,' Frances added. 'I'm telling you, being an actress is not for the meek. The moment you get a line on your face, you're asked to play somebody's mother.'

'Makes me mighty glad I'm a cook,' Tish noted.

'I'll say,' Celestine commiserated.

'Since you mentioned cooking, is there a place within walking distance where we can get coffee and breakfast in the morning?' Ted asked. 'Our trailers are all hooked up, so we're without wheels until the fair is over.'

'Well, the Bar and Grill is just around the corner and they do weekend brunch starting at ten o'clock. My café opens at seven, but it's about a mile or so down the road.'

'Hmm, we have a dress rehearsal at nine, so brunch is out, and the walk to and from your café would put us tight for time.'

'How about I deliver? Check out the menu on my café website.' She passed Ted a business card. 'Give me your order before I leave tonight, and I'll bring it by in the morning. No delivery fee.'

'Really?' Frances exclaimed. 'That would be terrific, but we don't want to put you to any trouble.'

'It's no trouble at all. A mile by car is far quicker than a mile on foot.'

As Ted and Frances packed up their coffee and bowls of stew and set off to discuss breakfast options with the rest of the troupe, Schuyler observed, 'Carry-out delivery service. Just what you need to be doing while juggling the café and the fair.'

'It won't be that bad,' Tish dismissed. 'Mary Jo and Charlotte are covering at the café all weekend. I just have to make sure the baking is underway before they arrive. Besides, how long could it possibly take to drive here and dole out coffee and breakfast sandwiches?'

THREE

Friday morning dawned cold and clear. Tish, armed against the wintry weather in her heavy black wool coat, leopard-print beret, and lined leather driving gloves, loaded an insulated jug of coffee and a reusable shopping bag filled with cooked egg dishes, breakfast sandwiches, and biscuits into the hatchback of her bright-red Toyota Matrix and drove off for the Hobson Glen Recreation Park. It was seven thirty and the sun had just begun to poke its head above the horizon, bathing the frosty, barren landscape in its watery glow.

Navigating the Matrix across the grass of the fairgrounds as she had done for the previous day's load-in, she brought the car to halt behind her food stall and, gathering the foodstuffs from the trunk, set off behind the stage toward the area of the park that, in summer, served as an RV park and campground, but which had been temporarily reopened to serve the needs of the theater group.

Striding into the makeshift camp, Tish was promptly greeted by Frances Fenton as she emerged from her Winnebago, the first in a line of ten camping vehicles assembled there. 'Good morning,' she welcomed in a singsong voice.

'Good morning. I bring nectar of the gods,' Tish announced as she lifted the jug of coffee above her head.

'Oh, bless you for doing this. If I had to go on to that stage this morning without my java, I'd probably be kicked out of the group.'

'Not a problem.' Tish followed Frances to a collapsible steel table that had been erected in the center of the row of camping vehicles. 'Cold time of year to be camping.'

'It's not too bad, actually. We all have gas heaters, which keep things warm and snug through the night. That said, I *am* glad this is the last performance of the season. We'll do two or three indoor venues through the winter, but when you're as busy as we are from March through December, it's nice to have some time off. Also, even though camping with one's husband for ten months of the year can be romantic, there are moments when one yearns to be alone with one's thoughts in someplace larger and more scenic than a cruise-ship-size bathroom.'

Tish plopped the jug of coffee and the bag of food on to the surface of the table. 'There are moments when my apartment above the café doesn't feel far enough away from work. At least I can hop in my car and drive somewhere.'

'Yeah, it does get tough at times, but so does any job. We're both lucky to be doing what we love.'

'I hear you on that one.' Tish took some recycled paper coffee cups and a bunch of sugar and sweetener packets out of the bag and directed Frances to help herself while she went about locating the containers of milk and soy milk she had brought from the café refrigerator. Once found, she then went about the task of distributing orders. 'What did you order again, Frances?'

'The Italian ham, egg, and pineapple-mango chutney sand-wich,' the actress replied as she poured two cups of coffee.

'Oh, yes, the *Tropic of Capicola*. And your husband is having the *Ham-elet*.'

'The *Ham-elet*? I don't remember seeing that on the menu. What is it?'

'A basic cheese omelet with ham. Not the most adventurous item I serve, but "To thine own self be true."'

Frances gave a hearty guffaw. 'Yep, that's Ted all right. Non-adventurous.'

'Hey, it takes all kinds. Let him know he can order off-menu, should he want something plain,' Tish offered. 'That is, if you don't have other breakfast plans for tomorrow.'

'No, it's the same schedule as today, so if you could deliver again, that would be fantastic.'

'You bet.'

'Thanks, Tish. I'll let Ted know about those menu options. As for the bill, Rolly will settle up.'

As if on cue, a man in his mid-fifties exited from the trailer beside the Fentons' Winnebago. He was tall and broad-shoul-dered, with dark hair that was graying at the temples, and a pleasant yet nondescript countenance that lent itself well to the parts of Scrooge, Orsino, and the countless other roles he must have played in his lifetime. 'Morning.' He waved.

Tish returned the gesture.

'Morning, Rolly. Just bringing Mr Ted his breakfast. I'll see you at rehearsal,' Frances bade before heading back to her camper.

'You must be Tish Tarragon.' Rolly approached the folding table with an outstretched hand. 'Rolly Rollinson, Director of the Williamsburg Theater Group.'

Tish accepted the hand and gave it a shake. 'Nice to meet you, Rolly. Yes, I'm Tish, owner of Cookin' the Books Café.'

'The Fentons told me all about you. Nice name for a restaurant owner, by the way.'

'Yes, I'm a born caterer.'

'You probably hear the name thing all the time, don't you?' Rolly blushed self-consciously.

'Occasionally.' Tish maintained a friendly smile.

'Sorry. We, um, we really appreciate you coming out here with breakfast. Normally, I'd unhitch my trailer and drive my truck into town for food and supplies.' He gestured toward the black pickup still attached to the trailer from which he had recently exited. 'But one of our sound guys called in sick, so I've been filling in as needed. I scarcely got the plumbing in the trailer hooked up before it was time for our first rehearsal.'

'No problem. I appreciate the business.'

'Speaking of which, how much do we owe you for this morning?'

Tish handed him a slip of paper.

'Do you accept checks?'

'I do, but if I'm doing breakfast again over the weekend, why don't we settle up at the end? No sense taking the checkbook out twice.'

'That would make accounting a lot easier,' Rolly deemed as he helped himself to a cup of coffee.

'What did you order, Rolly?' Tish asked as she rummaged through the bag. From the opposite end of the line of campers, Justin Dange approached.

'In my heart, the *Portrait of the Artist as a Young Ham,* but then I thought about my cardiologist and ordered the *Danielle Steele Cut Oats.* Come to think of it, put me down for that tomorrow as well.'

'Chin up, Rolly. You can live vicariously through me,' Justin teased and then quietly requested the aforementioned breakfast sandwich from Tish.

'Thanks, Justin.'

'Hey, a friend in need . . .' Justin turned to Tish. 'I want to apologize about last night. I hope we didn't embarrass you and your staff with our antics.'

'Not at all,' Tish dismissed. 'When people work together as much as your group does, there's bound to be arguments, just as there are in any family.'

'What "antics" are you apologizing for, Justin?' Rolly's voice took on the tone of a vexed parent.

'Just Frances sharpening her talons on Jenny again,' Justin grumbled. 'The way she goes after that girl.'

'So you leaped to Jenny's defense,' Rolly surmised.

'Of course.'

'Jenny isn't some helpless innocent, you know.'

'Don't you start on her, too.'

'I'm not starting anything. Justin, I rely upon your even temper in these situations. Between Bailey and Frances, there's enough hot-headedness in the group already. We don't need you flying off the handle.'

'OK,' Justin capitulated. 'I'll apologize to Frances, but you'd better do something to rein her in. Most of her spare time is spent wagging either her finger or her tongue.'

'I'll talk to her this morning,' Rolly promised as he made his way back to his trailer. 'See you later, Tish. Thanks again.'

'See you on the stage,' Tish replied. 'Well, I'd best deliver this food before it gets cold.'

'I can do that for you if you'd like,' Justin offered.

'That's most kind, but I'm not sure you'd be able to decipher my labeling system.'

'And I'm not sure you want to just "drop in" on everyone in our little encampment without having met them, so why don't I come with you?'

'That would be great,' Tish agreed and followed Justin to the end of the line of trailers.

'That's me.' He gestured to the black Travato camper van parked at the end of the row. 'Small, but plenty enough room for one person. It even has a kitchen.'

'Ah, so you didn't need my services this morning,' Tish presumed.

'I said I had a kitchen. I didn't say I knew how to cook.' His hazel eyes danced. 'And if I did, I'm not sure I'd want to cook for this lot, anyway. All I'd get would be complaints.'

'I'll be sure to brace myself for the backlash.'

'You have nothing to worry about. You're an outsider. This group is all about the infighting.' He pointed to the vintage 1950s Airstream camper parked beside his Travato. 'That belongs to Lucinda LeComte.'

'Wow, what a beauty.'

'Classy camper for a classy lady. We all purchase our individual trailers and campers. A means of retaining a sense of self while on the road.' He gave a quick rap to the camper door. 'Lucinda. Breakfast.'

Within a few moments, the door swung inward to reveal a woman who appeared to be in her late thirties. She had long, luxurious auburn hair, soft ivory skin and wide blue eyes, and was draped in a resplendent floral kimono. 'Perfect timing. I'm starving!' She addressed Tish, 'Hi, I'm Lucinda, by the way.'

'Hi, I'm Tish. I loved you as Olivia last night.'

'Thanks. That was my first time playing Olivia. In the past, I've always played Viola. I'm relieved I kept my lines straight.'

'You did more than that. You were wonderful.' Tish reached into her bag. 'So what am I bringing you this morning?'

'The *Belinda*.'

'Ah, yes, the "Good 'wich."'

'Sounds healthy,' Justin mocked.

'Egg-white omelet with avocado, kale, and sautéed shitake mushrooms on spelt bread,' Tish explained.

Justin gagged. 'Woman, eat some bacon.'

Lucinda laughed. 'I would if I didn't have a corset to wear later today. Now, I have to take the approach that my body is a temple. Ancient, crumbling, and in need of both preservation and restoration.'

Tish scoffed at the actress's self-deprecating remarks. 'You look fabulous.'

'Thanks, but that's only because I'm vigilant about not eating things like bacon.' She glared playfully at Justin Dange. 'Can I put in an order for the same thing tomorrow, Tish?'

'Of course. I can even add some smoked salmon to it if you'd like.'

'Hmm, yes, please. It's Saturday. That's my treat day.'

'To be clear, adding fish to a breakfast sandwich isn't a treat,' Justin ribbed. 'It's a punishment and possibly a crime in several states.'

'Oh, you.' Lucinda swatted him away with a laugh and a roll of the eyes. 'See you on the boards in a bit. And, Tish, thank you for the food.'

Justin and Tish moved to the next vehicle in the camp – a vintage 1970s' van with beaded curtains in the window and a bevy of decals on the rear bumper. 'Bailey Cassels's pied-à-terre. Presented without comment.' He knocked on the rear side door.

There was no reply.

Justin banged again. After a few moments' silence, he tried the door handle. 'Locked. Must have gone out somewhere. Strange, he knew breakfast was coming. Though he *can* be a flake.'

'We can come back again later. Let's deliver everything else before it gets cold.'

Justin nodded and led Tish to the small red-and-white travel trailer next door. 'This is Jenny. I loaned her the money to purchase it when she joined the group.'

'That was nice of you,' Tish remarked.

'Jenny,' he called and then leaned toward Tish to explain. 'Jenny can't stand people knocking on her door out of the blue. It startles her. You have to call her name first.'

When there was no answer from inside the trailer, Justin called her again. 'Jenny? Jenny, it's Justin. Breakfast is here.'

The call was met with silence. Within moments, a chilling breeze swept through the campground, grabbing hold of the door of Jenny's trailer, blowing it open, and slamming it shut again.

'It's not like her to leave her door unlocked,' Justin noted.

'We'd better go inside and make sure she's OK,' Tish suggested, even though she was reluctant to violate the young woman's privacy.

'Jenny, we're coming in to check on you,' Justin announced as he stepped inside, Tish close at his heels.

As Tish's eyes acclimatized to the dim interior, she was able to pick out certain features. The cool early-morning sunlight filtered between the slats of the Venetian blinds, while strands of multicolor Christmas lights draped along the ceiling cast the camper in a warm glow.

To the left of the door stood a single bed, lined with a bevy of sequined and animal-print cushions. The bed had been turned down, but the sheets were unwrinkled and the bed pillows plump and undisturbed.

'She obviously didn't sleep here last night,' Justin noted with a frown.

Meanwhile, Tish examined the rest of the trailer. Across from the bed, a narrow door led to a bathroom. And to the right, a single row of upper and lower cabinets, a mini refrigerator, a microwave, and a hot plate served as a kitchenette.

A wall-mounted foldaway table divided the kitchen from the sleeping area, serving as both extra counter space and an eating/work area. Given the presence of a laptop computer and empty fast-food containers, Jenny used the area for both purposes.

'We should probably get out of here.' Justin sighed. 'Wouldn't want Jenny to come home and find me here snooping around. She'd accuse me of interfering with—'

He was interrupted by a loud gasp. 'What is it?'

'Call nine-one-one,' Tish ordered, her voice quavering. Beneath the table, slumped against the far wall of the trailer, rested the body of Jenny Inkpen. Her mouth was agape, and her lifeless eyes stared blankly back at Tish. She was dressed in fuzzy pink mules and a pair of flannel pajama bottoms, but the gaping wound in her chest and the vast quantity of blood encircling it made it impossible to discern what she was wearing on top.

From his position at the head of the bed, Justin could not see what was hidden under the table. 'What? Why?'

Tish thought that she might be sick, but she steeled herself. 'It's Jenny. She's dead.'

FOUR

As Justin Dange was escorted into the back of a nearby ambulance to be treated for shock, Tish accepted a blanket from one of the paramedics and, wrapping it tightly around her torso, gave her statement to a member of Sheriff Reade's team. She had just finished her account when Reade approached.

'When I said that you catering the fair meant there might be a crime spree, I didn't expect you to take it as a personal challenge,' he joked.

Tish stared down at the ground beneath her feet.

'I'm sorry, Tish. Policemen are cursed with gallows humor. Are you all right?'

She shook her head.

Reade waved Tish to follow him. 'Come on. Let's get you some coffee.'

'Thanks, but I'm OK. Really.'

'You're not OK and I'm not arguing with you. I have a thermos in my car. You can warm up and we can talk about the case in private.' Reade eyed the scads of officers and forensics specialists scanning the campgrounds and questioning its residents.

Tish allowed Reade to guide her back to his squad car, which was parked in a grassy patch just outside the camp area. Once inside, the sheriff started the engine, cranked the heating system, detached the cap from his insulated canteen, poured a cup of coffee, and handed it to Tish.

Accepting the cup, she murmured her thanks and gave it a sip. 'This is really good,' she stated, the color returning to her face.

'It should be,' he smiled. 'I got it from your café. Mary Jo filled this thing to the brim just before I got the call.'

'*The call*,' she breathed. 'I don't know why I'm reacting this way. It's not like I haven't seen a dead body before.'

'No, but this one was particularly . . . gruesome. The medical examiner believes Jenny was killed by a shotgun fired at close range, but the injuries she sustained and the subsequent blood loss were far more extensive than those from any shotgun blast I've ever seen.'

'It *was* gruesome, but it's not as if Sloane Shackleford's death was any less brutal. No, I think this might be worse because Jenny was so young.'

'Twenty-two years old. A kid, really,' Reade commiserated.

'A "kid" with a future. She'd made a name for herself in the troupe, and critics were certain she'd soon move on to off-Broadway productions.' Tish drew a deep breath. 'Now it's all gone. Who would have done such a thing?'

'Could be anyone. This area is secured and patrolled during the day to prevent a wayward visitor from breaking into the trailers. But at night, during the off hours, it's the other way around. We leave this area in relative peace so as not to disturb anyone, but the rest of the fairgrounds are cordoned off and guarded to prevent vandalism or theft.'

'Do you really think someone snuck into the campground last night with the intent to kill Jenny?'

'No idea. I'm just saying that this could very well have been a stalker scenario. She was an attractive young actress with a huge online following.'

'She was also an attractive young actress who'd generated more than her fair amount of jealousy within the group,' Tish announced before taking another sip of coffee. The rich brew was going a long way toward making her feel semi-human again.

'Jealousy over Jenny being touted as the star of the group?'

'That as well as sexual jealousy. Justin Dange, the actor with whom I discovered the body, dated Jenny until she dumped him shortly after getting into the group. And Bailey Cassels, another young actor, made a move on her last night, only to have Jenny verbally chop his head off.' Tish drew another long sip of coffee. 'By the way, Bailey Cassels wasn't in his trailer this morning. Or, if he was, he wasn't answering the door.'

Reade was pensive. 'Hmm. I'll have to speak with him about that.'

'Also, the head of the group, Rolly Rollinson, is a bit suspicious. According to Ted Fenton, Rolly founded the group on the principle of equality; that all the players in the group would get their share of "star" time. He did a complete one-eighty when he met Jenny and gave her all the lead parts.'

'You think he might have had a thing for her, too?'

'Could be. It would be interesting to find out why he made the sudden about-face.'

'But why would he want to kill his leading lady?'

'Because, as I mentioned earlier, Jenny was going places. She might have been going there far quicker than Rolly liked.'

'Gotcha.' Reade nodded.

Tish suddenly pulled a face.

'What's wrong?'

'Jenny's position under the table. It looked as though she'd been cowering in fear.'

'Yeah, it did. Someone standing at your door with a shotgun will do that to you,' Reade deadpanned.

'Well, I just can't imagine anyone in this group being capable of instilling that much terror in Jenny. Even if that person was pointing a gun, Jenny would have been shocked or puzzled at first, wouldn't she? She wouldn't have immediately hidden under the table.'

'I think that would have depended upon the circumstances. If, for instance, Jenny had already experienced a physical altercation with her killer, she would have taken the presence of the shotgun as a legitimate threat.'

'That's precisely what I'm getting at. Jenny was already frightened of this person.'

'That's a very valid point,' Reade conceded. 'It also backs my stalker theory.'

'It does. And yet the stalker theory doesn't feel right to me. I saw Jenny after the show last night. She was cool, haughty, a bit aloof, but one thing she wasn't was afraid.'

'She was also a talented actress.'

'Granted, but to remain that calm and collected would have required nerves of steel. There was a sizable audience here last night. If Jenny had a stalker, that stalker could have been anywhere in the audience. Yet Jenny came out of her dressing room on her own, placed an order for coffee, spurned Bailey Cassels's romantic overtones, and then walked back to her trailer, once again alone. That's not acting, Clemson.'

'We'll find out soon enough, but only if I get back to the scene. You want me to give you a lift back to the café?'

'No, thanks. I have my car.'

'You've had a shock. Are you sure you're fine to drive?'

'Positive. The coffee and the car heater helped a lot. So did the conversation. Thank you.' She drank the last drop of coffee. 'I actually hadn't planned on going back to the café right away. I started the morning bake before I came here, and we were all so tired last night that I locked up without restocking anything. I'd like to get things in order before we open at eleven. That is, if we're still opening.'

'This is the town's biggest fundraiser of the year. It's also the one folks look forward to the most, so I've promised the interim mayor that I'll do what I can to keep it running. Since the crime was committed in a non-public area, I can uphold that promise. However, if we discover evidence in any of the public areas, I may have to make a difficult decision.'

'I don't envy you your job.' She sighed.

'Really? There have been times when I thought you were trying to take it over.' He laughed.

'Come now. I just helped with a couple of cases,' Tish replied sheepishly.

'You did more than help. Your investigative skills were vital to closing those cases. I appreciate all you've done for me – erm, I mean for the department. I, um, we, value your input.'

'Thanks. I doubt you'll be receiving much of that input this weekend, what with the fair. I'll probably be flat out the next two days.'

'I wouldn't bet on that.' Reade grinned. 'If I've learned anything from working with you, it's that you never fail to surprise.'

Tish and Reade stepped out of the squad car and walked back to the campground. In the time since Jenny Inkpen's body was discovered, the sun had given way to a thick cover of clouds and a damp northerly breeze. Yet, regardless of rain, sleet, snow, and even murder, the show, and indeed the fair, must continue.

Tish nodded a farewell to Reade and watched as he knocked on the door of the Fentons' camper. Tucking her hands into the pockets of her coat, she continued on her way to the folding table to collect her now-empty coffee urn. As she passed by Rolly Rollinson's trailer, she could overhear him instructing someone to 'get to Hobson Glen as soon as possible' and to bring their 'brother' as he would be 'the perfect understudy for the role of Sebastian.'

Tish paused. Calling someone to fill in for Jenny Inkpen was an urgent matter if the group was to continue with the day's performances, but why would Bailey Cassels need an understudy? Did Rolly know something no one else did? And was that 'something' related to why Bailey was missing earlier that morning?

Not wishing to be seen loitering outside Rolly's trailer, Tish hurried along to the folding table, collected the urn, and then went to check on Justin Dange. She found him seated in a camp chair positioned just outside the ambulance. He was enveloped in an emergency services blanket and sipping a steaming mug of tea.

'How are you?' Tish asked as she took up the camp chair alongside Justin's.

'Jenny's dead. I just can't wrap my mind around it. It doesn't seem real.'

'I can't imagine,' she sympathized.

'And you? How are you doing? You had a shock yourself.'

'I'm OK. Distracting myself with my duties for the fair.'

'Yeah, we're supposed to go on today as planned. Part of me thinks we should cancel. The other part is happy to get back to work. That is, if your local constabulary doesn't arrest us all.' Justin gestured as Sheriff Reade stepped into the Fentons' trailer.

'Sheriff Reade is excellent at his job. He'll find the killer *and* ensure there's a minimal amount of disruption to your group and to the fair.'

'Well, if you'd give Sheriff Reade a message from me, since given how you two walked over here together it would appear you have his ear and perhaps a few other things—'

'Oh, no, we're not—' Tish began to set the record straight about her relationship with Reade, but Justin was too quick for her.

'Tell him that he's barking up the wrong tree with all this questioning.'

'The sheriff needs to question the group in order to establish the time of death and to find out if anyone saw or heard anything out of the ordinary. For instance, did anyone hear the shotgun blast? Did they look outside their window and see the killer?'

'Doubtful,' Justin replied. 'Kids were setting off fireworks all night. The sound of a gun would have blended right in.'

Tish had slept soundly the previous night, but even she

could recall being awakened on more than one occasion by the sound of fireworks coming from the direction of the recreation park.

'You need to tell your boyfriend to back off—'

'He's not my—' Tish again tried to clarify the nature of her and Reade's relationship, but was again interrupted.

'No one in the group could have murdered Jenny. They're simply not capable of such a thing.'

'Even Frances Fenton?' Tish challenged with a raised eyebrow.

'Yes, even Frances Fenton. I know she can be loud and brash at times, and I know she and I got into it last night, but she's just looking out for my interests. She's always been like a crazy overprotective aunt to me. You see, I was a theater major at William and Mary when I started with the group. While my professors taught me the history of theater and acting techniques, Rolly, Edie Harmes – she's our costume designer – and the Fentons featured me in bit parts so I could build confidence. They had me designing the sound and lights for performances. They had me building sets. It was a totally immersive experience. When I graduated, I was tempted to move to New York or LA, but I found Rolly's offer to make me a fully-fledged partner too difficult to resist. This had become my family.'

'By fully-fledged partner, you mean . . .'

'I mean that as well as having a say and a hand in advertising, bookings, and day-to-day management, I take a share of the profits. Well, along with Rolly, Edie, the Fentons, and Lucinda, of course.' He gave a wistful laugh. 'I haven't thought of my early days with the group in years. You know, I had a huge crush on Lucinda in those days.'

'And now?' she smiled.

'Lucinda and I are good friends. I never had the guts to tell her about my feelings back then. However, she knows about them now. We laugh about it every now and then. You know, "what might have been" and all that nonsense. It was Jenny who most recently had my heart, but you probably already guessed that.'

'I suspected as much when you jumped to her defense last night.'

Justin sighed in exasperation. 'Stupid of me, I guess, given our age difference, but I truly cared for Jenny. If only Frances had known her the way I did, she wouldn't have said half the things she said last night.'

'If you don't mind me asking, if you still had feelings for Jenny, then why did the two of you break up?' Tish asked as delicately as she could.

'Jenny was a complicated human being. I know that sounds like a lame excuse, but it's the truth. She ran away from home when she was quite young, so she was used to being on her own and taking care of herself, instead of relying upon others. All of it made her seem hardened, in a way. But that wasn't the case at all. In fact, I think she probably felt things more intensely than anyone I've ever known.'

'Is that why you broke up, because she felt things too intensely?'

'I got too close. She was unaccustomed to trusting people, to letting anyone see the person she was, deep down.'

'What kind of person was that?'

'A deeply wounded one.'

Tish and Justin were interrupted by the sudden reappearance of Bailey Cassels. His dark hair was uncombed, and he was dressed in a heavy parka, flannel pajama pants, and work boots. A pair of dark glasses shaded his eyes and a series of fresh red scratches ran down the left side of his face. 'What's going on? What's happened?' he demanded in a panic.

'It's Jenny,' Justin answered. 'She's dead.'

'Dead?' Bailey shrieked. 'How? When?'

'We found her this morning,' Tish explained as she stood up and helped Bailey into the seat she had just occupied. 'She's been murdered.'

'Murdered? My God. Who would kill Jenny? And why?'

'Why don't you ask that of the claw marks on your face?' Justin braved.

Bailey brought a hand, absently, to his face. 'I went for a walk in the woods this morning to clear my head. I guess I must have caught myself on some branches.'

'An early-morning walk? I've never known you to get out

of your trailer much before rehearsal. And those scratches don't look like they're from any tree I've ever encountered.'

'What are you trying to say?' Bailey's tone was confrontational.

'I'm saying that Jenny came down pretty hard on you last night. I'm saying that, in retaliation, you stopped by her trailer and gave her a piece of your mind. Things got physical. You grabbed her. She scratched your face in an attempt to break free, and you lost your temper and killed her.'

'What? You're delusional. I'd never hurt Jenny, let alone kill her.'

'And yet she's dead.'

'Look, you're right about last night. I did see Jenny and things did get physical, but not in the way you described.' Bailey Cassels leaned back in his chair and nervously licked his lips. 'I went to Jenny's trailer because I didn't like the way we left things between us.'

'I'm sure you didn't,' Justin sneered.

Bailey ignored the comment and turned his gaze toward Tish. 'My timing in asking Jenny to join me for coffee at your booth couldn't have been worse. She'd just given a dynamic performance as the lead in a Shakespeare production and had no time to regroup, and there I was yapping at her heels like some needy little dog.'

'Finally, something we agree upon,' Justin added.

'So I apologized to Jenny for my poor timing and told her how much I respect her work as an actor, as well as how much I enjoy working with her.' Bailey fell silent.

'Yes?' Tish urged.

'Out of the blue, she pulled me inside the trailer, shut the door behind me, and began kissing me. It was completely unexpected, but it wasn't unwanted. I mean Jenny is – was – a beautiful girl.' He drew a deep breath. 'Things were going fast. She had unbuttoned my shirt and had removed her top and was about to remove her bra and lead us to her bed when she got all weird.'

'Weird?'

'Yeah, like hitting me and pinching me and biting me. Not fun or in a teasing way, but hard. I thought I'd done something wrong, so I stopped. That's when she told me – not asked but *told* me – to hurt her. I gave her a small bite on the neck and a light slap on her' – Bailey cleared his throat – 'erm, bottom . . . but that wasn't what she wanted. She wanted me to slap her across the face. I refused. I mean, I can't hit a woman. I just can't. Least of all a woman who's half-naked and kissing me.'

Justin leaped from his chair, overturning it in the process. 'You're a goddamn liar. Jenny wouldn't have gone near you. Not for one second.'

'But she did,' Bailey maintained. 'She was all over me until I refused to strike her. Then she got angry and demanded I leave.'

'What did you do?' Tish asked.

'I tried to explain that I was incredibly attracted to her, but that I couldn't hurt her. She didn't want to hear it. She was furious. That's when she clawed at my face.'

'That's it! I will not have you making Jenny out to be some sort of freak,' Justin shouted.

'I never implied she was a freak.' Bailey rose to his feet and stabbed a finger into Justin's chest. 'You're the one using that word. I simply said I was uncomfortable with her request.'

Tish inserted herself between the two men. 'What happened after Jenny clawed at you, Bailey?'

'I did as she asked and left, but the scene haunted me. I tossed and turned all night. When dawn began to break, I took a walk. That's where I've been since.'

'While you were awake last night, did you hear or see anything strange?'

Bailey shook his head. 'I didn't look out of my window, so I didn't see anything, but I did hear people shooting off fireworks. Some of them sounded really close.'

Tish frowned and stared down at her shoes as she thought about the significance of Bailey's statement.

Her reaction was not lost upon the young actor. 'Jenny . . . she was shot, wasn't she?'

'How do you know that unless you're the one who did it?' Justin Dange exploded. 'That's it. I'm getting the police over here.'

Justin, empty mug in hand, trotted off to the nearest uniformed officer, leaving Tish to answer Bailey's question.

'Yes, Bailey, Jenny was shot.'

'Then those nearby rockets I heard last night might not have been rockets. They could have been . . .'

Tish nodded. 'Yes, they very well might have been.'

FIVE

Tish returned to her booth to find Jules, wearing a heavy parka and a worried expression, waiting for her. Biscuit was in his arms, clad in a green-and-red tartan coat that coordinated with the heavy scarf wrapped around Jules's neck. 'There you are! You poor thing. How are you?'

Tish collected Biscuit from Jules's arms for a cuddle. 'I'm OK. Just hoping that getting ready for the day will erase the image of Jenny's face from my memory.'

'You want me to call Schuyler? I know he'd want to be here.'

Tish turned down the offer. 'He's attending a funeral and a will-reading up in Fairfax County. He'll be gone until late.'

'Should I take you back to the café? A good lie down might help.'

'Thanks, but no. What I really need is to get to work.' Her eyes narrowed as she cradled Biscuit in her arms and stroked his head. 'By the way, what are you doing here? The murder couldn't possibly have made the news yet.'

'Honey, I *am* the news. I'm covering the case for Channel Ten.'

'Really? Wow! That's quite a step up the ladder for you. Congratulations!' She threw her free arm around Jules's neck excitedly.

'Thanks.' He gave her a quick squeeze around the waist. 'It's actually not *that* exciting. I got the job by default.'

'Default?'

'Our crime desk guy took an early vacation so he could

spend time with his family over the holidays. His stand-in gets squeamish whenever he covers a case involving lots of blood. He practically fainted on camera once.'

Tish was about to ask how a reporter with hemophobia could have been assigned to the crime desk, but she was well aware of the Channel Ten newsroom's staffing idiosyncrasies.

'And the stand-in's stand-in owns a Dodge Ram 1500, so my boss doesn't want to reimburse him fuel and mileage at twelve miles per gallon.' Jules sighed and gave Biscuit a scratch around the ears. 'Especially as I'm already here . . .'

'And can cover the story at minimal expense,' Tish filled in the blanks.

'Exactly. Default.'

'It's still a good opportunity.'

'It is. So long as people tune in to watch me and not the major network news affiliates.'

'Of course they'll watch you! You have charm and sass and personality.'

'And a detective friend with connections to the sheriff's office,' Jules added.

'Jules,' she warned.

'I know, I know,' he reassured her. 'I was joking. Well, kinda . . .'

Tish flashed him another warning glance and placed Biscuit into his heated doggie bed.

'You know, Tish, I find it amazing that at the same time you launched your café business, you've also proven yourself to be a brilliant sleuth. You're like the Nancy Drew of the catering world.'

'Well, I wouldn't count on Nancy Drew to be digging up any clues on this case. Not with a fair booth to run and a renegade barman.'

'Renegade barman? Oh no, no, no. I'm not shirking my beverage duties.'

'But you're covering both the murder and the fair for Channel Ten,' Tish pointed out. 'This could be huge for you.'

'Yes, and there's no better place to cover both of them than right here at this booth.' Jules pointed at the ground beneath his feet. 'Not only did the murder take place just a few yards away, but Reade and his team will be here ordering their hot beverages and snacks. As I ply them with caffeine and Celestine's yummy cakes, I'll be able to get the scoop on case developments before the competition does.'

'You have it all worked out, don't you?'

'Sure do. The crew will be here at one to get some preliminary shots for both stories. Then we go live at five o'clock. The murder will be the lead story, natch. So I'll broadcast from the campground. The fair coverage, however, will emanate from here. I figure it would give you some great publicity.'

'That sounds terrific, as long as the fair segment doesn't run immediately after the murder coverage. I wouldn't want the visual association, if you understand.'

'No worries. The fair – featuring your lovely food booth – is the third story of the evening. The holiday sales season is the fourth. So there will be a nice festive theme to balance out the Inkpen story.'

'What's the second story?'

Jules referred to his phone. 'The opening of a new fertility clinic in downtown Richmond.'

Tish's and Jules's eyes met.

'Right. We'll just move the holiday sales story up to number three and you to number four.' He opened his email program and punched some digits into the phone. 'So can we discuss Jenny Inkpen's murder?'

'Off the record?'

'Completely. Utterly. Entirely.'

'OK, but there's not much to tell.' Tish began restocking the shelves of the booth with cups and food packaging. 'We only just found her this morning.'

'Rumor has it that this is the work of some madman.'

'Rumor? How can there be rumors circulating already?'

'Well, maybe the rumors were limited to the newsroom, but still . . . You know this town. I'm sure someone, somewhere, is spreading word of there being a homicidal maniac on the loose.'

Once again, Tish and Jules exchanged glances. 'Enid Kemper.' They uttered the name of the town eccentric in unison as if it were some magical incantation.

'No doubt that parrot of hers already has the story memorized,' Jules predicted.

'Langhorne is not a parrot.' Tish mimicked Enid's thin, reedy voice. 'He's a conure.'

Jules howled with laughter. 'You do that far too well.'

'I only hear that voice every Sunday afternoon when Enid and Langhorne come to the café after church for lunch. Enid always orders the *Zelda Fitzgerald* fried chicken and pimento cheese sandwich. And Langhorne gets a small portion of pasta with sesame seeds.'

'Good lord, you cook the bird lunch? You're too good to be true.'

'Nah, it's usually just leftover pasta, and I have the seeds for bread baking, but it makes Enid happy. I call it the *Big Bird Special*. It's not a literary reference, but it was the best I could come up with at the last minute. Enid has yet to call me out on it.'

'Lucky.'

'Don't I know it. So, getting back to those madman rumors . . .'

'Yes, and we're still off the record,' Jules reminded Tish as he passed her a stack of bright-red cups.

'Thanks,' she replied. It was unclear whether her response was for the cups or the invitation to speak freely. 'Sheriff Reade is looking into the possibility that Jenny had a stalker.'

'That's it?'

'What do you mean, "That's it?"? The girl's body isn't even cold yet.'

'I mean you typically lend a bit more insight when you report matters.'

Tish shrugged. 'You asked me whether or not a homicidal lunatic might be responsible, and I answered you.'

'You don't believe such a person exists, do you?' Jules surmised from his friend's reaction.

'I don't know. It stands to reason that an attractive young actress may have had a stalker, and yet there was so much going on behind the scenes that shouldn't be discounted.'

'Such as?'

'Well, namely, Jenny wasn't very well liked.'

'Successful young newcomer becomes audience favorite. Jealousy ensues,' Jules reasoned.

'Yes, Frances Fenton and Lucinda LeComte both lost leading roles to Jenny. And then there were Bailey Cassels and Justin Dange.'

'What did Jenny do to them?'

'She had dated Justin prior to making the group. Then she broke up with him.'

'And then Bailey hit on Jenny only to be rejected, as we witnessed.' True to form, Jules was eager to sink his teeth into the Williamsburg Theater Group gossip.

'Yes, that is, Bailey claims, until late last night.'

Tish described the scratches on Bailey's face and his description of the night's events.

Jules whistled. 'The cops are going to have a field day with him.'

'And well they should.'

'You mean you don't believe him?'

'I mean that it's all a little too Robert-Chambers-Preppy-Murder-Case for my liking.'

'Oh, I remember that case! A young woman was found strangled in New York's Central Park. The cops charged her boyfriend, but he claimed it was an accident. He said she liked being choked and the situation got out of hand.'

Tish nodded. 'However, he had scratches all over his face.'

'Just like Bailey Cassels. The police are definitely going to have a lot of questions for him.'

'Yeah, especially if someone saw him leaving Jenny's trailer in the wee hours.'

'Sounds as if you know something.'

'I don't, but Rolly Rollinson might. I overhead him arranging for understudies for both Jenny Inkpen *and* Bailey Cassels.'

'Why would Bailey need an understudy?'

'Precisely.'

'You think Rolly heard the gunshot and looked out to see Bailey leaving Jenny's trailer?'

'He may have seen Bailey, yes. But I doubt he heard anything. Some kids were shooting off rockets all night. It would have been difficult to discern a gunshot in the midst of all that racket.'

'Is that what that was? I was pretty out of it last night, but I remember waking up to something that sounded like a car backfiring.'

'Fireworks. *Twelfth Night*'s Lord of Misrule was alive and well.'

'But without hearing an actual gunshot, why would Rolly assume Bailey shot Jenny? There could have been a myriad of reasons Bailey was there – but murder? That's quite a leap.'

'Not as strange as the leap Justin Dange made just a little while ago.'

'What's that?'

'When I mentioned that someone in the group might have murdered Jenny, he was adamant that the crime had been committed by an outsider. But when Bailey told us about the incident in Jenny's trailer, Justin flew into a rage and began accusing Bailey of shooting her.'

'Justin was probably jealous and angry. Jealous that Bailey might have nearly gotten it on with his former flame and angry that he may have assaulted her.'

'Was he, Jules? Or was Justin happy to find a scapegoat so he could divert suspicion from himself? Or possibly someone else he wanted to protect?'

SIX

Whatever might have inspired the decision, Rollinson's call for an understudy to replace Bailey Cassels was a prudent move, for the young actor was taken into police custody shortly before the curtain was to go up at noon. Despite initial panic and a fair amount of last-minute adjustments, Jenny Inkpen's and Bailey Cassels's understudies filled in for the roles of Tiny Tim and the Ghost of Christmas Future, respectively, to thunderous applause.

For the evening performance, the group opted to place the

primary roles in the hands of the major players. Lucinda moved into the part of Viola, Justin took over the part of Orsino, leaving Rolly to try his hand at Malvolio, and the group's costumer, Edie Harmes, to slide into the role of Olivia. With a background in musical theater, Jenny's understudy, Martina, was a natural for the role of Feste, the fool, while her brother, Lawrence, took over for Bailey in the part of Sebastian.

The show was a triumph.

Although the previous evening's performance was delightful, the energy level of the reordered cast was near explosive, with each member hitting their marks and timing their lines for maximum comedic value. However, the star of the evening was, without doubt, Lucinda LeComte.

Whether dressed in the doublets and trousers of Cesario or the lace gowns of Viola, Lucinda was luminous, dominating the stage yet remaining gracious and generous to her fellow cast members, so that they too could shine. It was the performance of a highly skilled, finely polished, veteran actress.

Indeed, so successful was Lucinda's performance that when she took to the stage for the curtain call, the audience rose to their feet, cheered, and applauded wildly.

Unlike the previous evening, wherein the group dispersed to their individual trailers, this time the actors waited just until the majority of the crowd had dispersed to emerge from behind the stage, stopping to sign autographs and pose for selfies with the more gregarious members of the audience.

With their publicity tasks complete, they gathered at Tish's booth for well-earned refreshment. The mood was practically giddy.

'Oh, how I've missed performances like that,' Frances Fenton rejoiced. 'It was just like the old days.'

'It was very much like the old days,' Lucinda agreed.

'I'm loath to say this, given the circumstances, but it did feel pretty darn good up there,' Justin Dange admitted.

'Felt even better to see Rolly step down as Orsino,' Ted interjected. 'Every time I saw him in the part, I wondered if Viola was marrying him so she could steal his social security checks.'

The group broke into raucous laughter.

'Funny, Ted. Very funny,' Rolly answered. 'Personally, I enjoyed the challenge of playing Malvolio. There's nothing quite like embracing one's inner villain.'

The group laughed again, this time uneasily. Bailey Cassels, it seemed, had embraced his inner villain and was now, perhaps, paying the penalty.

Tish was eager to change the subject. 'What a terrific performance! Simply wonderful! But I must say, Edie as Olivia might be the biggest surprise. I thought you were the costumer for the group, which requires talent enough, but you're also quite an accomplished actress.'

'I originally joined the group as one of the players,' Edie explained. 'Rolly and I were friends in college.'

'She was in *all* our productions,' Lucinda added gleefully as she draped an arm around Edie's right shoulder and gave it a squeeze.

'The three of us used to call ourselves Rolly's Angels,' Frances rejoined as she flanked Edie on the left. 'But, of course, we all knew Edie was, and still is, Rolly's one and only angel.'

'Oh, Frances.' Edie blushed.

'Well, you are.'

'That's because she's fabulous,' Lucinda asserted. 'The best actress of all of us.'

Edie blushed even brighter at this compliment. 'Anyway,' she continued her story, 'even when I was acting, I'd always done the costumes for the group, but as we got more bookings and tried to vary our offerings, the costuming became more of a full-time position. Mind you, I'd still take on a role here and there if it was juicy enough or provided a challenge. But when Rolly hired Jenny, I bowed out completely. Didn't make much sense for four of us to be fighting over the good parts, did it?'

'I still think you made the wrong choice,' Frances opined. 'As Lucinda said, you're the best actor in the group. It was a shame to lose you. But that's all over now, isn't it? Everything is back to normal.' And with that, Frances Fenton grinned a satisfied grin and sunk her teeth into a slice of *Twelfth Night* cake.

*   *   *

'That woman did it,' Jules insisted when the group had retreated to their trailers, leaving Tish, Jules, and Celestine to clean up for the night.

'Who?' Tish asked, as she counted out the till.

'That Frances woman. She murdered Jenny Inkpen. Did you see how she devoured her cake with not even a thought for the poor girl? Cold.'

Celestine packed up the few remaining cakes in wax paper. 'Ice cold,' she echoed. 'Her aura is dark red, too. Lots of anger.'

'Aura?' a shocked Jules and Tish replied in unison.

'Yeah. I told you how I have trouble sleeping, Tish. Well, for an early Christmas present, Mr Rufus gave me some meditation sessions with a yogi fella in Ashland. I still haven't slept a full night, but I've learned that my aura is orange, which is creativity and vitality, and Mr Rufus's is dark blue, which is fear of expression. Together, our aura is brown.'

Tish strained to remember what she knew about auras. 'Is there such a thing as a brown aura?'

'Nope. That's part of the problem.'

Tish wondered how to respond to Celestine's marital aura conundrum in a manner that was sensitive yet didn't delve too deeply into the subject, as it was late, she was beyond tired, and Jules was still eager to discuss Frances Fenton's guilt. Thankfully, the arrival of Sam Noble rescued her from the need to make any comment at all.

'Hey, Tish. Can I talk to you for a second?' Dark-haired and bearded, the fifty-something owner of the Hobson Glen Bar and Grill nervously wiped his hands on the grease-streaked apron he wore over an insulated plaid flannel shirt and corduroy work pants.

'Sure, Sam. What is it?'

'I, um, I wanted to apologize for the way I reacted to you getting the library's endorsement to cater the theater events. My wife brought our daughter, Lily, to the show this afternoon and she ate one of your *Tiny Tim* lunches – the grilled cheese and alphabet soup. Not only did she eat every bite, but she wouldn't stop talking about it. Do you know how many meals I make that Lily won't eat?'

'Smart kid,' Jules whispered to Celestine.

'My wife said she even ate the orange. I've never been able to get her to eat fruit.'

'Aw, I'm so glad she enjoyed her lunch, Sam.'

'Yeah, she and my wife have been reading the book that came with the lunch too. Can you believe it? My nine-year-old is reading Dickens.'

'That's awesome, Sam. It's good to know the program is doing what it should.'

'Thanks to you. You were the right person for the job, and I was wrong to give you so much guff. I want to apologize and make it up to you.'

'That's not necessary.'

'Yes, it is. I'd like to extend an invitation to you for a free dinner.'

'Oh, that's—' Tish tried to beg off the invitation.

'You've never been to my restaurant, have you?'

'Actually, my boyfriend Schuyler and I had our first date there back in August.'

'That was before the new menu. You and your boyfriend should try it now. I put the grill back in the Grill with ten different varieties of burger. And there's a whole section of the menu dedicated to smoked meat.'

'Because nothing says love like a plate of burnt ends and beans,' Jules quipped to Celestine, who shooed him away while trying to refrain from laughing.

Tish was gracious. 'That's very kind of you. I'll run it past Schuyler and see when we might have some time to take you up on your offer.'

'Excellent. I'll see you tomorrow.' Sam Noble said good-night as a weary Reade approached the booth.

'You look the way I felt this morning,' Tish remarked.

'It's been a long day with very little to show for it.'

'Did you have dinner?'

'No dinner. No lunch. Wasn't time.'

'I have some stew left. Beef, not root veggie,' she offered.

'At this point, I wouldn't care if it were roadkill stew.'

'Are you off duty, Sheriff?' Jules asked.

'Yeah, finally.'

Jules lifted a stainless-steel canteen and poured some steaming red liquid into a hot cup. 'A little mulled wine. Most of the alcohol's burned off by now, but I'll refill it with coffee afterwards, so no one's the wiser.'

'I'm not much for bending an elbow after work, but with the day I've had, I'll make an exception.' Sheriff Reade helped himself to the wine.

'You realize Jules is just plying you with liquor in order to get a scoop,' Tish warned as she ladled some beef stew into a recycled paper bowl and garnished it with a sizable hunk of sourdough bread. 'He's covering the Inkpen case for Channel Ten news.'

'Congratulations. That's a nice step up from the weather desk.'

'Thanks. If I could get an exclusive, I might be able to make the position stick.' Jules flashed an alluring smile.

'I'd be happy to give you an exclusive, if I actually had something to tell you.'

'I thought you had Bailey Cassels in custody?' Tish questioned.

Reade's eyes slid silently toward Jules.

Tish followed his gaze. 'There's a picnic table a few yards from here, over near the stage. Why don't we bring your food over there so you can eat in comfort?'

'Good idea,' Reade acknowledged as he grabbed his bowl and cup and bid adieu to Celestine and Jules with a nod of the head.

'Discussing the case in private? Now that's not right, y'all,' Jules shouted after them. 'Where's the love?'

Tish took a seat upon one of the table's attached benches, her back toward Jules. 'He's still watching us, isn't he?' she asked as Reade slid on to the bench opposite.

'Yeah. You know, I was telling the truth about giving Jules an exclusive. I'm just not in a position to do that right now.'

'Don't worry. It's sort of fun to see him foaming at the mouth.'

'He doesn't know how to read lips, does he?'

'No, but if there's someone here at the fair who can, he'll hire them in a hot second.'

'Fortunately, I didn't see lip reading on the entertainment roster.' Reade took a mouthful of stew. 'Mmm, so good. Even better than the veggie.'

'That's because you're famished.'

'No, this is seriously good. How do you do it?' He plunged his spoon into his bowl again.

'Practice,' she dismissed absently. 'So what happened with Bailey Cassels?'

'He's clean. Not a trace of gunshot residue or blood on him.' Reade took a bite of bread. 'Mmm, did you bake this too?'

'Yes, I mix and knead a large batch of dough, freeze in loaf sizes, and then bake when needed,' Tish explained. 'Bailey could have been wearing gloves, couldn't he? It's certainly cold enough to warrant them.' Reminded of her own leather driving gloves, Tish reached into her coat pockets, extracted them, and pulled them on to her hands.

'Sure, but there would have been some traces of residue or blood on him somewhere, especially considering the size of that blast. Hair, clothes, forearms – something – but he was totally clean. The DNA swab from Cassels's mouth, however, wasn't. It matches the skin underneath Jenny's fingernails, but the preliminary coroner's report showed no signs of sexual assault.' He took another giant bite of bread. 'God, this is good.'

'So Bailey's story checks out,' she presumed.

'Not completely. We still have only his word that Jenny Inkpen invited him inside her trailer. He could have pushed his way inside and forced himself on her – hence the scratches. We're holding him on assault charges, but I doubt they'll stick. There's simply not enough evidence.'

'What about a possible stalker?'

'Jenny had her share of online admirers, many of whom made lewd comments on her Instagram posts and Tweets, but Jenny neither engaged nor blocked them. Some fans over on the theater group Facebook page could get nasty. They'd pick apart her photos – nose too wide, eyes too far apart, looks like she'd gained weight, probably had plastic surgery, that sort of thing – but none of the comments on any of her or the group's social media pages ever threatened her with violence.

Our IT people are checking her phone for emails, text messages, and DMs, but Jenny never reported anything to the police or to any of the social media sites she frequented. Of course, many victims don't report these matters to the authorities for fear of being shamed or blamed, so we can't rule the theory out just yet, but we can't substantiate it either.'

'You're right, you did have a frustrating day,' Tish sympathized.

'You haven't heard the best part. Jenny Inkpen doesn't exist.'

'What?'

'I ran a search through our system, so that we could notify the victim's next of kin, but found just two Jenny Inkpens in their twenties, one located in Alberta, Canada, the other living in Inkpen village, Berkshire, England.'

'That's not entirely shocking. Many actresses use a stage name.'

'Granted, but typically there's a paper trail leading back to the legal name associated with that stage name or pseudonym. Not this time. We searched for Jennifer Inkpen. Virginia Inkpen. Nothing. We even changed the spelling of Inkpen in case it was an Anglicized version of a foreign name. No dice.'

'What about her driver's license and social security card?'

'Oh, she had them. They list her name as Jennifer Inkpen and are obvious fakes, but they allowed the victim to drive a car and open a small checking account at her local Chesapeake Bank.'

'How could she get a job with the group with a fake social security number?' Tish questioned.

'Easy. Rolly Rollinson probably isn't using a background referencing service. Not only doesn't he hire often enough to warrant paying the monthly service fee, but when he does hire, he's hiring based upon talent. Once Jenny was on the payroll, it could take twelve to eighteen months before the Internal Revenue Service noticed that Jenny's number either didn't exist or belonged to someone else.'

'How long had Jenny been with the group?'

'Just eight months.' Reade punctuated his reply by dabbing the corners of his mouth with a napkin.

'Jenny was probably counting on being with another group by then,' Tish noted.

'Even if she wasn't, the IRS would initially conclude that the number was inaccurately reported and the onus would be on the employer to rectify the problem. If Rollinson reported the number as a fake, the IRS would then report it to the Social Security Administration, who would go after Jenny. By that time she could be long gone and living under a different alias.'

'But why? Why, if Jenny was trying to hide, would she seek out a profession that puts her in the spotlight?'

'There's something to be said for hiding in plain sight,' Reade speculated as he used his bread to mop up the last traces of stew from his bowl. 'You also need to keep in mind that Jenny joined an independent, traveling theater group based out of Williamsburg, Virginia, not some established Broadway company where her face might be splashed across a New York City billboard. Although she'd become quite the star on Virginia's summer stock and festival circuit, the odds that Jenny would been seen by someone outside the Tidewater area were slim. And if someone did recognize her, she'd already be on to the next town.'

'Do you think she might have been part of the witness protection program?' Tish suggested.

'As crazy as that idea might seem, I already checked. She wasn't.'

'Justin Dange did say that Jenny had run away from home as a girl. It's probably as simple as that.'

'I don't think so. Jenny Inkpen did more than just run away. She left her entire past hanging somewhere in the ether.'

'Well, there has to be some way to find out who she really was.'

'There is. As soon as Jenny's photo runs in the papers and on TV – I'm hoping Jules will help out with that – someone will step forward.'

'Along with a whole bunch of false identifications.'

'Now you know why I was so grumpy when I arrived. But, thanks to you and your food, I'm feeling much better.'

'A simple matter of low blood sugar,' Tish replied with humility.

'What I'm not feeling better about,' he went on as he pushed the empty bowl aside, 'is the fact that a twenty-two-year-old woman has been shot dead.'

'I know. It's haunted me all day. Twenty-two. When I was that age, I had just graduated college and was preparing to get married. We all know how that panned out.'

'I had just graduated college and was preparing to attend med school. We all know how *that* panned out.'

'Jenny had so much living and learning yet to do. What on earth was she running from?'

Reade threw his hands up in the air and shook his head.

'You know, it might be interesting to hear how Justin met Jenny,' Tish continued.

Reade leaned forward and perched his elbows on the table. 'You're right. He was her entry into the group. What was she doing when their paths crossed?'

Tish mirrored Reade's stance. 'And where was she doing it? Did they meet in Williamsburg or somewhere else? Even if that "somewhere else" wasn't her hometown, it would at least give us a fragment of her background and might lead to something else.'

'It would also be interesting to learn about Rolly's first meeting with Jenny. She never completed a formal job application – we checked – but did she mention prior theatrical experience? What companies had she performed with and where? The most successful liars often pepper their stories with factual elements and shades of the truth. More importantly, did Rolly ever suspect that she wasn't who she claimed to be?'

'While you're at it, someone needs to ask Rolly how he knew Bailey Cassels wouldn't be available for today's performances.'

'What do you mean?'

'I mean that Rolly Rollinson called for an understudy before Bailey Cassels was even taken into custody.'

'Rollinson did that?'

'Yep, I overheard him on the phone this morning on the way to pick up my insulated coffee jug. That understudy took to the stage just forty minutes after you took Cassels to headquarters.'

'I'll question both Dange and Rollinson on those matters first thing tomorrow,' Reade resolved.

'Or . . .' she started.

Reade raised a questioning eyebrow.

'*I'll* talk to Justin and Rolly, as I'll already be at the camp delivering breakfast and might be better equipped to ask questions.'

'Better equipped?'

'Justin already felt comfortable enough to talk to me about Jenny. I could nonchalantly ask him how and where they met, and I doubt he'd think twice about it. As for Rolly, he was coveting your favorite breakfast sandwich today, but opted to remain healthy and order the *Danielle Steel Cut Oats* instead. If I brought along a slider version of that sandwich—'

'Tish,' Reade uncharacteristically interrupted, 'you're a grown woman and capable of making your own decisions, but I don't think you should be questioning anyone in that theater group. I didn't tell you yet, but the wound in Jenny's chest wasn't from some ordinary shotgun. It was from a Colonial-era rifle.'

Tish tried to wrap her mind around the significance of Reade's statement, but words failed her.

'The Richmond Revolutionary Re-Enactors' fife and drum band has been storing their weapons in an equipment shed near the baseball field for the duration of the fair, so that they didn't need to transport them here for their daily drills. The shed was deadbolted and padlocked, but someone still broke their way in and stole the murder weapon.'

'But I thought the re-enactors used blank cartridges for their drills and parades.'

'They do, but they were also giving rifle-loading demonstrations this weekend, so there was a generous supply of both gunpowder and bullets – or, in this case, minié balls. They spin rapidly as they're fired from the barrel and tear up everything in their path.'

'That's why there was so much damage to Jenny's body,' Tish whispered at the memory of the young woman's wounds.

'I'll get you some water,' Reade offered as he rose from his seat.

Tish drew a deep breath and forced the image from her mind. 'No, that's OK. I'll be all right. So, anyone who saw that rifle-loading demonstration could have fired the fatal shot.'

Reade sat back down. 'Yes, but not everyone would have known where the rifles were stored. The baseball field is cordoned off to the general public.'

'The baseball field is only a few hundred yards from the campground. And the equipment shed is even closer.'

'That's why I'd prefer you didn't get involved in this case. Whoever shot Jenny wasn't taking chances. They wanted her out of the way, permanently, and they knew the rifle was the best way to do it. Whoever broke into that shed didn't use a pair of bolt cutters and a lock pick; they broke the door down. It was as if the murderer flew into a rage and needed to get that rifle at any cost.'

'I understand your trepidation, Clemson, but it's not as if I'll be alone. You and your team will be at the campground the entire time I'm delivering breakfast.'

'Tish, everyone knows you run the café down the road. The murderer could just wait until you're back there to strike. Look what happened to Jenny. Look what happened to you during the Sloane Shackleford case.'

'I don't want to risk a repeat performance of either event, but if the murderer is as angry and violent as you describe, shouldn't we be doing everything in our power to stop him or her? We don't know the motive behind Jenny's murder, so we can't say that this person won't kill a second time.'

'I agree, but—'

'You said yourself that my involvement in both the Broderick and Shackleford cases made a difference. Let me make a difference again.'

Reade drew a deep breath. 'Look, I truly value your investigative skills and I would like nothing more than to have you on the case, but I need to be honest here. If something were to happen to you—'

Schuyler Thompson suddenly appeared at their table, dressed in a black overcoat and suit. 'Jules told me I could find you two over here, talking shop.'

Tish smiled broadly before standing up and planting a kiss

on the attorney's lips. 'Hey, you. I didn't expect to see you tonight.'

'I didn't expect to be here, but I tried calling you and kept getting voicemail, so I thought I'd pop by on my way home. Hi, Clem.'

'Hey, Schuyler,' the sheriff returned the greeting.

Tish reached beneath her coat and pulled her phone from the back pocket of her black denim trousers. 'I'm out of charge. Sorry about that.'

'That's OK. I thought it was probably something silly like that, but I still wanted to check and make sure.' He glanced between Tish and Reade. 'Things seemed pretty intense when I came over here. Is something going on?'

'No,' she nervously denied. 'I mean, yes . . . a member of the theater group was murdered.'

'Tish found the body while delivering breakfast this morning,' Reade added.

'You discovered the body?' Schuyler turned to Tish, his eyes wide. 'Are you OK? Why didn't you call me?'

'You were at a funeral. I didn't want to disturb you. Nor did I think it was appropriate for your cell phone to ring, in the event you had forgotten to turn off the sound.'

'I actually had my phone switched off.'

'Then I wouldn't have gotten through to you anyway.'

'But I would have gotten your message when I checked my calls later in the day.'

'What good would that have done? It would only have caused worry and there was no need for it. I'm tired, but fine.'

'You need any help packing up?'

'No, I'm going to balance out the till, take home the dirty pans, run them in the dishwasher, and take care of everything else in the morning.'

'Well, if you don't need me for anything, I'll go talk to a few of the town council members – I saw them over by Sam Noble's booth – then maybe we can leave together? I mean, that is if you and Sheriff Reade are finished.'

Tish looked at Reade, her face a question.

'I don't have anything else to discuss,' Reade replied.

'Neither do I. So, I'll see you at the campground in the morning, Clemson.'

'The campground?' Schuyler questioned.

'Yes, I'm delivering breakfast.'

'Ah,' he dismissed with a smile.

Reade, meanwhile, remained silent.

SEVEN

Despite the day's events and Reade's warnings of danger, Tish slept soundly – almost as if her mind and body had been pushed to their limits and were in desperate need of restoration. She awoke a few minutes before six in the morning, just before her alarm went off.

As was her habit, she went downstairs, switched the coffeemaker on, and preheated the oven for the morning bake before heading upstairs for a quick shower. Before she could make it to the top of the stairs, she heard the sound of keys jangling in the kitchen door.

Expecting to see Celestine, as the baker often stopped by for coffee and chitchat on the mornings she couldn't sleep, Tish took a few steps back and peeked around the stairwell wall to say hello. She was greeted by the puffer-jacketed figure of Mary Jo Okensholt stepping over the threshold.

'MJ? Are you OK?' Tish asked as she descended the stairs.

'Yeah . . . no . . . I've been up all night. Can't sleep.'

Tish put the kettle on and placed a bag of Mary Jo's favorite licorice tea into a mug. 'The divorce?'

'The bills.' Mary Jo hung her purse and coat on a hook behind the kitchen door. 'I don't know how I can ever make it all work. I got a one-hundred-and-ninety-dollar gas and electric bill in the mail yesterday. One hundred and ninety! That's almost half of what I earn in a week working part-time for you and part-time as Augusta May's assistant.'

'Did you try one of those switching sites where they estimate what you'd spend with other utility companies?'

Mary Jo sat down at one of the counter stools. 'I did. The lowest estimate was one hundred and twenty. I made the switch already, but it's still more than I can afford to spend. I spoke with the kids about conserving and they've been really good about things – Kayla's been wearing sweaters instead of turning up the thermostat, and Gregory has even been timing his showers – but I don't know what else to do. I've even been washing the laundry and doing the dishes with cold water, but it's still not enough.'

'The fair has been quite successful so far and business has improved since the cold weather set in. I can float your bill for this month.'

'Thanks. I may need to take you up on that.' Mary Jo frowned. 'But it still doesn't get to the root of the problem, which is that most of the bill is from heating a house that's way too big for us. Glen's office is empty, and now that my parents don't visit, we don't need a fourth bedroom. The three of us barely get the chance to sit together at the kitchen table, let alone use the dining room.'

'Sounds like you need to sell the place.' Tish's statement was offset by the sound of a whistling kettle. 'There's a cute little ranch house for sale on the edge of town. Something like that would be perfect for you and the kids.'

'I would love to move and have a fresh start, but since Glen is paying the mortgage and both our names are on the deed, I can't sell without his consent. And his girlfriend might want to live in the place.'

'Then let them live in it.' Tish poured the steaming water from the kettle into the mug and then passed it to Mary Jo. 'He can buy out your share and you can use the cash to get something smaller.'

'And therein lies the problem. Because I haven't held down a full-time job since before the kids were born, I don't have enough income history to even rent a place, let alone buy one. Nor do I have credit. Even though my name was on the mortgage, everything else at the old place was in Glen's name.'

'Oh, MJ . . .' Tish poured herself a cup of coffee and sat down beside her friend.

'Now you know why I can't sleep. If I pay the heat and electric bill, I may not be able to pay for groceries.'

'Schuyler, Jules, and I would never let that happen.'

'I know, but I just can't see a way out of this hole I'm in.'

'Did you speak to Glen about it? Kayla and Gregory are his children, too. He should share the responsibility for feeding them and keeping them safe and warm.'

'I did talk to him. He's already paying the entire mortgage and the property taxes. He's also paying for Kayla's horseback-riding lessons as well as all the equipment fees so that Gregory can stay on the football team. He said he can't afford any more and still be able to maintain his and Lisa's apartment and other living expenses.'

'Did you mention your troubles to your attorney? He should be able to negotiate some more money when the divorce goes through.'

'Yeah, I put a call in to him yesterday. He'll do what he can to negotiate the best settlement possible. In the meantime, I just need to sit tight. The problem is, if the negotiations don't work out, the divorce is delayed and so is any possible solution to my financial predicament.' MJ sighed. 'Oh, Tish. I really feel as though I'm at the end of my rope this time.'

Tish placed a consoling arm around her friend's shoulder. 'This might sound crazy, but why don't you all stay here?'

'What? You only have a two-bedroom apartment.'

'You stayed here once before.'

'For a couple of nights. Not on a permanent basis.'

'I know, and it will be tight at first, but hear me out. Right now, I have enough beds for everyone, if you and Kayla don't mind sharing the guest bedroom and Gregory doesn't mind being on the sofa bed for a week or two.'

'Just a week or two? How's that possible?'

'Well, you know how I've been wanting to convert that stock room in the back into an office? This is the perfect opportunity. I'll invest in a storage unit to go behind the café and move all the racks out there. Then we can give the storage room a fresh coat of paint. Voila! An extra bedroom. That can be Gregory's room for now.'

'And when Gregory goes off to school?'

'You can have one bedroom, Kayla can have the other, and I'll take the sofa bed.'

'No, we are not putting you out of your bed. That's final.'

'It makes sense for me to be on the sofa. I get up earlier and stay up later,' Tish reasoned.

'Tish, you're a grown woman. What if you need privacy? What if you and Schuyler need privacy?'

'Schuyler has his own place. We can hang there. As for me, the kitchen is my refuge. As long as no one's sleeping on my countertops, all's good. Besides, this isn't a long-term arrangement. With you not paying rent and only paying me for the difference in utility bills, you should be able to save enough for first and last month's rent before Gregory even graduates.'

'If someone is willing to rent to someone without credit.'

'This is a small town. I'm positive that someone in the community would be willing to overlook your credit rating in order to help you out of your situation. And if they don't, then we'll get creative. Either Jules or I will co-sign your lease. In the meantime, you and the kids will be safe and warm – if a bit cramped – and you won't be panicking over a one-hundred-and-ninety-dollar heating bill.'

'No, I'll just be panicking that my kids might eat one hundred and ninety dollars' worth of your food in one sitting.'

'Nah,' Tish dismissed with a smirk. 'They could never eat that much. I buy wholesale.'

With a stomach full of seeded-sourdough avocado toast, the morning bake safely underway, and Mary Jo in a far better headspace than when she first arrived at the café, Tish showered and dressed, prepared the theater group's breakfast order, and headed to the campground.

As she had done the previous morning, Tish deposited the insulated urn and the coffee accoutrements on the central folding table before delivering her breakfast orders. From the corner of her eye, she spotted Sheriff Reade talking to a uniformed police officer outside Jenny's trailer.

Reade looked up and gave a nod in her direction. She returned the gesture before knocking on the Fentons' door.

The morning loomed gray, overcast, and damp, with more than a hint of snow or sleet in the air. Tish shivered and hoped someone would open the door soon, so she could either get out of the cold or move on to the next delivery. Within moments, her wish was answered as the stubbly face of Ted Fenton appeared in the doorway.

'Morning, Tish. Happy to see you haven't been scared off by the police in our backyard. I was afraid one of us might have to walk to the gas station convenience store and see if they had some of those miniature boxes of cereal.'

She smiled. 'I could never allow you to succumb to such a fate.'

From inside the trailer, the voice of Frances Fenton called, 'Ted, don't let that girl freeze out there on our doorstep. Let her in.'

Ted did as he was told and opened the door wide to allow Tish admittance. Stepping into the warm interior of the Winnebago, she was instantly greeted by Frances Fenton. Lounging on the sofa, Frances was dressed in a hot-pink chenille bathrobe and a pair of matching slippers. Her blonde hair had been piled on the top of her head so as not to interfere with the thick layer of moisturizing cream she had spread over her face. In her right hand, she held the television remote control, in her left, a Bloody Mary. 'Come, sit.' She pointed the remote toward the adjacent dinette. 'Have a drink.'

'I'd love to, but I'm afraid I'm on a tight schedule.' Tish placed her bag of food on the dinette table, upsetting a stack of magazines in the process. 'Oh, I'm sorry. Clearly, I'm in need of another cup of coffee.'

'Or a Bloody Mary,' Frances suggested with a husky laugh.

Tish flashed a polite smile and then bent down to recover the periodicals from the tiled kitchen floor. As she stacked them neatly back on the table alongside her bag, she was shocked to discover that each of the periodicals featured an antique firearm on the covers. 'Seems you're quite the military history buff, Ted.'

'Buff is an understatement,' Frances snickered. 'He's a fanatic. Back at home, Ted has an entire room full of guns and Revolutionary and Civil War memorabilia. He'd take over the entire house if I let him.'

Ted Fenton thrust his hands into the pockets of his plaid flannel pajama pants, which he wore with a white T-shirt that accentuated his middle-age paunch. 'It's a hobby. Guy needs something to fill his time when he's not working.'

'You could spend that time and money taking a vacation with your wife.'

'Fran,' he sighed, 'we travel enough for work all year. When we finish work for the season, I don't want to go anywhere.'

'But you go to antique gun shows,' she argued.

'They're relaxing to me. I wander around the booths and talk to other enthusiasts.'

'You could also wander around an art gallery or a garden. Those can be relaxing, too.'

'Maybe to you.'

'The point is, we could choose activities where we could spend time together.'

'We already spend time together.'

'Yes, working time. That's not the same as leisure and relaxation time.' She took a swig of her Bloody Mary.

Rather than get in the middle of a marital dispute, Tish busied herself with retrieving the Fentons' orders from the bag. What was it, she wondered, that made people open up to her about the most intimate details of their lives? She was a cook, not a therapist – a cook who needed to steer the conversation back to antique firearms.

Thankfully, Ted Fenton accommodated. 'Gun shows and battle re-enactments *are* my source of leisure and relaxation.'

Tish handed Ted his breakfast. 'Scrambled eggs, bacon (not overly crisp), sausage links (not patties), white bread toast, and a side of ketchup.'

'Perfect. Thank you, Tish.' Ted grinned.

'My pleasure. You know, it's strange I should stumble upon these magazines today.'

'Strange, how?'

'Well, rumor has it the gun that killed Jenny Inkpen was a Colonial rifle.'

Tish typically wouldn't have disclosed details about the weapon just yet, but she wanted to see the Fentons' reactions.

'Really?' Ted appeared intrigued by the information, but not shocked.

Frances Fenton, on the other hand, tried a bit too hard to make a joke out of the news. 'Ted! Are you certain you left *all* of your collection at home?' She laughed nervously.

'Under lock and key,' he affirmed.

Tish passed Frances a cinnamon bun the size of a small child's head. '*The Bun Also Rises*,' she announced.

'Yum!' Frances cried as she attacked the pastry greedily. 'As you can see, it's my cheat day.'

'So where did the killer get such a rifle?' Ted continued the conversation. 'I find it hard to believe a collector would have done such a thing. We have respect for our weapons.'

'The members of the fife and drum band that opened the fair were keeping their weapons and instruments in an equipment shed on the baseball field. That shed was broken into.'

'Remarkable that the fife and drum band would have active ammunition here.'

'They were performing rifle-loading presentations throughout the fair and brought the gunpowder and bullets for authenticity's sake. They never intended to actually fire the rifles.'

'Really? I had no idea such a thing was going on at the fair; otherwise I would have made time between performances to witness one of the demonstrations.'

'Yes, it does sound as though it's something a gun lover like yourself would enjoy.'

'Guns, guns, guns! All the time, guns,' Frances declared, sending tiny crumbs of cinnamon roll flying from the corners of her mouth. 'Although, if it *was* one of those antique firearms that took out Jenny Inkpen, I might have found a new respect for them.'

'Frances,' Ted chided, 'that's a horrible thing to say.'

'Well, she was a horrible person,' Frances replied drily. 'The six of us were tight before she came along. We were like the Fleetwood Mac of festival theater – without the drugs and partner-swapping, of course.'

'Of course.' Without the drugs and partner-swapping, Tish failed to see any parallel between Williamsburg Theater and the seventies music group, but she played along. 'But there were seven of you before Jenny joined, weren't there?'

'Huh? Oh, you mean Bailey. Yes, er, yes, but he's never been much of a serious actor. And he's only been with us a few months longer than Jenny.' At the mention of Jenny's name, Frances seethed. 'Oh! How Justin could have been so stupid to introduce her to the group is beyond me. Although I shouldn't be at all surprised. That girl had all the men in the group wrapped around her finger.' Frances's eyes slid toward her husband. 'All of them.'

EIGHT

Deeming it wise to leave the Fentons' Winnebago before another spat ensued, Tish knocked on the door of Rolly's camper. Within moments, the group's founder appeared in the doorway, clad in a white T-shirt, a long, heavyweight terrycloth bathrobe, and a pair of flip-flops.

'Hi, Rolly,' Tish greeted. 'Got your breakfast.'

'Morning, Tish. Why don't you come in,' he invited, pushing open the door. 'It's a nasty one, isn't it?'

'It is. Feels like it might sleet or even snow.' She reached into her canvas tote bag. 'So, I have your oatmeal.'

'Terrific.' Rolly rubbed his hands together in anticipation and then held them out to receive his breakfast.

'I also have a surprise.' She placed a wax paper parcel into his waiting hands.

'What's this?'

'I know you coveted Justin's *Portrait of the Artist as a Young Ham* breakfast sandwich yesterday, so I made you a smaller, lighter version using turkey bacon instead of pork, nitrite-free ham, a poached – rather than fried – egg, wholegrain mustard in place of butter, and a wholewheat seeded bun.'

'You could have skipped all that.' Rolly laughed. 'I'd have eaten it regardless.'

'Perhaps, but I wanted to minimize the guilt you might feel.' Tish paused at her choice of words. 'The next time you see your cardiologist,' she quickly added and passed Rolly his bowl of *Danielle Steel Cut Oats*.

He put the oats aside and dove straight into the sandwich. 'Mmm. Delicious. Thank you.'

'Thank *you* for producing two terrific performances yesterday. When I heard Bailey Cassels had been taken into custody just before the afternoon show, I thought for certain the production would be lost. But it turned out brilliantly.'

'Yes, it did. And the evening production was a triumph,' he gloated as he plopped on to a threadbare recliner. 'So good to feel like we're back to normal.'

'Yes, everyone seemed quite jubilant last night. Even Martina and Lawrence fit in quite well.' Before Rolly could comment, Tish noted, 'Lucky for you that Martina's brother was available to fill in for Bailey. That must have been a frantic, last-minute phone call.'

Rolly's mood suddenly darkened. 'Nothing last minute or lucky about it. I asked Lawrence to come here with his sister when I phoned her about Jenny. As I told you, I was already down a lighting guy. I thought an extra pair of hands might come in handy.'

Edie Harmes emerged from the camper bedroom and joined Rolly on the sofa. She was wearing an oversized sweatshirt – presumably Rolly's – that stretched to her knees and a pair of argyle knee socks. 'Morning,' she yawned. 'What's going on?'

Rolly's disposition grew rosier. 'Morning, honey. Tish and I were just discussing our understudies.'

'Yes, I was just saying how lucky you all were to get Martina and Lawrence on such short notice,' Tish explained as she retrieved Edie's pesto-and-spinach-filled *Green Eggs and Ham* omelet from her bag.

'Oh, that wasn't luck. Not with Rolly.' She beamed at her lover. 'He's an excellent planner. He's had Martina and Lawrence on standby for other productions. We've just never needed them until now.'

'It's a shame they were needed,' Tish lamented, 'but they were enjoyable to watch, nonetheless.'

'And sweet, too,' Edie exclaimed as she dug into her breakfast. 'Jenny used to poke fun at my costumes. She'd refuse to wear what I designed for her, but Martina thinks my designs are brilliant. She wants to look at my sketchbook in between shows.'

'Sounds as if you may have found a new permanent cast member.'

'What? Oh, no, there's no need for that.' Edie smiled at Rolly, 'We've agreed that I will be in all the performances from now on. Just like old times.'

'We're going to give *Evita* a shot, with Edie in the lead role. Once we discuss it with the group, of course.' He returned Edie's smile.

'I'm going to get to work on the costumes right away. The gown for the balcony scene will look magnificent on our new posters.'

Not wishing to ruin Edie's visions of grandeur with questions about Rolly's first meeting with Jenny – and suspecting Rolly might not be completely truthful with Edie in the room anyway – Tish made her way to Justin Dange's Travato and knocked on the door.

She was greeted not by the actor himself but by the faint sound of his voice instructing her to enter through the unlocked door. Tish complied.

Stepping into the darkened van, she spied Justin flopped upon the bed. His face was unshaven, his hair uncombed, and he bore the expression of a man in genuine grief.

'Are you OK?' Tish asked, although she was quite certain of the answer.

Justin shook his head. 'I should have protected her. I should have protected Jenny.'

She placed her bag on the nearby dinette table. 'I'm not sure how you could have done that.'

'I shouldn't have let her break up with me. If I hadn't, I might have been with her last night. I might have—'

'You might have been shot, too.'

'I don't think so. The killer would have had no reason to shoot me.'

'You know the killer's motive?'

'If the killer was Bailey – and we all know it was – then, yes. He was sick of Jenny constantly rejecting him and decided to make her pay.'

'And if Bailey isn't the killer?' Tish challenged.

'Of course Bailey's the killer! If not him, then who?'

'You tell me.'

'What do you mean?'

'I mean that it doesn't look as if you slept well last night,' she guessed.

'You're right. I didn't.' He sat up and kicked the covers away, revealing his night-time ensemble of a dark long-sleeved T-shirt and gray track pants.

'I'm no psychologist, but I think if you genuinely believed Bailey killed Jenny, you might have slept better knowing he was locked away in a holding cell. Yet you didn't.'

'I don't know. It's all so confusing. I just kept thinking about Jenny. How she always seemed . . . haunted, for lack of a better word.'

Tish handed Justin the breakfast sandwich and carton of orange juice he'd ordered. 'Eat up. It'll help you feel better.'

Justin obeyed Tish's instructions. After a few bites of food and some juice, the color had returned to his face.

As Justin was starting to feel better, Tish asked the all-important question. 'How did you and Jenny meet?'

'I was in Savannah, Georgia, for a friend's wedding and decided to stay on a few days for a bit of a vacation. It was my first day of sightseeing and I noticed a crowd of people gathered near the fountain at Forsyth Park. At first, I thought they'd gathered to admire the fountain – it is a landmark – but they'd gathered to watch this young street performer give a rather manic one-woman, thirty-minute performance of *Romeo and Juliet*. That street performer was Jenny.

'It was absolutely brilliant. She played all the parts herself and her only costumes were these hats which she'd change to denote each character, although she didn't need the hats because she had all the different voice inflections and mannerisms down pat,' he went on. 'I was completely blown away and was tempted to say something to her after the performance, but she was inundated by fans and tourists taking selfies, so I went on my way. Still, I couldn't stop thinking about her, so that evening, before dinner, I took a stroll around Forsyth Park on the off chance she was still around, but she was nowhere to be seen.

'Figuring she'd gone home for the day, I walked over to The Olde Pink House for a drink in their basement bar before grabbing some seafood by the river. Well, I'd only just stepped foot on The Olde Pink House steps when I heard the voice of a young woman reciting lines from *A Midsummer Night's Dream.* It was Jenny. She'd brought her show to Reynolds Square.

'I watched, enraptured, just as I'd done at Forsyth Park. This time, however, when Jenny finished, I approached her. I was astounded to learn that she actually remembered me from the afternoon audience. Which, in itself, was remarkable. Jenny was always completely wrapped up in her performance. I'd sometimes laugh about an odd thing I'd spotted in the first row of the audience and Jenny was oblivious to it.'

'She lost herself in the character,' Tish paraphrased.

'Yeah, that's exactly it. Anyway, I introduced myself to Jenny and told her I was an actor, too. We started chatting about acting and, eventually, I invited her to continue the conversation at The Olde Pink House bar. She declined and suggested we continue the discussion over *dinner* in The Olde Pink House restaurant instead. Seemed the manager so appreciated Jenny entertaining the restaurant guests outside waiting for tables that he'd give her a free meal between shows. Occasionally, she could even invite a friend to join her.'

'Wait a minute. You ate dinner *between* shows? You mean she was putting on multiple shows in the evening?' Tish was impressed by Jenny's dedication and work ethic.

'Yeah, and during the day. I was totally in awe of Jenny's schedule, too. Until I learned the reason behind it. Jenny was homeless.'

Tish felt her jaw drop.

'Yeah, that's pretty much how I felt. The second night I

saw her, I offered to walk her home, and she led me to some youth outreach center. That free meal from The Olde Pink House six nights a week was the only decent meal she was getting. The tips she earned from her performances went toward purchasing toiletries, makeup, hygiene products, a few articles of clothing, and supplies to create and repair her hats. She'd managed to save up a hundred dollars. She showed it to me to prove she wasn't on the streets because of drugs, but because she'd run away from home before graduating high school.'

'Where did she live before running away?'

'She never said. Somewhere south of Savannah, though. I remember her stating that the second she turned eighteen she took a bus north. So maybe Florida?'

'That must have tough for Jenny. Living on the streets.'

'Yeah, and she wasn't out there for lack of trying. She'd worked at fast-food joints, but her minimum-wage earnings allowed her to either make rent or eat but never both, so she turned to her life's passion to make money and get herself out of the hole.'

'Then you came along.' Tish smiled warmly.

'Yes, then I came along. She was so talented, so vivacious. I couldn't just walk away from her. Not only did she deserve to be acknowledged for her craft, but I knew she couldn't keep on doing what she was doing. I needed to get her out of her situation. Fortunately, I had the means to do so. I told Jenny about the group and suggested that she join us. She was reluctant at first. Very reluctant. Although she wasn't at all happy with her living situation, she was pleased with what she was doing artistically. She had autonomy and control over her work – plus, she was the star.

'I'm sure other members of the group will have mentioned Jenny's love of the spotlight,' he acknowledged. 'It's true – she thrived on being the center of attention – but I think it was less about ego and more about a need for approval.'

'Makes sense,' Tish agreed. 'Even those of us who didn't run away from home still look for our parents' approval.'

'True,' he remarked before taking another bite of sandwich.

'How did you convince Jenny to join the group?' she asked after Justin washed down his sandwich with some orange juice.

'I busked with her. Joined her on a couple of her shows. Demonstrated how nice it could be to work with another actor. It was a hard sell, but she and I had fun, and she eventually agreed to travel home with me to Williamsburg so she could have an audition with Rolly. If Rolly took her on, she'd stay in Williamsburg with the group; if not, I'd pay for her to return to Savannah.'

'You took a chance,' Tish noted. 'You might have lost the girl you were falling in love with.'

'Falling? I'd already fallen – hook, line, and sinker. And I really wasn't taking much of a chance. I knew Rolly would both recognize and appreciate Jenny's talent. I just had to keep the fact that she was homeless under wraps; otherwise, he might question her motives. So I told him she was a family friend I'd reconnected with during the wedding I attended.'

'And Rolly believed you,' Tish presumed.

'He had no reason not to. I'd never lied to him. Plus, he knew I had a thing for Jenny. Heck, he might have had a small crush on her, too. In addition to being amazingly beautiful and talented, she could be quite charming when she wanted. I even caught faithful old Ted Fenton casting an eye in her direction every now and then. That's probably the real reason Frances was so sour toward her. And yet . . .' Justin stared off into space.

'Everything OK?' Tish prompted after several seconds of silence had elapsed.

'Yeah, it's just that when Jenny broke up with me, I thought it was because she felt trapped. Jenny had been out on her own for so long and was so accustomed to doing things her own way that even though she was making a fairly decent living and had a safe place to sleep, she probably felt stifled by the whole situation. Whether it stemmed from her childhood or her time on the street, Jenny had difficulty trusting people, and the more she stayed here with us – with me – the more she was expected to share of herself. The prospect terrified her, I think, so she isolated herself emotionally. And yet there's part of me that questions if I wasn't being too generous in that assessment. I wonder if perhaps the other members of the group were right, after all.' Justin's eyes grew steely.

'Maybe Jenny Inkpen wasn't a damaged, lost young woman trying to find her way in the world. Maybe she was, in fact, just a cold, calculating, manipulative little shrew.'

'He deserved better,' Lucinda LeComte declared as she presented Tish with a steaming cup of detoxifying tea.

'Thanks,' Tish readily accepted, as she felt quite chilled – a result of the weather and, most likely, too much insight into the inner workings of the theater group members. In exchange for the tea, Tish handed Lucinda her egg-white-omelet sandwich with kale, avocado, shiitake, and salmon.

'Oooh.' Lucinda rubbed her hands together excitedly. 'Lean protein, isoflavonoids, calcium, D, complex B-vitamins, and fiber in one delicious package. If only there were cheese on there, it would be perfect.'

'There is cheese on there. Just a sprinkle of feta.'

'Tish, I think this is the beginning of a beautiful friendship,' Lucinda quoted as she sunk her teeth into the sandwich.

'I second that motion,' Tish agreed as a mouthful of deliciously gingery pomegranate-scented tea traveled down her esophagus and into her stomach, bringing much-needed warmth to her body's core.

Looking up from her mug, Tish followed Lucinda's gaze out of the window of her Airstream camper.

'How is he?' Lucinda asked, her eyes fixed on the black Travato van parked next door.

'Justin? He was in a state when I first stopped by, but food and a chat seemed to help him. Still, he's having some difficulty coping with it all.'

'Yes, well, he was in love with Jenny, wasn't he?' She flashed a sardonic smile.

'And you? How did you feel about her?'

Lucinda directed her focus back toward her breakfast. 'I wasn't as vehemently opposed to Jenny's presence as some other members of the group,' she replied as she tore off a small piece of kale from her sandwich and ate it. 'I was excited at the prospect of having a young actress in our merry little troupe. Apart from providing a nice transfusion to this aging bunch, the presence of a new actress granted me an opportunity to share the lessons I've learned during my twenty-plus years of stage experience – a chance to mentor someone the way I'd been mentored when I was a fledgling thespian.' Lucinda frowned. 'Unfortunately, Jenny would have none of it. She was Jenny Inkpen, entertainer extraordinaire! She had little use for advice – disdained it, actually. I confess I had much the same attitude as a young actress, but I at least remained receptive to suggestions. Then again, I didn't have as much confidence – or shall I say haughtiness – as Jenny did when I was her age, which is probably why I got knocked up at age twenty-three.'

Tish felt her mouth drop open, not because Lucinda had accidentally become pregnant at a young age, but because she would share such an intimate detail with a virtual stranger.

'Yes, I know, I "let it all hang out," as they say,' Lucinda affirmed in response to Tish's reaction. 'I see no reason to hide who I am. Plus, it's relevant to my relationship with Jenny. The daughter I gave birth to – and subsequently put up for adoption – all those years ago would have been the same age as Jenny, thus providing me with another reason to want to mentor the girl. And another reason to be disappointed when she rejected my input.'

Something about Lucinda's timeline didn't quite add up. 'Um, you said you became pregnant at age twenty-three, but the playbill for the show says—'

'That I'm in my late thirties,' Lucinda completed the thought. 'The playbill lies. I'm forty-five. Why do you think I've restricted carbs and drink this ridiculous tea?'

'I rather like the tea,' Tish replied honestly, but, then again, perhaps she liked it because she wasn't far behind Lucinda in age.

'You're right, it isn't bad,' Lucinda acknowledged as she stared into her teacup. 'But when you sip it all day long in order to prevent middle-aged belly bloat and an expanding waistline, the flavor can start to wear thin.'

'Well, whatever you're doing is working, Lucinda. You look terrific.'

'Thanks. I only hope I can stave off the ravages of time until I'm ready to retire. I've dedicated my entire life to acting and I've finally reached the point where I feel that I've hit my stride. I'm still learning, of course, but I'm enjoying stepping out of my comfort zone and stretching my boundaries. You can't do that when you're assigned to play the part of someone's mother or grandmother.'

'But you wouldn't always play someone's mother or grand-mother, would you? I mean, you might once or twice a year, but then, eventually, you'd play the leading role again.'

'As long as the audience will still have me, in theory, yes.' Lucinda took a bite of sandwich.

'In theory? But I thought the group was founded on the principle that everyone has something to offer, and therefore everyone in the group takes turns playing the lead,' Tish posed.

'It was,' Lucinda confirmed. 'However, it's hard to make that argument when you're losing roles to a young Audrey Hepburn lookalike with a nineteen-inch waist.'

'And Justin?'

'What about him?'

'Do you feel as though you lost him to Jenny, too?'

The color rose in Lucinda's cheeks. 'What on earth do you mean?'

'I could be wrong, of course, but it strikes me that you possess a certain tenderness for him.'

'We're friends,' the actress protested. 'Just friends. Justin was quite green when he joined the group, so I took him under my wing.'

'A mentorship like the one you discussed earlier?'

'No, not quite. I'm older than Justin, but not *that* much older. When he came on board, I still had much to learn myself. I helped him whenever I could, but a lot of what we learned through the years, we learned together. True, he had a crush on me back in the day, and I rather enjoyed flirting with him, but a seven-year age difference is tough to overlook.'

'I don't know. I don't think seven years is much of a difference,' Tish stated.

'It is when you're the one who's older. I know, I know,' Lucinda sang. 'The world is supposedly a different place now, but an older man getting involved with a younger woman is still far more socially acceptable than an older woman getting involved with a younger man. Older men don't get labeled as "cougars." Look at Justin and Jenny. Look at how many years stood between them, but no one in the group, aside from Frances, batted an eye over their age difference or accused Justin of being a cradle snatcher.'

'Not even you?' Tish challenged.

'No . . . well, maybe I did question his motives. I mean, what was he trying to prove by dating someone that young? But that quickly dissipated, most likely due to the nature of their relationship.' Lucinda explained her change in opinion. 'Whereas one would assume the older party was the predator, it was clear from the start that Justin was the innocent in that relationship. Jenny was a player who only cared about her career.'

'A player?' Tish questioned.

'Yes, she played up to Justin so that he'd introduce her to the group. Once in, she played up to Rolly until he cast her in a leading role. Then, knowing that Ted Fenton is in charge of designing our marketing materials, she fluttered her fake eyelashes in his direction.'

'Wait? Jenny made a move on Ted Fenton?'

'Not a move, just general flirting and flattery. Trying on various costumes – costumes not designed by Edie, by the way – and sashaying around Ted under the guise of seeking his "artistic opinion" as to which skimpy outfit looked best. Well, guess who wound up on this season's posters, pamphlets, and local television ads shortly afterwards?'

Tish raised her eyebrows.

'That's right. Then, after she'd sowed enough seeds of division here and decided it was time to move on, she charmed poor Bailey Cassels into pitching her name to his parents, who are agents.'

'Wait. I saw both Jenny and Bailey after Thursday night's show. She completely shot down his attempts to make a move on her.'

'That was for the sake of appearances, I'm sure of it. No,' Lucinda dismissed with a wave of her hand, 'I overheard them talking on Thursday morning outside the campground showers. Jenny was thanking Bailey for getting his parents to sign her to their agency because they'd gotten her an audition with a repertory theater in Maryland over the Christmas break.'

'So Jenny *was* looking to leave the group,' Tish uttered as her mind processed all the possible ramifications of such a decision.

'That or she was positioning herself to approach Rolly for more money, more influence, and maybe even a partnership.'

Did Rolly know Bailey had conspired to help Jenny leave the group? Was that why he arranged for Bailey's understudy – because he had plans to fire the young actor? 'Did you tell anyone what you'd overheard?'

'Just your sheriff when he was here yesterday. Between dress rehearsals and our first show that night, I didn't have time to warn Rolly. I'd planned to say something to him yesterday morning, but then Jenny was discovered dead.'

If Lucinda LeComte hadn't notified Rolly of Jenny's possible departure, who, if anyone, had? Did Rolly have other reasons to replace Bailey Cassels? Or had he actually told Tish the truth about wanting help with the lighting? Perhaps this didn't involve Rolly at all. 'Is it possible anyone else might have overheard that conversation?'

Lucinda pulled a face. 'Bailey and Jenny weren't what I'd call discreet, but they weren't exactly loud either. And I didn't see anyone else around as I snuck back to camp.'

Tish silently sipped her tea, her mind awhirl with questions.

'I know what you're thinking.' Lucinda's eyes narrowed. 'But if you suspect Rolly, you're wrong. That's not just coming from a loyal member of the group – that's coming from someone who knows his flaws all too well. Rolly has never been the most attentive boyfriend, and he would have made a terrible father to our child, but he's not a murderer.'

Tish felt her jaw drop once again. 'Father?'

'Yes, the daughter I told you about. I put her up for adoption mostly because I thought raising a child would hamper my artistic aspirations, but also because Rolly didn't want to be tied down to a family. It was a long time ago. Long before Rolly and Edie ever became an item,' she reassured Tish.

'Everyone's fully aware of the relationship, but not the product of our little tryst, as I took a sabbatical in Florida during the last few months of the pregnancy. So if you wouldn't mind not letting it get around to the rest of the group.'

'I won't,' Tish promised, before sighing and taking a long sip of tea.

Lucinda echoed the sigh and took a bite of sandwich. 'You see what I mean now, though, don't you? About Jenny? She was poison. Had she stuck around, Justin might have lost his mind, the Fentons' marriage might have broken up, the entire group might have imploded. As much as I'm sorry Jenny went the way she did, she needed to go. She desperately needed to go.'

NINE

'Hold on a minute,' Clemson Reade requested from his spot at the counter of Cookin' the Books Café, where he had met with the caterer for a post-breakfast-delivery debriefing. 'Are you telling me you think Jenny might have been Rolly and Lucinda's child?'

'No,' Tish answered as she poured them both coffee from a glass carafe. The café was unusually quiet for a Saturday morning – a result, no doubt, of the townsfolk conserving both their energy and their money for the afternoon and evening festivities. 'Well, maybe . . . Jenny had dark hair and eyes like Rolly, fair skin and a lithe figure like Lucinda, and she definitely inherited the acting bug from someone. I might also point out that Justin said Jenny had hailed from somewhere south of Savannah. Lucinda had her baby in Florida, so it's not outside the realm of possibility.'

'I'll look into births and adoptions related to Lucinda LeComte in Florida at the time, but I highly doubt we'll find anything. I mean, seriously? Jenny grows up, runs away to Savannah, and just happens to meet Justin Dange, who just happens to invite her to join him in working for her birth parents' theater company? That's an awfully big coincidence.' Reade was skeptical.

'It is, and yet awfully big coincidences occur all the time.'

As if summoned by Tish's words, Jules barreled through the front door of the café. He was dressed in a heavy green parka zipped to his bronzed chin and a matching green velvet elf's cap. Beneath his left arm, he held Biscuit, dressed in a coordinating red velvet Santa suit. 'Tish, Sheriff Reade. Just the two people I wanted to see.'

Mary Jo glared at Jules over the bridge of her reading glasses as she rang up the café's only customers and bid them a good day. 'It's lovely to see you too, Jules,' she quipped.

'Sorry, Mary Jo,' Jules apologized breathlessly before returning his attention to the couple at the counter. 'You won't believe this, but I saw the dead girl last night.'

'Jules, how many times have MJ and I told you not to watch *The Sixth Sense* by yourself? You know it gives you nightmares,' Tish admonished.

'I didn't watch *The Sixth Sense*. I'm telling you, I saw that actress who was just murdered – Jenny Inkpen. She was down at the Piggly Wiggly last night.'

Tish, Sheriff Reade, and Mary Jo exchanged puzzled glances.

'What were you drinking last night?' Mary Jo snickered.

'Nothing. I was stone-cold sober.'

'Are you sure?' Tish joined her friend. 'Back in college, you once spotted Elvis in Leggett's Department Store after drinking half a bottle of Riunite Lambrusco.'

'Elvis?' Octogenarian and neighborhood eccentric Enid Kemper shouted as she hobbled through the front door of Tish's café. 'Never cared for Elvis. But I saw Liberace at The National back in fifty-nine. Now *that* was entertainment.'

'Here for your morning tea, Miss Kemper?' Mary Jo asked. Enid nodded.

'Where's Langhorne?' Tish enquired, concerned by the green conure's absence from his owner's shoulder.

'Too cold for him today. Can't dress a bird in a sweater or a hat or whatever folks put their pets in nowadays.' She slid a judgmental eye in Julian and Biscuit's direction.

'It is a cold one. Are you and Langhorne set for the weather?'

'Oh, yes, Langhorne and I always manage to do just fine,' Enid reassured her, but Tish had her doubts.

Wrapping a couple of miniature quiches in a wax paper bag, Tish slid the parcel across the counter toward Enid. 'There's plenty of vegetables in those. Just to make sure Langhorne keeps up his strength.'

'Oh, Langhorne doesn't need anything so fancy—'

'On the house. You'll be doing me a favor. As you can see, there's no one here to eat them.' It was a blatant lie. Tish could easily have sold the quiches at the fair.

'Well, seeing as you need my help and all . . .' Enid shoved the bag into her tapestry tote and picked up her steaming to-go cup of tea. As she made her way toward the door, she spied Sheriff Reade. 'You're not here to close the place down, are you?'

Reade stood up from the stool before addressing the woman. 'No, Miss Kemper.'

'Good. Only place in town where I can get a halfway decent cup of tea,' she declared before shuffling off into the cold.

'OK,' Tish prompted Jules once Enid was at a safe distance from the café, 'tell us about this Jenny sighting.'

'I left the fair last night and realized on the way home that I needed milk for my morning cereal and some treats for Biscuit, so I stopped at the Piggly Wiggly just a few blocks away from the park. The place was packed with other fairgoers picking up odds and ends, so I left Biscuit in the car rather than risk him being trampled. Well, I was in the beer and wine aisle—'

'Knew it!' Mary Jo joked.

Jules wrinkled his nose and bared his teeth in mock anger. 'Since it had been an ex-*haust*-ing day, I was looking at a nice Malbec to enjoy with a hot bath. While I was reading the wine label, I suddenly felt someone jostle my shoulder. I looked up and it was her! It was Jenny.'

'You mean it was someone who looked like Jenny,' Reade corrected.

'No. I'm telling you, it was her. She had no makeup on, her hair had been cut really short, almost like a buzz cut, and she was dressed in a hoodie, jeans, and a down vest, but it was definitely her. She had the same doe eyes and delicate features, and she even moved the same way. I watched as she walked away. It was definitely Jenny.'

'That's impossible,' Tish reasoned. 'Jules, Jenny is dead.'

'On a slab, in the morgue,' Reade added.

'Are you positive you weren't drinking?' Mary Jo reiterated.

'For the last time, I wasn't drinking. You can bet I did when I got home, though. And I do understand how preposterous the whole thing sounds, Sheriff. I'm a journalist, for heaven's sake. But I'm telling you the truth. I saw Jenny Inkpen alive last night.'

'If I'm ever resurrected from the dead, I hope I have somewhere better to go than the local Piggly Wiggly.' Mary Jo sighed.

Jules nodded. 'I know. And buying boxed macaroni and cheese and Pop-Tarts of all things.'

'Kid's food,' Tish lamented.

The group fell silent for several seconds at the stark realization that Jenny Inkpen wasn't very much older than a child.

'I'm going to bake more bread for the fair.' Mary Jo excused herself and retreated to the kitchen.

'I believe you saw what you say you saw, Julian,' Sheriff Reade addressed in a quiet voice. 'But it couldn't have been Jenny Inkpen. There has to be some logical explanation for it.'

'Yes, I know,' Jules agreed. 'Are y'all sure the woman in the morgue is Jenny and not someone made-up to look like her?'

'Positive,' Tish asserted. 'I found the body. She and I had come face to face at the booth the night before her death. It was definitely Jenny lying dead in that trailer. I'll never forget her face.'

'And I won't forget the face of the girl in the Piggly Wiggly. I saw Jenny the night before she died too – I served her coffee. And I'm telling you, if it wasn't Jenny I saw last night, then it was someone doing a mighty fine impersonation.'

Reade drank some of his coffee before interjecting, 'OK, Julian. I'll investigate this doppelgänger at the Piggly Wiggly. However, I need you to promise you won't breathe a word of it to anyone who isn't in this room. That especially includes your news broadcasts. The last thing I need is the entire town thinking I lost a corpse.'

'Oh, believe me, honey, I'm not about to go on the air with any of this. People already think I'm crazy for getting wiped out by a snowplow outside the Edgar Allen Poe Museum last winter. Telling them I saw a dead girl buying Kraft Dinner would get me banned from the newsroom and a six-year stint in the sanitorium.'

'Good. I'll send an officer around the Piggly Wiggly to see if anyone knows the young woman you described or has noticed her shopping there before. For all we know, she could even be a relative of Jenny's.'

'Didn't you already notify her relatives?'

'No.'

'Why not?'

'Um, off the record?'

'Absolutely.'

'We have no idea of the victim's identity.'

'You have no idea . . .' Jules's hazel eyes flared, and he wagged a warning finger. 'I come in here saying how I saw Jenny Inkpen at a convenience store last night and y'all tell me I'm wrong because Jenny Inkpen is dead, on a slab, in the morgue. Then, in between asking me if I've been drinking, y'all treat me like I'm your crazy old Aunt Velma who crochets toilet-paper cozies, smells like mothballs, and talks to squirrels. Now you're saying the dead girl might not even be Jenny Inkpen, after all. Are y'all gaslighting me or what?'

Tish quieted her friend. 'What Sheriff Reade meant to say is there is no Jenny Inkpen. She doesn't exist – at least not this incarnation of her.'

Jules narrowed his eyes. 'Then who's in the morgue?'

'We don't know,' Reade confessed. 'The ID in the dead woman's trailer was forged and we've yet to get a lead on who she was or where she came from.'

'What do you think? Was she FBI, CIA, M6?'

'That's MI6,' Tish corrected. 'The M6 is a motorway in England.'

'Oops! Hey, you don't think Jenny was KGB, do you, Sheriff? The Russians are everywhere these days, you know.'

'No.' Reade's facial expression swayed between disbelief and amusement. 'I think she was simply using an assumed name.'

'Hmm, guess we should have seen that coming. Inkpen? What kind of name is that? Oh!' Jules exclaimed. 'Maybe Inkpen is an anagram of her real name. Let's see . . . Pinken? Penink? No, that's just as bad as Inkpen. Knipe? No, that's missing an "N."'

'Jules,' Tish interjected. 'I don't think—'

'Oh, I know! Inkpen is a substitute for her real name, which is similar to that of a manufacturer of ink pens. Let me think, who manufactures pens? Parker . . . Cross . . . Faber-Castell? No, they're just pencils, aren't they? Papermate . . . no, that doesn't work. Bic . . . could be short for Bickford. Yes, Jenny Bickford.'

'I'll, um, be certain to look into those possibilities,' Reade stated. 'In the meantime, if you could help out by broadcasting Jenny's photo, asking her family members to call my office, I'd greatly appreciate it.'

'Consider it done.' Jules smiled. 'On that note, I'd better stop by the newsroom and add that to tonight's schedule. Tish, are you heading to the fair right now?'

'No, I thought I'd warm up a bit first,' she replied between sips of coffee.

'Good move. I have an electric heater I keep by my desk. I'll bring it by the booth later. I'll see you in, say, an hour or so?'

'Sounds great. I just hope it doesn't snow,' she added to get Jules's proverbial goat.

'It won't. There's absolutely no snow in the forecast. It's meteorologically impossible.' And with Biscuit tucked beneath his arm and more than a bit of smugness, Jules made his exit.

'Thanks for your patience,' Tish said to Reade after Jules left. 'I know Jules's outside-the-box, stream-of-consciousness ramblings can seem odd to those who aren't well acquainted with him, but those strange ideas of his can be quite helpful. You know, he actually suspected Callie Collingsworth was named after a soap star two minutes after meeting her.'

Reade laughed. 'Sounds like maybe I should ask him to join the team.'

'Only if you don't mind him interviewing your deputies on live TV and hanging a disco ball over his desk.'

'The disco ball is fine. The interviewing? Not so much. But, seriously, I don't mind his odd suggestions. A change of perspective can help you view things in a different light. And, quite frankly, the idea that the name Inkpen was derived from the victim's real name isn't too far out there. As I said to you yesterday, liars pepper their stories with elements of the truth. That said, I won't hold my breath for a Mr and Mrs Rollerball to step into my office, asking to identify their daughter.'

'How about the Montblancs?' Tish grinned.

'They're sketchy, too.'

'Sketchy?' she groaned.

'Hey, Tish,' Mary Jo called from the kitchen. 'You want to check this gingerbread you made? I don't want to overbake it.'

Tish excused herself and joined Mary Jo in the kitchen. She returned with a half sheet pan of deeply aromatic molasses-colored cake.

Reade smiled and shook his head. 'My God, I haven't had real gingerbread – the cake, not the cookie – since my grand-mother was alive.'

'Really? Every year I debate whether I'm going to make it, but then as Christmas gets closer, I start to crave it. Not just the taste, but the smell.' She placed the hot tray on a wooden trivet.

'The smell is incredible. Is it a family recipe?'

'No, my mother and grandmother weren't big into cooking or baking. They put healthy meals on the table and had their specialties, but they weren't as obsessed as I am. When I was in junior high, my folks separated and my mother went back to work, so I pitched in getting dinner ready on weeknights. Then, when I was sixteen, she fell ill with a degenerative muscular disease. She could barely lift her arm to brush the hair on her head, so I took over all the cooking, as well as the cleaning, and the laundry. My grandmother would come by the house to nurse my mom until it all became more than she could handle.'

'I'm sorry.' Reade stared down into his coffee cup.

'Don't be. I taught myself to cook because of it. I discovered my passion.'

'If you don't mind me asking, where was your father during all of this?'

'Oh, he and my mother reconciled after her diagnosis and he moved back into the house, but he did shift work at the local factory, so he was rarely home.'

'Still, it must have been comforting to have him nearby during that difficult time.'

'It was. Until I discovered he was having an affair with my mother's nurse.' Tish bit her lip and refilled their coffee cups.

'I'm sorry your mother had to endure that in addition to her illness.'

'My mother never found out. I never told her.'

'I'm sorry *you* had to endure that.'

'Don't be. Had I told her, it would have broken her completely. That would have been worse.'

'Families.' Reade exhaled noisily.

'Families.' Tish raised her mug high in salute. 'And what about yours? You've spoken of your grandmother twice since I've met you, but you've never mentioned your parents.'

'The last time I saw my parents was Christmas morning, 1983. I woke up anticipating presents under the tree, but instead found them unconscious from a mixture of pills and booze, surrounded by parts of the bicycle Santa was supposed to bring me. I went into the kitchen and called my grandmother. She arranged for the local police to bring me to her house and I never went back.'

'I'm so sorry, Clemson. Had I known, I wouldn't have—'

'No, please, don't be sorry,' Reade soothed. 'It was a turning point in my life, and a good one. My grandmother was on a fixed income, but I always knew she was there to love and support me. And those cops who collected me? I'm one of them now. Granted, I started out wanting to be a doctor, but I have no regrets about where I am now. I haven't rescued any kids from negligent parents, but I like to think that I help out the community by enforcing the law while not trampling on anyone's rights or souls.'

'Well, I haven't been here long, but I think you're doing a great job.'

'I've lived here nearly twenty years, and you've done a terrific job,' Mary Jo shouted from the kitchen, prompting Tish and Reade to laugh.

'Well, since you've both given me a high job approval rating, may I have a slice of gingerbread?' he asked.

'Sure. I usually top it with cinnamon-scented whipped cream, but it's still too warm for that.'

'I don't care. I never could wait until it was cool – which is why my grandmother dubbed me "asbestos mouth."'

Tish grabbed a serrated knife and sliced into the warm cake. 'Would you like some, Mary Jo?'

'Oh, I shouldn't. I had cookies last night.' Mary Jo emerged from the kitchen, wiping her flour-dusted hands on her apron. 'But you know how I love your gingerbread.'

'I do.' Tish positioned a square of gingerbread on a white plate and handed it to Reade before slicing another one.

'The first time you ever baked it for me was sophomore year of college. Neither of us could afford to go home for Thanksgiving, so we drove Jules home to West Virginia and had dinner with him and his mother, then we returned to the dorm Friday morning and, in between studying for exams, decorated our room with Christmas lights and used the shared kitchen to bake treats.'

'Feeding people even then,' Reade remarked and plunged a fork into the gingerbread.

As Reade and Mary Jo chatted and devoured their gingerbread, Tish spied Schuyler in the parking lot. Excusing herself, she left the counter and greeted him at the door with a kiss. 'Good morning.'

'Morning.' He returned the kiss and slid both arms around her waist. His face was cold, but cleanly shaven and redolent with musky aftershave. 'I thought I'd try and catch you before you headed off to the fair.'

'I'm glad you did. Can I get you some coffee?'

'No, thanks. I filled my travel mug in the Keurig before I left the house. But something smells good.' He inhaled deeply and undid his cashmere scarf and unbuttoned the top two buttons of his navy Chesterfield coat.

'Gingerbread. Fresh from the oven.'

Reade and Mary Jo looked up from their plates and gave a wave in Schuyler's direction.

'Yum. Looks like I'd better act fast. Would you mind if I steal a piece to go with my lunch later?'

'Of course not. Where are you headed?'

'Well, unless you need me to help out today, a town council meeting. There may be some zoning law changes coming next year and I want to be prepared. But if you need a hand, I'm more than happy to stick around.'

'No, I should be fine. I have Jules and Celestine, and since the café has been super quiet, I'll probably bring MJ along. I know Charlotte's just seventeen, but she's learned enough to hold down the fort here.'

'Sounds as though you're covered, then.' Schuyler wrapped his arms around her waist and bestowed upon her another kiss.

'Yeah, um, speaking of Mary Jo' – her voice sank to a whisper – 'can I talk to you?'

'Yeah, sure.'

With a quick word to Mary Jo and Reade, Tish led Schuyler upstairs to her apartment. 'As you know, Mary Jo has that great big split-level she's now running on her own. Although Glen is paying the mortgage and for the kids' activities, Mary Jo's responsible for all the utilities and taxes and she's falling behind.'

'Yeah, that's a tremendous burden. Does she need a loan? I'd be happy to give her one.' As if to show his earnestness, Schuyler reached under his coat and into his trouser pocket.

'No.' Tish rethought her words. 'Well, yes . . . but I already promised her one. Just to cover this month's gas and electric bill.'

'Can you float that on your own? I mean, you're just getting your business off the ground.'

'I can float it, for now. What I wanted to tell you, as my landlord, is that I invited MJ and the kids to stay here until they can get back on their feet.'

'I think that's an excellent idea. It gives her a fresh start in a new environment, some breathing space from the bills, and an additional person to help with her parenting duties or just for support. The only problem it doesn't fix is the property tax, for which MJ will still be responsible, even if she's living here, but filing for an abatement should resolve that.'

'An abatement,' Tish repeated. 'Could you help us with that, or do we need to contact an accountant?'

'It's a simple form. I'll pick one up while I'm at the town hall for the meeting.'

'You're wonderful. Do you know that?' She smiled.

'I'm not wonderful. Just in love with you.' He returned the smile and pulled her close. 'If it's OK with you, I'll have a new lease drafted to include MJ. That might sound finicky to you—'

'Not finicky, just "attorney-ish."'

'But it's protection for all of us. With her name on a lease, MJ can get a renter's insurance policy that will protect her belongings in case of fire or theft. Likewise, with her name on the lease, my insurance will cover any damages should her kids accidentally break through a wall with a field hockey stick. But, more importantly, a lease gives MJ more security. If she's a co-tenant, she can go on living here even if you don't.'

Tish was dumbfounded. *Live somewhere else? When her business, blood, and livelihood was rooted in the kitchen and dining area downstairs?*

Schuyler watched Tish's face and broke into a broad grin. 'That last part wasn't an eviction. It was a proposal.'

'A proposal?'

'Will you move in with me?'

Tish was thunderstruck. 'What?'

'Move in with me.'

'I–I don't understand.'

'I'll try to make it clearer. Move in. With me. Move. In. With. Me. I've changed the pacing, but you're still looking at me with a question in your eyes, so maybe I'll change the words. Please share my humble abode. The two of us cohabit-ating at my dwelling place would give me great pleasure. My house is empty without you in it. Have you got the idea now?'

'But my business, my café, my kitchen are all here.'

'And they'll still be here, even if you live elsewhere. You'd simply need to drive your little red car five miles or so to get to them.'

'I don't know, Schuyler. I've only just begun to get settled into this place.'

'But now with Mary Jo and her kids moving in, you'll be "unsettling." That's the wrong word, I know, but everything you've put into place is going to be undone. Not intentionally, of course. It's just the nature of the beast.'

'I know.' Tish meandered over to the sofa and plopped down on to it.

'Let them have this place to themselves. You'll still be around to help them through things; you'll just be outside the chaos. In fact, although you'll have to drive to work in the mornings, you'll gain more time in the end. Those Monday mornings you spend catching up on laundry? I'll have done it on the weekend. Those days when you're running the café and a catering job simultaneously and are too tired to even think of cooking anything else?' Schuyler waved his hand in the air and sat down beside her. 'Your boy here will have fixed your favorite salmon supper or have ordered from that Italian place in Ashland that you like so much. And did I mention the foot rubs?'

'That does sound tempting,' Tish conceded as she leaned her head on Schuyler's shoulder. 'I appreciate your offer – your very sweet, very lovely offer – but I'm just not sure I'm ready.'

'But you're ready to share this space with three other people?'

Tish looked Schuyler in the eye. 'In theory, yes. In practice, it will be difficult. I was thinking of moving my storage room to an outbuilding and then converting the storage room to an office/bedroom.'

'Orrrrr,' he sang, 'you could move in with me. I have three bedrooms, one of which could be your office. You can have free rein in the kitchen, too. Rearrange it to suit you and your needs. Hell, make over the whole condo – I don't care. All I want is you.'

Tish teared up. 'I love your proposal. I love you. I just feel as though it's too soon.'

'My parents got married two weeks after meeting each other.'

'You're talking about two different people living in a

different time. When you and I met, we said we wanted to take things slowly.'

'We did. And we have. In a way.'

'Moving in together after only four months of dating isn't taking things slowly.'

'Maybe not,' Schuyler acknowledged. 'But I don't think that's a valid reason for saying it won't work.'

'I never said it wouldn't work. I said I feel rushed.'

'And maybe that's the answer. Maybe we "unrush" you. How about you spend a little more time at my place this January? Get used to being there, tweak some things to make it feel more like home. Feng shui the living room, alphabetize my refrigerator—'

Tish laughed. 'I've already organized it by height.'

'That's true. Then we'll buy a houseplant together or something.'

'Oh, you don't want to have a houseplant with me. My cooking skills never have translated to gardening skills.'

'Well, then we'll get some throw pillows or a new mixer. In the meantime, you'll still have your time here in the café, with Mary Jo, Jules, and the kids. Let's make it a slow transition with an eye on you eventually moving in with me, instead of a sudden move. Would that work?'

'That sounds perfect. Thank you for being so understanding.'

'Why wouldn't I be? I want you to move in with me, but I'm not going to strong-arm you. As long as we're in agreement that you'll eventually move in, I can wait because you're worth waiting for.'

TEN

'I can't believe you turned him down,' a perplexed Mary Jo told Tish as the former replenished the small change of the fair booth till. 'It's like you're actually looking forward to being crammed into an apartment with me and two teenagers.'

'Well, I think it's romantic,' Jules broadcast while stirring his famous mulled wine. 'Him willing to wait for you until you're ready.'

'It's not romantic. It's what real men do,' Celestine announced. She had brought along a fresh batch of cakes and was loading them into the glass countertop case.

'Aww, did Mr Rufus wait for you?' Mary Jo posed.

'Nah, I got pregnant just about a second after he looked at me,' Celestine guffawed. 'Nine months later, though, he waited with me and held my hand through twelve hours of labor. He waited with me for the births of the other three as well, but they took no time at all.'

'Amazing, isn't it? Gregory's delivery was so difficult, I swore I'd never have another child. I did, of course, and Kayla's delivery was a breeze.'

Celestine nodded. 'Mine got easier with each go. Number four was so fast, Mr Rufus likened her to an airplane passenger zipping down one of those inflatable emergency evacuation slides.'

'Mr Rufus has a way with words,' Tish noted.

'And, apparently, his eyes,' Jules joked.

Amidst boisterous laughter, Tish set about adjusting the temperature beneath her kettles of stew and alphabet soup. As her friends continued to discuss children, marriage, and life in general, she took note of Sam Noble approaching the booth. He was dressed in his usual outfit of insulated flannel work shirt, jeans, and apron, and in the company of a young girl.

'Morning, Sam,' she greeted.

'Mornin', Tish.'

'And who do you have with you?'

'This is my daughter, Lily. Seeing as she enjoyed your lunch so much, I thought she should drop by and say thank you.'

Tish bent slightly at the waist so as to be closer to eye level with the youngster. 'Hello, Lily. Nice to meet you.'

The raven-haired girl dug her hands deep into the pockets of her bubblegum-pink, fur-trimmed puffer jacket and stared at Tish with wide brown eyes but said nothing.

'Lily, what do we say to the nice lady who made you that delicious lunch yesterday?' Noble prompted.

'Thank you,' Lily recited in a near-whisper.

'You're welcome. I'm glad you enjoyed the lunch and the show. Will you be here for another show later today?'

Lily nodded.

'Good. Now that I know who you are, I'll make sure Mom doesn't pay for your lunch. And maybe we'll have a special treat in store, if Mom approves.'

'I can't let you do that, Tish,' Noble argued.

'Don't be silly, Sam. Had I recognized your wife and daughter in yesterday's lunch crowd, I wouldn't have charged them in the first place.'

'That's mighty kind of you.'

'We both own restaurants in this town and we're both vendors at the fair. I know had I or any member of my staff popped over to your booth, you'd have done the same.'

'I would have, but I still thank you.' Sam looked down at his daughter. 'What do you say we get set up for the morning?'

Lily nodded and the two walked off hand in hand. 'See ya, Tish,' Sam called.

'Bye, Sam. Bye, Lily.'

At mention of her name, Lily turned around and stared over her shoulder at Tish, until a gentle nudge from her father urged her to look forward.

Tish watched as they walked toward Sam's booth and her thoughts went instantly to Jenny Inkpen. Had Jenny, in her childhood, ever felt safe clutching the hand of a caring parent or adult? Or had her early years been filled with neglect and abuse? What had occurred in her short life to drive her away from family and home, to change her name, bury her life story, and seek sanctuary in the streets? What trauma had Jenny endured to make her consider a homeless shelter a safer place than home?

Home. Once again that word came flooding into Tish's consciousness.

Although her parents' separation and her mother's subsequent death had brought pain and uncertainty into Tish's young life, there was always a sense of home. Be it the apartment she shared with her mother, her grandparents' Cape Cod house, or even the noisy inner-city flat her father rented after the separation, there was at each residence a sense of safety and security. So strong was this sense of security that, on difficult days, Tish still longed to crawl on to her grandparents' well-worn sofa, snuggle beneath one of her grandmother's crocheted afghans, and watch one of her grandfather's favorite detective films.

And yet the word 'home' had a connotation of loss and sadness as well. After ten years of marriage, Tish split from her husband and sold the Richmond home they shared together. The silver lining of that loss was that the money from the sale enabled her to start the café. The café that was her lifelong dream. The café she had just started to call home – the home that Schuyler was asking her to leave.

Perhaps that was the real reason Tish was reluctant to agree to move in with Schuyler. She had, after her divorce, been seeking another 'home' and she thought she had found it in her little apartment above her beloved café, but now she was being asked to leave that space before she could finish putting down roots.

It wasn't as if Tish doubted her ability to 'root' at Schuyler's condo. Indeed, she liked the idea of seeing him each evening and recounting the day's events over dinner, but she was concerned how her absence would affect the 'home' her café offered to its employees and patrons.

Tish was roused from her thoughts by the sound of the ladle Jules used to serve his mulled wine crashing upon the counter. 'What's *he* doing here? I thought the police had him in custody.'

Tish looked up to see Bailey Cassels entering the fairground from behind the stage. His hair was uncombed, his face unshaven, and he wandered the grounds like a lost soul, with his head hung down and hands thrust deep into the pockets of his navy-blue parka.

'Mind if I remove my barman hat and replace it with my newsman cap?' Jules asked.

'Only if I can play detective first,' Tish replied.

'Even better. Then I can really get the scoop.' Jules rubbed his hands together.

'You can listen in, but the conversation will be off the record.'

Jules threw his hands down at his sides. 'You know, people in this town really have to start being more open.'

Tish cast him a side-eye before calling out to the forlorn actor skulking down the fair midway. 'Bailey! Bailey Cassels!'

The young man was stirred from his reverie and looked up at Tish, his face quizzical.

'Come here,' she beckoned.

He obeyed and approached the booth, albeit with trepidation. 'Hi, Tish. Look, I'd love to talk to you, but if you're going to ask me about my stay with your illustrious police force, then "Bye, Felicia."'

'Who's Felicia?' Celestine demanded.

'It's a way younger people tell someone to get lost or go to hell,' Mary Jo explained.

'Why not just tell them to get lost or go to hell?'

'Umm . . .'

'I was actually going to offer you coffee and food,' Tish explained.

'Oh. That's nice of you,' Bailey said appreciatively. 'You're not even open yet, are you?'

'A formality. Everything's been prepared ahead of time. You're just getting in before the rush. So, Jules will get you a beverage: tea, coffee, cocoa, flavored coffee, soft drink . . .'

'A medium gingerbread coffee, please,' Bailey ordered. 'With soy milk. Do you have soy milk?'

'I do. Now for food, would you like a turkey, apple butter, sage, and cheddar sandwich or a modified ploughman's lunch of salad, Stilton, and bread?'

'I'll go with the turkey. What sides do you have with that?'

'It comes with an orange and two Christmas pudding bon-bons.'

'Can I swap out the dessert for a cup of soup?'

'Sure. I have Peter Cratchit's alphabet soup – which is a vegetable soup with alphabet-shaped pasta – and Jacob Marley's bean and barley.'

'Seeing how I've recently been called "childish" on occasion, I'll go with the alphabet.'

Tish refrained from comment and ladled a portion of soup into a recyclable cardboard container. When finished, she packaged it with the rest of the boxed lunch and some bamboo cutlery.

'How much do I owe?' Bailey asked.

'Nothing. Compliments of the interim mayor's office for all group members.'

'I, um, I'm no longer with the group.'

'What? Really?'

Bailey nodded. 'Fired. Effective immediately. Rolly's orders.'

'On what grounds?'

'Does Rolly need grounds? He's the head of the group. What he says goes.'

'So he didn't provide grounds for your firing?'

Bailey added soy milk and sugar to his coffee and took a sip. 'Nope. I figure he was jealous because I was tight with Jenny.'

'Oh? Rolly had an interest in Jenny?'

He unwrapped his sandwich. 'Rolly thought he owned Jenny. That's what she was trying to break free of.'

'She was trying to leave?'

'She wasn't at first, but when Rolly re-upped her contract for next season and didn't offer her a raise, she decided to do whatever was necessary.' Bailey took a bite of sandwich and Tish gestured for him to sit at a nearby picnic table.

He gathered up his food while Tish grabbed his coffee cup and escorted him.

'Jenny had been with the group less than a year,' she pointed out as she took a seat. 'I'm not familiar with the entertainment business, but in every other profession, it's customary for an employee to wait at least one year to expect a raise. Perhaps Rolly was going to give Jenny a bonus on her anniversary date?'

Bailey sat down and bit, once again, into his sandwich. 'Mmm, this slays, by the way.' He chugged some coffee to wash it down. 'Rolly was always on the cheap side, but he was extra when it came to Jenny and me. All the money from ticket sales was divided between him and the five older members of the group.'

'Well, they're all partners, aren't they? At least, that's my understanding. They've all been working together for years.'

'Yeah, and it's cool Rolly has their backs, but when you think of how much Jenny did for the group, it was pretty ungrateful of him not to compensate her at all.'

'I know Jenny was the lead in a few productions as of late, but did she play another part within the group?'

Bailey opened the soup container and plunged a bamboo spoon into it. 'Yeah, she was the face of Williamsburg Theater Group. Prior to Jenny being on the billboards and posters, the group's performances only attracted families and blue-hairs. Once Jenny came on the scene, we started selling tickets to millennials, thirty-somethings, and even some teens. And what did she get for it? She got trolled on social media.' He slurped down some soup. 'This soup is lit.'

'Um, thanks?'

'It's a good thing. It means . . . outstanding.'

'Ah, I'll be sure to include that in the café's marketing materials and maybe I'll attract a new audience as well.' Tish smiled. 'So, what did Jenny intend to do about it?'

'Wasn't much she could do.' He bit off another hunk of sandwich. 'I followed her on Instagram, Twitter, Snapchat, and Facebook, and all I ever saw were jealous hags calling her names or old people saying how much better the group was before Jenny was in it. There were even a few who implied she'd slept her way into the group. Jenny reported some of the trolls for online harassment, but it wasn't really abuse per se. More like things to be filed under "Hashtag: Bitter."'

'I'm sorry. I didn't make myself clear. I meant, what did Jenny intend to do about the situation with Rolly?' Tish clarified.

'Oh, that.' Bailey slurped down some more soup. 'Mmm. You know, if my parents had served me this kind of alphabet soup instead of the canned stuff, I probably would have thrown far fewer tantrums as a kid.'

Tish was not at all surprised to learn that Bailey was the sort of child to throw tantrums. 'Thanks. Um . . . getting back to Jenny?'

'Yeah, she, uh, she was auditioning with a company in Maryland over Christmas break. If they made her an offer, she was going to confront Rolly and see if he was willing to match it.'

'And if he wasn't?'

'Then she'd take the better offer and leave.'

'Did Rolly know this?'

'No, we kept it completely confidential.'

Bailey's words were the opening Tish needed. 'How did you know about her audition?'

Bailey went pale and, for the first time during their conversation, he stopped eating. 'How? Because we were seeing each other. I cared for her and she . . .'

'Cared for you?' Tish filled in the blanks.

Bailey dropped his spoon into the container of soup and covered his face with his hands. 'No, I don't think she did. I mean she said so at first, and made a great effort to appear to, and then it all got weird.'

Tish pushed the cup of coffee toward him. 'Here. Drink up. It will help.'

Bailey took the cup between his hands and drew a large sip.

'Better?' she asked.

Bailey nodded. 'Like the audition, Jenny wanted to keep our relationship secret. She knew we'd get backlash from the group, so she went out of her way to put me down in front of them. I'd go out of my way to act like the spurned lover, and then we'd meet after everyone went to bed. That's what happened the night she was killed. When things got weird.'

'And she scratched you on the face,' Tish surmised.

'Yeah, but it wasn't exactly like I told you and Justin,' he blurted. 'Jenny freaked out when I told her that if she was leaving the group, I was going with her. I tried to settle her down, but she was absolutely furious. That's when she scratched my face.'

'That's a far cry from the rough-sex claim you made earlier,' she noted.

'I know. I know I was wrong for saying all that, but Justin – well, I guess I was competing or something. As for the police, I stuck with my story because I didn't want to seem like a loser, and I was afraid if I changed it, they'd detain me.

God, what an idiot I am.' Once again, he buried his face in his hands.

This time, she directed Bailey back to his cup of soup.

He devoured the remnants of the container before speaking again. 'Jenny and I were never intimate. She and I kissed a few times and she made promises, but looking back at how she behaved that last night, it's clear she thought I was inadequate.'

'Then why lead you on?'

'My parents own a theatrical agency. They were the ones who got her the audition. They were also the ones who made certain that if the new company signed Jenny, taking me on as a player would be part of the contract.'

Tish pursed her lips. 'So, when you told Jenny you were going with her if she left, it wasn't—'

'Stalkerish?' He grinned. 'No, it was the truth.'

'But why didn't your parents just allow you to audition?'

'You mean, instead of making me an addendum? Because the last time they left auditions in my hands, this was the best offer I got.' He polished off the rest of his sandwich.

'Once again, do the police know about all of this?'

'No, because, once again, the whole situation made me look like a complete loser.'

'Bailey, this is a murder case, not a men's locker room. If what you've told me is the truth, then you need to share it with Sheriff Reade.'

'Of course it's the truth, but I don't see what difference it makes now. Besides, if I go to the sheriff and change my story, he'll probably detain me again.'

'He won't detain you without the physical evidence to do so,' Tish argued. 'You need to tell him what you told me. This is a murder case. Every detail matters.'

'OK, I'll talk to him after I finish my orange. Murder,' he repeated. 'I can hardly believe it. It seems like a nightmare, and yet—'

'Yes?' Tish prompted.

'Yet it's not surprising. It always felt as though part of Jenny was already dead.'

ELEVEN

'Have a second?' Reade asked of Tish as the twelve o'clock production of *A Christmas Carol* was just getting underway. The opening of the fair had been much quieter than anticipated as families trickled in after a Saturday morning spent sleeping, taxiing children to the final sporting events of the year, and finishing last-minute holiday shopping. It was, to be certain, merely the calm before the storm.

Tish confirmed that she had several seconds to spare and led Reade to the picnic table she had occupied with Bailey Cassels just an hour earlier.

'Ten different email addresses. Ten different user accounts on each of the major social media platforms using said email addresses. All the accounts were accessed via two IP addresses: that of an iPhone 8 used as a wi-fi hot spot and the other a Cox Cable Broadband account. Both the iPhone and Broadband accounts are registered to Mrs Frances Fenton of Williamsburg, Virginia.'

'Frances was Jenny's troll,' Tish deduced.

'There were others, but Frances was the primary commenter and chief rabble-rouser. Most of her comments disparaged Jenny on her appearance and acting abilities, but the nastier ones called her a "tramp," a "whore," and asked, "Whose husband did you sleep with to get your ugly face on a billboard?"'

'Ouch. Well, Lucinda did say Jenny played up to Ted to get her face on the marketing.'

'She did a little bit more than that. We checked Jenny's phone and Ted was texting her.'

'Texting or sexting?' Tish queried.

'Texting.'

'Whew!' She pretended to wipe sweat off her brow with the back of her hand.

'Yeah, I know.' Reade seconded the sentiment. 'His texts

sound relatively innocent. Telling Jenny she looked great during rehearsal or that she gave a strong performance.'

'Um, these texts do correspond with rehearsal and perform-ance times, right? I mean, he wasn't using the "performance" as a euphemism, was he?'

Reade laughed and shook his head. 'You and our IT guy think alike. Yes, the times and dates of the texts align with the performance and rehearsal schedule posted on the Williamsburg Theater website. In addition, Ted's messages never said or implied any impropriety between them. He didn't even comment on the clothes she wore. The texts read more like Ted Fenton was secretly coaching and cheering Jenny Inkpen. As I said, relatively innocent.'

'Unless you're Frances Fenton and you believe your husband is more in love with guns, acting, and theater marketing than he is with you,' she remarked.

'What's your take on the situation?'

'I don't know, but I wouldn't necessarily describe a fifty-odd-year-old man secretly texting a twenty-two-year-old woman as innocent.'

'Valid point,' Reade conceded.

'Did Jenny reply to these texts?'

'No.'

Tish raised her eyebrows.

'Do *you* think they were having an affair?' he asked.

Tish recalled the descriptions of both Justin's and Bailey's relationships with Jenny. 'A physical affair? No, I don't. A "mental" affair – the thrill of someone and something different? The promise and tease of what's to come? Yes.'

'Do you think she strung him along like she did Bailey Cassels?'

'Oh, Bailey went to see you,' Tish assumed.

'He did. Thank you.'

'No worries. Just thought he needed to set the record straight. You didn't detain him, did you?'

Reade shook his head. 'No need. Not only is he innocent, but I'd already ordered him not to leave town.'

'Camping alongside one's former boss,' Tish noted. '*That* should be interesting.'

'Murder does make the strangest bedfellows. So, getting back to Jenny,' he prodded.

'Do I think she was stringing Ted Fenton along? I'm not sure she actually strung Bailey along, or if she was simply afraid of people getting too close, as Justin suggested. But to answer your question, I think she probably laughed at Ted's jokes, listened to his stories, made him feel interesting and clever. All the things Frances hasn't done in a long time.'

'Sad.' Reade frowned.

'It is. For both of them. What do you plan to do about Frances Fenton?'

'I'm going to bring her in for questioning.'

'And Ted?'

'Same thing.'

'Today?'

'As soon as they both get off that stage.'

'There's another performance an hour and a half after this one. If you bring them in, Rolly will have to call yet another two understudies. And I'm not sure they'd arrive in time.'

'So?'

'So, that's not exactly following the interim mayor's orders of allowing the fair to go on without interruption. And unless you plan on making an arrest, you'll have taken three of the seven theater members into headquarters, yet still have failed to solve the case. Not exactly great optics.'

'OK, what do you propose I do?'

'You interview Ted back at the camp and I' – Tish smiled broadly – 'talk to Frances.'

'You're right about the optics thing, but I think *I'll* interview both Frances and Ted, separately, at the camp.'

'Is there a reason you don't want to include me on this one?'

'Tish, you know I don't feel comfortable with you getting so involved in this case.'

'Yes, you say you feel uncomfortable and yet when I give you a lead, you devour it.'

'That's not fair. I've included you in this investigation as I always do. I simply don't want you being in harm's way.'

'And you think I will be with Frances?'

'Frances lives in a house full of antique firearms. She was jealous of Jenny. She created ten different email accounts and numerous online identities just to slander the girl on social media.'

'You think Frances killed Jenny?'

'I think it's entirely possible, especially if Jenny learned about Frances's online activity and confronted her about it.'

'I suppose you're right,' Tish allowed, 'but you know I'll be careful, Clemson. If I get a whiff of anything wrong while talking to her, I'll call you.'

'You actually believe someone like Frances would give you a warning before she murdered you?' Reade challenged.

Several moments elapsed while the pair stared at each other in silence.

'Well, well, there's quite the atmosphere in this little corner of the fair.' Tish and Reade looked up to see Opal Schaeffer, Hobson Glen's resident romance author, approaching their table.

'Sorry,' Tish apologized, her face a pale shade of crimson.

'We're discussing the Inkpen murder,' Reade explained.

'Oh, don't be sorry. It gave me the best idea for the cover of my next book. It's about a cop who falls in love with a prisoner and then tries to rehabilitate them.' Opal tugged the flaps of her knitted bobble hat over her ears excitedly. 'It's the first of my novels to blend romance and suspense.'

'Opal, I've told you a thousand times, I can't pose for your book covers. People don't want to see their law enforcement officers acting like Fabio.'

'You don't have to pose, I took a photo.' She held her phone aloft in a fleece-gloved hand.

'I can't let you use that photo. Not when you're portraying me as a policeman engaging in unethical conduct.'

'You're not the police officer. She is.' Opal pointed at Tish, prompting the caterer to burst into laughter.

'Oh, I think I might need to read this book,' Tish chuckled. 'When does it come out?'

'Alas, not until summer. But I'll save you a copy. It's called *The Shawhunk Redemption*.'

'Sounds like an interesting departure for you.'

'It is, and it will be even nicer when I can give my artist a great concept photo for the cover,' Opal's expression was hopeful.

'I'm sorry, Opal, but I'm afraid I can't oblige. I don't want café patrons to think I'm also in the business of re-habilitating hunks. I hope you understand how embarrassing that could be.'

'It could be fun, too. Sifting through applicants.' She tucked a wayward strand of silver hair beneath her hat with a smile.

Tish felt her face go red. 'Maybe for someone else.'

Thankfully, Opal dropped the conversation. 'So many people expected at the fair today. It's wonderful fodder for me, as you can imagine. I've captured the most interesting faces these past couple of days. They really inspire my stories – faces. Like the two of yours when I first arrived here. Intense, at odds, combative, and yet unified.'

'Against a common enemy,' Reade disclosed.

'Yes, that poor murdered girl. There wasn't a photo included in the article I read, and I didn't see her perform – I've been too busy snapping photos! – but I trust she was quite beautiful. If so, you might want to look for an ex-lover, Sheriff. There are many men out there who try to possess and diminish a young woman who has both beauty and talent.'

'Words from an observer of the world?'

'Words of personal experience. I wasn't always seventy years old,' she added with a wink. 'And I wasn't always married to the love of my life, God rest his soul. No, to find him I had to kiss a lot of toads. Sometimes I had to flee those toads as well, if you catch my meaning.'

'I do and I'll be sure to look into it,' Reade promised.

'Good man,' Opal proclaimed. 'Tish, my winter cabbage is nearly ready to harvest. Would you be interested in some for the café?'

Opal, an avid gardener who produced more vegetables than her single-person household could consume or pickle, often sold her excess produce to Tish.

'Absolutely. I can add it to soups and stews, and a stuffed cabbage special would probably go over well,' Tish replied.

'Wonderful, I'll bring some by the café late next week.'

'Great. Let me know how much I owe you.'

'Nothing. Except perhaps a vegan version of that stuffed cabbage.'

'Consider it done.'

Opal leaned in to give Tish a hug before departing. Her Sherpa clothing and hair smelled of cigarette smoke and patchouli. 'And maybe that photo on a book cover,' she teased.

'Nothing doin'.' Tish laughed.

'Still a nope from me,' Reade rejoined.

'That's OK, darlings. I have a different photo I can use. I came across a doozy at the rifle demonstration the other day.' Opal held her phone aloft for the pair to see.

The photo showed Ted Fenton posing with his finger on the trigger of an antique rifle. Standing at the end of the rifle, with her hands in the air pretending to plead with Ted not to shoot her, stood Jenny Inkpen.

'Ted lied,' Tish gasped. 'He *did* get to see a demonstration.'

'And he wasn't alone, either,' Reade added.

TWELVE

As the day's first performance of *A Christmas Carol* drew to a close, Tish braced herself for the onslaught of hungry audience members and new fair arrivals, while readying herself for her next investigative assignment. Leaving Mary Jo, Jules, and Celestine to serve the first round of fairgoers, Tish supplied the theater company members with their lunches so that they could finish eating before the next curtain call, just a brief ninety minutes away.

Corralling the group behind the booth, Tish doled out their orders. 'Ted. Chicken salad on white, no lettuce or tomato, coke, and a bag of chips,' she called.

Ted Fenton retrieved his lunch to his wife's jeers of 'Boring. Boring!' Seconds after claiming the brown paper bag of food, he was whisked away by Sheriff Reade.

Frances watched as her husband was escorted to the mobile

crime unit. 'Where's your sheriff taking my husband?' she demanded of Tish, who continued to hand out lunches. 'Oh, what has that man done? What has he gotten himself into?'

'I'm sure he's fine,' Lucinda reassured. 'The sheriff probably wanted to double-check something in his statement.'

Frances continued to fret. 'Oh, he's done it now, hasn't he?'

Tish intentionally held Frances's lunch for last, dispensing it after the other cast members had wandered backstage for their break.

'Done it? Done what?' Tish asked as she handed Frances a bag containing the *Ebenezer Scrooge* meal and a bottle of water.

'Killed Jenny,' she sobbed. 'He was infatuated with her. Her youth and beauty, the way she looked at him, how she smiled while he nattered on about guns or search engines or whatever entered his mind.'

Tish led Frances to her car, which was parked just a few yards away. 'If Ted was infatuated with Jenny, why would he kill her?'

'Because she rejected him.'

Tish opened the passenger door and gestured Frances to enter. 'It's warmer and more private.'

Frances nodded and shimmied her way into the passenger seat.

'Jenny rejected your husband?' Tish continued the conversation after sliding behind the driver's wheel and shutting the door behind her.

'Of course she did. She rejected all of them in the end, didn't she? Justin. Bailey. They meant nothing to her. You think Ted would be any different?' She began to sob again. 'My dear, sweet, stupid, lovable, gullible Ted. How could he ever have thought that Jenny might fall in love with the likes of him?'

Tish passed a tissue and the bottle of water from the lunch bag to Frances, who accepted both eagerly. 'But *you* fell in love with Ted.'

'That was years ago, when we were both young and fearless and the world was full of opportunity.'

'And now?'

'We're old, fat, balding, and life is flying by.' She blew her nose into the tissue and wept. 'But I still love Ted, even though we seem to be drifting farther apart by the day.'

'I'm sorry, Frances.'

'I am, too. Oh, the things I've done. My God . . . but I was just so angry.'

'What did you do, Frances?' Tish asked, albeit slightly fearful of the answer.

'I tried to make Jenny's life miserable, so she'd leave the group. Leave Williamsburg. Leave Ted to me. I had no idea things would end this way.'

'How did you make her life miserable?'

'Any way I could I think of while still remaining anonymous. I stuffed our comments box full of negative remarks about Jenny's performances. I left online reviews of our shows stating how much better the group was before Jenny signed on. I harassed her on social media. I even sent Rolly a few emails and letters complaining about how the quality of the performances had gone downhill. I always used assumed names, different handwriting, and different email accounts so I couldn't be tracked.'

'You put a lot of time and effort into your—'

'Campaign?' She flashed a cutting smile. 'It's not like I had anything else to do with my time. Ted was always going to gun shows or re-enactments or working on the group's marketing. So, in the evenings, when Ted would hop on his computer to create a new poster or a post on Facebook, I'd get on my laptop and trash Jenny. He thought I was playing games and looking at costume ideas and recipes on Pinterest, but all the while I was pushing for Jenny's departure. It was a lot of work, though. I loved it when other people would join in on one of my posts because it meant I could sit back and take it easy for a little while.'

'Did Jenny find out what you were doing?'

'No, I don't think so. If she had, she'd have said something. I was also very careful. It made me feel empowered, being able to fool her. I'd see her swan about the stage or the campground and laugh to myself . . . thing is, now that Jenny's gone, I realize how stupid I was. I thought if I could get Jenny out of the group and out of our lives, things between Ted and me would improve. I thought he'd become more attentive, more spontaneous. I was silly enough to think we'd enter a second-honeymoon phase. But she's gone and it's the same as it ever was. Yet somehow emptier.'

Tish passed Frances another tissue and then her salad. 'Here. You should probably eat something before you take to the stage again.'

'What? No one grieves over salad,' Frances dismissed.

'No, I suppose you're right.' She retrieved the wedges of Stilton and Brie from the bag and spread each of them on a half of warm baguette.

'That's more like it,' the actress approved, eating heartily between sniffs. The food and water both calmed her considerably. 'Thank you, Tish.'

'I didn't do anything but give you your lunch.'

'No, you listened. And you've been kind.'

'That's nothing,' Tish dismissed, feeling horrible for imposing on the Fentons' private domestic drama.

'No, it isn't. I've been feeling very much alone these past few years. I'm friends with the gals in the group, but when your husband is also a member, you can't really tell them anything for fear of people taking sides. It's been good to talk to an objective party.'

'I think we've all felt alone from time to time.'

Frances ate more Brie, her gaze fixed upon some indeterminate spot in the distance. 'I was so afraid of losing Ted that part of me just cracked, I guess. When I think of everything I did . . . the times I'd sneak into the bathroom of our RV to scribble comments on our feedback forms, each in a different hand. And online, all the different accounts and passwords. I actually spent money on a program that would remember all my passwords. Can you believe it? I must have been insane. Obsessed. Just as Ted was obsessed with Jenny, I became obsessed with her, too. I wanted her gone. I even wished her dead, and now she *is* dead. Oh, God.' She broke down again.

Tish placed a consoling arm on the woman's shoulder and tried to calm her. 'Frances, do you honestly think Ted murdered Jenny?'

'I don't know for certain, but I'm afraid he might have, yes.'

'Because Jenny was using him?'

'Precisely. Ted appears quite calm and cool and almost bland at times, with his plain food and clothes, but he loves intensely. Finding out that Jenny was stringing him along to get her face on a billboard might have driven him over the edge.'

'But Ted would need proof that Jenny's intentions weren't sincere. As far as I can tell, she never let on that they might not be.'

'Oh, but she did.' Frances's lips curled into a Cheshire cat-like grin. 'Ted saw Jenny kiss Bailey Cassels and then invite him into her trailer the night she died.'

'How do you know?'

Frances looked Tish straight in the eye. 'Because I saw her, too.'

Reade escorted Ted Fenton to the sheriff's department trailer and ushered him inside. Once there, Reade directed the actor to be seated in one of two tubular metal chairs positioned on either side of the Formica-topped table currently serving as both Reade's desk and break area. Tellingly, Ted chose the chair nearest to the door.

Reade offered Fenton a cup of coffee, which the actor declined, citing the coke in his lunch bag. 'Feel free to eat your lunch, if you like. We'll try to have you back on stage for the next performance.'

Ted eyed Reade dubiously, but eventually popped open the bag of chips and ate one. Reade, meanwhile, emptied a cup of coffee from the automatic drip maker into his mug and added milk. Allowing a suspect to eat during questioning wasn't standard protocol, but since Tish had been so successful in leveraging information with food, he thought he might as well give it a try himself.

'Ms Tarragon makes some great stuff, huh?' Reade nodded toward the sandwich Ted Fenton was unwrapping.

'She does. She's also been very accommodating to my fussy eating habits.' Ted nervously tucked into his chicken salad sandwich.

'She aims to please.' Finding the small talk a bit awkward,

Reade cleared his throat. 'I brought you here to let you know we found your text messages to Jenny Inkpen.'

Ted Fenton sighed. 'I was afraid you might.'

'Then why not tell us about them in the first place?'

'I was hoping you'd think they didn't matter. There were no threats in them. Simply positive messages to encourage Jenny to keep up the good work. She was a talented actress, you know.'

'"Positive messages." That's all they were?'

'Yes, you read them.' Ted nibbled the corners of his sandwich.

'Did your wife know about them?'

Fenton swallowed. Hard. 'Frances? Um, well, no.'

'Why not?'

'Jenny was an attractive young woman. Frances wouldn't have understood our relationship. She can be jealous at times.'

'I'm pretty open-minded. Why don't you tell me about your relationship with Jenny?'

Ted Fenton set his sandwich aside. 'To start with, I want it to be put on the record that I've been faithful to my wife our entire marriage. I've never broken that vow.'

'That's a relief,' Reade quipped.

'Doubt me if you will, but I started talking to Jenny because I felt badly for her. She didn't seem to have anyone to talk to other than Justin, and they'd broken up soon after Jenny joined, so I thought that might be awkward. I love our group, but they can be a bit catty at times. So I approached her and told her that if she had any questions about her work, the performances we were putting on, or even Rolly, I was happy to help.'

'Did she take you up on your offer?'

'No, she was shy, withdrawn.'

'But you texted her anyway?'

'It wasn't like that. Rolly insists that cast and crew members exchange cell numbers, so that if any one if us is running late or gets sick, we can notify each other immediately. As Jenny had just joined the group, we were all provided with her number. One day during rehearsals, Frances and Edie were being particularly mean, standing off in a corner giggling while she was on stage. It seemed to be affecting Jenny negatively, so I texted her a note of encouragement to help her along.'

'She didn't reply,' Reade noted.

'Not by text, no, but she approached me afterward, when no one was looking, and thanked me. She told me she had no friends or family to speak of and that she appreciated my kindness.'

'So you continued to send her text messages.'

'Well, I really couldn't be seen approaching her, could I? If Jenny were to approach me and start talking, that was one thing, but if I were to seek Jenny out after rehearsal or a performance, Frances would have given me hell. Texting was the only way to drum up a conversation, to check in and see how Jenny was doing.'

'These "conversations" – did they turn into anything more?'

'Sometimes we'd take a walk together, so that we could talk where we were unseen.'

'And all you did was talk?'

'Yes. I did grow to care for Jenny, but I never acted on my feelings. I'm older, married, and I was raised to be a gentleman. I was also afraid how Jenny might respond if I did act. I felt that she cared for me too, but I wasn't one hundred percent positive.'

'So you were never intimate with the deceased?'

'Never. We hadn't even kissed. I just enjoyed being with her. She was young and beautiful. She listened to my battle re-enactment stories and even asked questions. She was interested in what I did for the theater group in a marketing capacity. She thought she should learn every part of show business, which, of course, I encouraged. It was during one of our marketing talks that I decided that Jenny should be the "face" of Williamsburg Theater.'

'And she liked the idea?'

'She loved it. Thought it would open us up to a new audience, which it did. I also think she enjoyed being photographed in some of her more glamorous costumes.'

'Even though you described her as shy and withdrawn?'

'Yes, acting allowed Jenny to come out of her shell. It gave her a chance to be someone else for a little while. Almost like a little girl playing dress-up, except that Jenny wasn't a little girl. She was an extremely talented actress.'

'So, this photo . . .' Reade opened Opal's photograph on his iPad and showed it to Ted. 'Care to tell me what's going on?'

'We were just goofing off after our dress rehearsal on Thursday.' Ted shrugged, but it was clear from his face that he took the matter far more seriously than he let on.

'With the same type of rifle that killed Jenny just hours later.'

'I'm a gun and military history aficionado, Sheriff. I couldn't resist seeing a demonstration.'

And yet Ted Fenton had claimed he had no inkling such a demonstration was occurring at the fair, according to what he had told Tish. Reade, however, could not call out Fenton on the issue without revealing the identity of his informant.

'When I asked you about your movements the day of the murder, you never mentioned the demonstration.'

'I told you, I didn't want my wife to find out about my relationship with Jenny.'

'The relationship where all you did was "talk"?' Reade scoffed.

'Are you married, Sheriff?' Fenton challenged.

'No, I'm not.' Reade braced himself and listened to the same "If you're not married, you don't understand women" argument presented to him by his married friends, bandmates, and coworkers. Reade readily admitted that he would never win an award for his long-term relationship skills, but he was savvy enough to realize that if one were blessed with the presence of a really good woman in one's life – a woman like Tish Tarragon, for instance – one shouldn't risk losing her affection by entering a texting 'friendship' with a twenty-two-year-old girl.

But perhaps that was the difference between the two men. Ted Fenton clearly was no longer in love with his wife, whereas Clemson Reade found himself completely beguiled by the blonde caterer.

The sheriff ignored Ted Fenton's insights on marriage and the feminine psyche and continued his investigation. 'During this demonstration, did you also happen to learn where the rifles were stored?'

Fenton remained silent.

'You do realize I can ask the re-enactors, don't you?

It would reflect better upon you if you told me yourself,'
Reade urged.

'OK, yes, I did. When the demonstration was over, I left
Jenny to wander the fairgrounds while I returned to the campground. The two of us returning together would have raised
some eyebrows. As I cut across the baseball field, I saw the
quartermaster stocking the rifles in a shed. Seeing an opportunity to talk guns again, I stopped and lent him a hand.'

'And got a good look at the shed lock in the process.'

'I get where you're going with this, but I had absolutely no
reason to murder Jenny.'

'No? So you still "cared for her" on the night of her death?
No arguments, no disagreements?'

'I was with my wife and on stage all evening. There was
no opportunity for Jenny and me to have a disagreement.'

'What about Bailey Cassels?'

'What about him?'

'I'm sure you've heard by now that he was in Jenny's trailer
just before she was shot. Apparently, he had also – how did
you put it? – "grown to care for her."'

Ted's eyes flashed. 'I highly doubt Bailey's feelings for
Jenny emanated from anywhere above the waist.'

'Those sound like the words of a jealous man.'

'I'm not jealous.' Fenton's voice rose. 'I'm disappointed
that Jenny would have chosen to associate on a personal level
with someone like Bailey.'

'How are your feelings for Jenny now? I mean, after learning
about Bailey.'

'I'm shocked and horrified by the manner of her passing
and saddened by the fact that I'll never again get to talk to
her or make her laugh or watch her give a great performance.
However, before Jenny's death, I'd realized that I'd made an
egregious error in starting any sort of relationship with the
girl. I'd let myself become infatuated with her without giving
a single thought to what might happen next. Did I sincerely
think Jenny would run away with me? It was stupid. Downright
idiotic. If Frances had found out, it would have destroyed my
marriage, and I couldn't allow that to happen.' Ted Fenton
looked up at Reade with a determined face. 'I simply couldn't.'

THIRTEEN

'So, Ted Fenton *did* see Bailey Cassels enter Jenny's trailer that night.' With Ted Fenton gone, Sheriff Reade spoke freely over his cell phone.

'Yes, Frances was in the bathroom when she saw Ted get up and look out of the bedroom window. She, in turn, looked out of the bathroom window and saw Jenny kiss Bailey and then bring him inside,' Tish explained as she stepped away from the booth for privacy. 'Ted went to bed right afterwards. She said he had the same expression on his face as when they had to put their dog down a few years back.'

'Heartbroken,' Reade remarked.

'Young girl dashes older man's dreams? That's one way to explain it, but what Ted told you could be the truth as well. When he saw Jenny with Bailey, he could have realized he'd made a mistake. It might have occurred to him that he nearly sacrificed his marriage for a pipe dream.'

'Yeah, I don't buy it. If the guy felt anything for his wife, he wouldn't have texted Jenny in the first place. He gets no sympathy from me.'

'Wow. I can see you'll take your afternoon coffee black, with no added sprinkles of opinion needed,' she teased.

'Sorry, but if you're fortunate enough to find a woman you want to marry, you don't neglect her while you shop for a newer model.'

'Yeah, well, tell my ex-husband that,' she said. 'I'd like to add, however, that it's not always so cut and dried. Husbands and wives sometimes drift apart. One partner grows and finds interests the other partner doesn't share and, as a result, the other partner feels left behind.'

'You paint a sad picture of love,' Reade remarked.

'No. Love can be sad, of course. We lose loved ones all the time. I've lost my fair share, but I have no regrets, because love itself is amazing. I just don't think love sticks to a specific formula. It's something nebulous. Something you can't quite explain, and it makes you do some crazy things at times. That's where Frances Fenton has been: the crazy side. Ted had this whole world outside his marriage, while Frances – well, all Frances wanted was Ted.'

Tish was met with silence on the other end of the connection. 'Reade? Hello?'

'I'm here,' he replied.

'Do you think Ted Fenton killed Jenny?'

'I think it's quite possible. Did Frances Fenton hear her husband get up in the middle of the night?'

'No, she said she slept very soundly and woke up only twice. The first time to use the bathroom. That's when she saw Jenny. The second time she was awoken by the sound of fireworks. Her husband was beside her.'

'Ted said the same thing. He woke up twice and otherwise slept through the night.'

'Doesn't prove or disprove anything, does it?' Tish complained.

'No, but Ted had a motive and knew where the rifles were stored.'

'To be fair, anyone with access to the campground or the area behind the stage could have seen where they were stored. The re-enactors are wearing Revolutionary-era clothing. It's not too hard to spot them returning the rifles to the shed after a demonstration.'

'Are you saying you don't think Ted Fenton did it?'

'No, I think he very well could have. I also think it could have been Frances. She was already out of her mind with jealousy and she wished Jenny dead. Also, she'd seen enough antique firearms in her own house that she might have known how to fire a rifle.'

'I have a team searching the Fentons' camper for the instrument that broke the shed lock and door. So far, the woods behind the campground have turned up empty.'

'Let me know what they uncover. I have to get back to my booth. There's a swarm of people trying to get lunch before the next performance.' With a quick goodbye, Tish disconnected the call and returned to her food booth.

There she found a long queue, at the head of which stood Edwin and Augusta May Wilson. 'You have quite the crowd here,' the library board director noted.

'I know. I'm sorry. I've been juggling a few things,' Tish apologized.

'No need to be sorry. You're slated to sell out of books by the end of the day. I've had to overnight a batch to have enough for tomorrow's crowds.'

'Do you have enough money left for that?'

'No, but John Ballantyne has been generous enough to cover the costs of the extra books.'

John Ballantyne, father of Charlotte, the high school junior who was currently keeping things running at the café, had turned his life and business around since selling his late mother-in-law's home, Wisteria Knolls.

'Just Dickens?'

'No, Shakespeare's in there too.'

'The bawdy Bard? So, after all her efforts to purge the library of books she deemed to be of questionable moral content, part of Binnie Broderick's estate is being used to purchase books she would have deemed to be of questionable moral content,' Tish noted.

'Ain't karma grand?' Augusta May grinned. 'Now, how can I help you folks?'

'Oh, we've got this. But thank you.'

'Yeah, this is our second lunch wave,' Jules explained. 'We got through the first round just fine.'

'Yes, but the next show starts in less than thirty minutes,' Edwin announced.

'We need to get people to their seats as quickly as possible to prevent a rush. Edwin and I will serve the lunches while you folks take and assemble orders,' Augusta instructed. 'That way there's less of a traffic jam here at the counter and most folks will be seated when the performance starts.'

Augusta's plan worked. Two minutes before the curtain was due to come up, the crowd hovering around the booth had been whittled down to just two families of four. As Tish and company assembled their food orders, Augusta May took to the stage to quiet the noisy audience members.

'Ladies, gentlemen, boys, and girls. Thank you for coming out on this blustery Saturday to make the Hobson Glen Holiday Fair the best-attended event in the region. We thought you'd come out in droves for some holiday fun, but we never anticipated this turn-out. Give yourselves a round of applause as I turn you over to Hobson Glen's interim mayor, Laurie Villanueva.'

Ms Villanueva, tall, slender, dark-haired, and festively dressed in a long red wool coat and knee-high quilted riding boots, took the microphone and gave a brief speech introducing herself, thanking the community for a warm welcome, reminding Hobson Glen residents that the election for a permanent mayor would take place in April, and wishing all present a beautiful holiday season.

Amid cheers and applause, Augusta May took to the microphone again. 'Thank you, Ms Villanueva. I would also like to extend a sincere thank you to the fair planning committee for all their hard work and our wonderful vendors, re-enactors, and volunteers for making this a fun and food-filled weekend. And a special thanks to Tish Tarragon and the staff of Cookin' the Books, for putting together a menu that complements the incredible performances of the Williamsburg Theater Company.'

As a swathe of sunlight broke through the low-lying clouds, Augusta May gestured toward Tish's booth. While Jules blew kisses to the cheering crowd and Mary Jo and Celestine bowed their heads humbly, Tish shielded her eyes against the sun with one hand and gave a friendly wave to the audience with the other.

It was then that Tish saw her. She was standing across the field, on the other side of the audience, to the right and several yards in front of the stage. She was dressed in a dark hooded sweatshirt topped with a navy quilted vest, a pair of fitted black jeans ripped at both knees, and a pair of Converse high-top sneakers. In the warmth of the sun, she peeled back her hood, revealing a head of dark peach fuzz.

It was Jenny Inkpen.

Not wanting to cause a scene, Tish waited until Augusta and Mayor Villanueva had vacated the stage and the curtain had lifted on the first act to give chase. Judging it more expedient to travel around the perimeter of the audience than to try to cut a path through the crowd, Tish dashed out from behind her booth and ran along the U-shaped arrangement of food stalls and gift sellers that surrounded the theater area until she had reached the approximate spot where she had seen Jenny standing.

Not surprisingly, the young woman was gone.

Tish scanned the neighboring booths for a sign of the girl, but the sheer number of visitors combined with the vast amount of dark-colored winter clothing put the search on a par with the proverbial hunt for a needle in a haystack.

Tish hastened back to the booth where she was met with the questioning stares of her friends. 'I saw her,' a breathless Tish explained. 'I saw Jenny Inkpen.'

'You did?' An excited Jules reached out and took Tish's hands in his.

'Yes, she was wearing the same hooded sweatshirt and jeans you described.'

'Same buzz cut?'

'Yes, but she was wearing sunglasses, so I couldn't see her eyes. Still, she seemed lost.'

'Of course she looked lost,' Celestine inserted. 'She's supposed to be dead, ain't she?'

'Where was she?' Jules asked.

'On the other side of the field, just there, to the right of the stage.' Tish pointed. 'I ran as fast as I could to try to catch her, but I was too late. She just disappeared into the crowd.'

'That's what she did at the Piggly Wiggly, too. It was as if she just vaporized.'

'I'd better call Reade,' Tish resolved.

'Yes, you should,' Jules agreed with a giggle.

'What's with you?'

'It looks like you're Aunt Velma now.'

'If you and your staff could refrain from seeing dead people for the next forty-eight hours, it would be greatly appreciated,' Reade half joked as he arrived on the scene.

'If it helps, we weren't too happy about seeing them – um, her – either.' Tish folded her arms across her chest with a shiver.

'Must have been a shock. Are you OK?'

'Yeah, a little creeped out. Otherwise, just sorry I didn't catch her.'

'That's all right. I'll go over and poke around, see what I can see, and ask some of the vendors if they've seen her. One of my deputies is talking to the Piggly Wiggly manager and looking at the surveillance camera footage. For now, that's the best I can do. My department is already maxed out controlling fair traffic, trying to find Jenny's killer, and tracking down who she was while she was alive.'

'No, I understand, Clemson. You're doing plenty.'

'Thanks. I, uh' – Reade glanced over Tish's shoulder – 'I have some news.'

Tish exited the booth and led Reade toward her car. 'What is it?' she asked when they were away from listening ears.

'I ran a search on all the baby girls born in Florida twenty-two years ago to a mother named Lucinda LeComte. I couldn't find a single match for the name LeComte, but I did find a number of Lucindas. One of those Lucindas – according to the birth certificate, a Lucinda Gilcrease, aged twenty-three – gave birth at Tallahassee Memorial on February twenty-third, 1998. The name of the child's father was not given. The baby girl in question was adopted several days later by a couple from Pensacola.'

'The age of the mother and the location of the birth line up perfectly with Lucinda's story,' Tish noted. 'Also, as Rolly didn't want to settle down, she'd hardly list him as the father.'

'The Pensacola adoptive family lines up with what Jenny told Justin about catching the bus north to Savannah,' Reade added.

'Do you think the baby was Jenny? And do you think Lucinda and Rolly were her parents?'

Reade shrugged. 'We've reached out to the adoptive parents to ask them about their daughter. We're waiting to hear back from them. I will say, if Jenny was Lucinda and Rolly's child, then her meeting up with Justin Dange seems like one hell of a strange coincidence.'

'Unless it wasn't a coincidence. If Jenny had run away from

home because of a traumatic childhood, she might have been looking to meet up with her birth parents.'

'Then why not go to her mother directly? Why rig some weird, seemingly random meeting with Justin? How would she have known he would be in Savannah and see her show?'

'It would have been easy to link Lucinda to the theater group. And the theater group, in turn, has a website and a social media presence. So does Justin Dange. He was at a wedding. He may have posted photos. As for seeing her show, Jenny performed at the major tourist sites in Savannah. It would have been hard to miss her.'

'Still sounds like a crapshoot to me. Why not just approach her birth mother?'

Tish pursed her lips as an idea flashed across her mind. 'Perhaps she did.'

FOURTEEN

As the second performance of *A Christmas Carol* ended and the cast gave autographs and posed for selfies, the audience dispersed on to the adjacent fairgrounds, inundating the Cookin' the Books team with orders for late-afternoon drinks, cakes, and snacks.

As per usual, Tish, Jules, Celestine, and Mary Jo kept up with demand and cleared the queue just in time for the cast members to put in their orders for post-performance refreshments and, since the additional Saturday performances put time at a premium, their evening meals, to be delivered to their trailers later.

Lawrence, the young understudy, still dressed in his long black Ghost of the Future robe, was first in line. 'Can I have a cocoa, please?' he asked of Jules.

Jules reeled back in mock surprise. 'Y'all can talk? I was expecting you to point a bony finger at the menu item you wanted.'

'Yeah, I can talk,' Lawrence chortled. 'Since it's my first

role in one of Rolly's productions, I don't think he trusted me to do a lot of it onstage, though.'

'Yes, Rolly told me he called you down with your sister so you could lend a hand with the stage work,' Tish stated. 'Lucky for everyone you were here to fill in.'

Lawrence's brow wrinkled in confusion. 'Stage work? No, I don't know a thing about stage production. I've performed in small community theater, which is why Rolly thought I could fill for Bailey, but I'm majoring in music composition at Old Dominion.'

'I must have misunderstood.' Tish excused herself and took Lawrence's dinner order.

The rest of the cast and crew having been served, it was finally Lucinda's turn. She passed her empty mug to Jules, who refilled it with Christmas chai scented with cinnamon, cardamom, and ginger.

'What about dinner?' Tish asked.

'Oh, that vegetarian stew sounds divine, but can I do something other than bread with it?' Lucinda requested.

'I have salad greens.'

'Lovely. I'll have that. See you in a little bit.' Lucinda, in her silver Ghost of Christmas Past costume, gave a wave and sashayed toward the campground.

A little over an hour later, Tish stood on the steps of Lucinda's Airstream camper, her right hand on the door and her trusty insulated bag in the other. After a loud metallic clang, Lucinda appeared in the doorway. She was dressed in her customary kimono and her ghostly makeup and pale wig had been shed in favor of red cheeks, red lips, a set of false eyelashes, and her natural auburn tresses.

'Sorry to make you wait, but I've been making sure my door is bolted tight these days.' She invited Tish to enter and shut the door behind her.

'Can't say I blame you.' Tish removed the cardboard tub of stew from the hot compartment of the bag and the foil container of salad and vinaigrette from the cold and passed both to an eager Lucinda.

'Tea?' the actress offered.

'I'd love one, but it has to be quick. I have other orders to deliver and then I need to get back before the dinner rush – oh, and Jules's news broadcast. He's featuring me in his report of the fair.'

'That should be good for business.' Lucinda poured a mug of tea from a ceramic pot.

'Yes, it should. Thanks.' She accepted the mug from Lucinda and perched on the edge of the kitchen banquette while Lucinda flopped on to the plush pull-out sofa and put her feet up.

'This smells incredible.' Lucinda removed the lid from the stew and inhaled.

'Perfect evening for it, too. It's a cold one out there.'

'Mmm, I was happy to have my brocade gown on this afternoon, with extra petticoats. Tonight it's a velvet tunic, but I'll be wishing my tights were wool.' She ate a spoonful of stew. 'Fab. Just fab.'

'I'm glad you like it,' Tish acknowledged. 'Lucinda, since we spoke this morning, something has been nagging at me.'

'Oh?' With her stew balanced on her lap, she took the bitter greens salad from the nearby table and drizzled it with dressing.

'Well, the times and dates, and everything you told me got me thinking. Did you ever wonder if Jenny Inkpen might have been your daughter?'

'Of course not,' she rejected out of hand. 'I mean, she made me think of my daughter and what she must be like today, but Jenny's family was friends with Justin's family or something like that. Anyway, he'd known her since she was a baby growing up in North Carolina and they reconnected at some wedding.'

'It's true that Justin met Jenny while he was attending a friend's wedding in Savannah, Georgia, but she wasn't a family friend. She wasn't even a wedding guest. Justin saw her busking at Forsyth Square and was so impressed he introduced himself. He then brought her back to Williamsburg.'

The spoon in Lucinda's hand dropped into her stew, splashing her kimono with specks of red. 'Busking? You mean she was a beggar? What about her family?'

'Jenny was a runaway. Living on the streets. Sheriff Reade is still trying to track down her family.'

'You're working with the sheriff?'

'In a strictly amateur capacity.' Tish saw no reason to lie.

The color drained away from Lucinda's face and she suddenly aged several years. 'If you're working with the sheriff, then maybe you know. Was . . . was Jenny adopted?'

'So you *did* wonder,' Tish ventured.

Lucinda put her food on the table and leaned back in her seat, looking utterly exhausted. 'I didn't wonder, but I hoped. Earlier this year, when I heard a twenty-two-year-old actress had auditioned for Rolly and was coming into the fold, I hoped it was her. I hoped – no, I prayed – it was my daughter. It's silly, I know, giving her up and now wishing to see her again, after all these years. But I did.

'When Jenny appeared, well, she had Rolly's dark hair, dark eyes, and shrewd mind, and my stubbornness, fair skin, and flair for being a diva. She knew how to work an audience, how to make them laugh and cry. She knew it intuitively, as any child of theater stock would. And yet, given what Justin had told me, I figured it couldn't have been her. Not to say that she couldn't have been adopted, but it seemed highly unlikely, so I let it go.

'Nevertheless, every time Jenny and I worked together, I thought of the child I'd given up.' A single tear trickled down Lucinda's cheek. 'I have no regrets, mind you. I would have made a lousy mother. Married to the stage and my career, managing my waistline and wrinkles instead of a household. And I do prefer it that way. I'm happy in my life, but there are moments when I wish it had been different, when I wonder what my life would have been like if I had kept her. I think of the missed snuggles and kisses. The laughs and cries we might have shared.' Lucinda dabbed at her tears with a napkin and gave a soft laugh. 'Then I think of the lost sleep and the dark circles under the eyes. Oh, I probably should have waited before applying these false eyelashes.'

'May I help you?' Tish offered as she stood up to get a glass of water.

'No, believe it or not, you've already helped quite a bit. Aside from my aunt and my mother, who died last year, no one else knows about my past. About the baby.'

'You never told Rolly you were pregnant?'

'No.' Lucinda picked at her salad and stared at the other end of the trailer. 'I was fearful of how Rolly might react. I'd already cried my eyes out when I got the test results back from the clinic. I didn't want to be pregnant. I wasn't ready to be a mother. I didn't feel ready to be anything. Rolly would have been even less ready. He wasn't even ready to be a steady boyfriend. He had things to do. Plans. The last thing he needed was a woman and baby clinging to him.'

'So you never named Rolly as the father of your baby,' Tish asserted, recalling the birth certificate Reade had found.

'No, I couldn't. I needed his social security number to do that. Rolly and I were intimate enough to have a child together, but we weren't *that* intimate.'

'I'm sorry, Lucinda.'

'Don't be. It was my decision and I stand by it. I just get a little weak from time to time.'

'I don't think it's weak to wonder what might have been. You're only human. Did Jenny ever mention anything to you about her past?'

Lucinda moved her head from side to side. 'She was always very guarded. I, however, once made the mistake of telling her that I had a daughter around her age. It was shortly after she'd joined the group. I'd invited her to my trailer for some wine, cheese, and "girl talk" by way of a welcome. I don't know what came over me. I hadn't even drunk a full glass of wine, but looking at her, sitting right where you are, my thoughts went to the child I gave up and the words just came tumbling out of my mouth.'

'How did she react?'

'She didn't. She looked at me and said, "Oh," and then went on to how she did during the day's rehearsal. "Oh." That's all I got from her. That's as far as my sharing got me. A disinterested, "Oh."' Lucinda broke down into sobs. 'Sorry,' she sniffed, regaining her composure. 'I don't know why her reaction cut me so deeply, but it did.'

Tish found a box of tissues in the trailer bathroom and delivered it to the woman on the sofa as she sat beside her. 'Here.'

'Thank you. Again, I'm sorry for being so emotional.'

'Don't be. Lucinda, where did you give birth to your daughter?'

'Such a pointed question.'

'You needn't answer it, if you don't want to.'

'No, I pride myself on "letting it all hang out," don't I? I gave birth in Tallahassee, Florida. I had an aunt living there at the time, now deceased.'

'And your last name?'

Lucinda became indignant. 'LeComte, of course.'

Tish smiled. 'Your *real* last name.'

'Oh, cripes. Do we really need to? Oh, all right. Gilcrease. Lucinda Mary Gilcrease. Why?'

FIFTEEN

'Oh, this looks and smells like a poem!' Edie Harmes, already dressed in a black velvet Elizabethan gown for her role as Olivia, held the bread bowl filled with vegetable stew to her nose and inhaled.

Tish, meanwhile, couldn't help but gawk at the decor of Edie's circa-1970s' camper. Filled with neon lights, art deco furniture, plush throw rugs, and a vast collection of movie posters and photos, the space was a mash-up of a Planet Hollywood restaurant and the set of the Olivia Newton-John movie *Xanadu*. The only difference was that, unlike Planet Hollywood's pristine memorabilia, Edie's collection featured certain elements circled in red.

Edie, eating at the counter of the camper's kitchenette so as not to wrinkle her gown, followed Tish's gaze. 'This camper is more than just living space; it's a mobile inspiration board. I'm sure it looks strange. Rolly won't sleep here. He says all the stuff on the walls gives him a headache. That's why I always stay at his trailer or his apartment when we get together.'

'May I ask what all the red circles are?' Tish ventured.

'Those denote style elements I'd like to emulate in my future costume designs.'

'Kind of like me bookmarking recipes in cookbooks and magazines.'

'Very much the same, yes.' She tore off an edge of the bread bowl and dipped it in the stew before consuming it.

'You're quite dedicated to your craft.'

'Well, the costumes are what got me involved in theater to begin with. I simply love them. As you can see.' She presented herself with outstretched arms. 'I don't have to be dressed for another hour, but I can't resist putting them on in advance. The feel of the fabric, the way they drape and hang.'

'Was Lucinda's gown this afternoon your handiwork?'

'Yes. It was difficult to get the right balance of etherealness and frostiness. I'm not sure I pulled it off.'

'Oh, but you did. I half expected her to fly across the stage. The gown and the makeup were both gorgeous. Lucinda told me how much she appreciated the heavy brocade you chose.'

'That's an important factor in costume design. Especially when you're designing for actors performing outdoors. Our Southern summers are humid and hot enough as they are, but when you factor in the lights, it's not uncommon for the temperature on stage to exceed one hundred and ten degrees Fahrenheit. But then you take that same humidity and apply it to the winter. Although forty degrees is mild by northern standards, the dampness really gives the air a bite.'

'Practicality as well as style,' Tish remarked with admiration.

'I have to be a slave to both. If a cast member comes down with heatstroke or pneumonia, Rolly has to call in an understudy. And he hates calling in understudies.'

'And here he's had to call in two.'

'Yes, Martina couldn't be helped, given Jenny's death—'

Tish noted that Edie avoided using the word 'murder.'

'But I was surprised Rolly called in Lawrence. He's the lead guitarist in a rock band. Not precisely Dickens or Shakespeare material, but he's doing OK so far. I can't believe our luck having him here when Bailey was detained.'

'Detained and now fired,' Tish amended.

'Yes, I have no idea why Rolly fired him. Bailey wasn't the finest of actors, but he certainly wasn't the worst I've seen either. He tried very hard to please. He was always on time for rehearsal and he was always polite. I feel a bit sorry for him, actually.'

'Did you ask Rolly why he fired Bailey?'

'Yes. Rolly mentioned something about loyalty, but beyond that he wouldn't say.'

Tish found it strange that Rolly wouldn't confide in his paramour, but she refrained from commenting. 'I'd love to see more of your designs.'

Edie's tanned, angular face beamed like that of a mother who's just been asked to show photos of her children. She set the bread bowl of stew on the counter and moved toward the closed bedroom door, the train of her magnificent gown trailing behind her. Turning the knob, she swung the bedroom door inward and gazed proudly upon her creations. Four dressmaker's mannequins, wearing costumes from the Regency, Belle Epoque, Victorian, and Jazz Age eras surrounded a built-in full-sized bed.

'These are incredible,' Tish gushed. 'But this might be why Rolly is reluctant to sleep here. I have no phobias about people or things lurking under or near my bed but even I'd be a bit freaked out.'

'Yeah, I know. I sometimes get startled when I get up to go to the bathroom. Rolly's reluctance to stay here, however, goes deeper than a few dressmaker's dummies.' Edie's brown eyes grew misty. 'He's never been completely comfortable with the idea of me dedicating my time to costuming. There's always a gap to be filled within the group. Administrator, lighting, sound, character actor, extra – I've done it all. When Jenny came along, we planned for me to take the extra and character actor parts off the table and then, when Jenny learned the ropes, the lighting and sound parts too. But Jenny was too much of the diva. She wasn't interested in the bit parts or what goes on behind the scenes. She wanted to be a star.'

'At least you were able to spend more time on your designs,' Tish mentioned.

'Doesn't do much good when the leading lady doesn't want to wear them. Jenny wanted to ditch costumes entirely. She said younger audiences wanted to see characters that dressed and spoke like them, so she started assembling her "costumes"'

– Edie drew quotes in the air – 'from charity and Goodwill shops. It was absolutely absurd. I'm all for some performances being "street," but even street clothes need to be carefully curated to match the theme of the work and suit the personality of each character in it. Moreover, some works simply don't translate well to a "street" interpretation. I mean, does anybody really want to see Tiny Tim in a Gap T-shirt?'

'Only if it's worn with a backwards baseball cap,' Tish teased.

'Oh, don't even joke about that! Jenny might have done it, if left unchecked.'

'So, Rolly did try to keep Jenny's wardrobe in check.'

'He was able to call her off the idea of the group performing only in street clothes, but she still refused to wear anything I made for her. We did *Cinderella* at some camps over the summer. Jenny bought a used prom gown. The outfit she wore when Viola masquerades as Cesario? Those were leggings from a sporting goods store and a blouse from Victoria's Secret.'

'I thought it looked out of place, especially when compared with the other costumes.'

'That's precisely it. Some people automatically assume that because we don't work out of a permanent theater, we're second-rate talent giving cheesy community theater performances. That's why we strive for professionalism in all we do. Upping the ante with costumes and sets removes the prejudices people might have about festival theater being a lesser art form than Broadway theater. But Jenny was undermining all of that. All our years of hard work would have been for naught had she had her way. When I think of it, I just get so angry I—' She brought her hands to her temples and shut her eyes.

'Well, thank goodness your costumes are both needed and valued once again. Now that Jenny's gone, you'll also be spending more time on stage,' Tish commented after several seconds of observing Edie's face turn from white to pink to red and then back to white again.

'Yes, I will be on stage more often.' She sounded less than enthusiastic.

'I thought you were looking forward to playing the lead.'

'Oh, I said that for Rolly's sake. I don't have the heart to tell him that it's all about the costumes. Eva Peron is a fine character, but I'm more excited about designing and then wearing her gowns.'

'I thought Evita was your dream role.'

'No, it's my dream *wardrobe*. I take the parts to help out Rolly and the group. I enjoy the camaraderie with the girls and Ted and Justin, and it's fun to have a laugh after a performance, but truth be told, I'd rather help fit their costumes than be on stage. My mannequins and sewing machine are far more comforting to me than audience applause.'

'Don't you think you should tell Rolly?'

'Tell him what? That the man who loves the theater above all else is in a relationship with a woman who'd rather be at home stitching fabric than acting?'

'If you try talking to him, maybe—'

'Maybe he'll give me a boot out the door,' Edie completed the sentence. 'You don't understand, Tish. Jenny was young and beautiful, yes, but Rolly's preoccupation with Jenny stemmed from her love of the stage. They were both completely obsessed with theater and performing. It was almost as if the same blood ran through their veins. And, oh, how I hated Jenny for it.'

'Beef stew,' Tish announced as she presented the bread bowl to Rolly, who was nestled into his velour recliner reading *Variety*. Clad in a pair of heavy sweats, he had already applied his makeup, false mustache, and powdered silver hair color for his role as Malvolio.

'Mmm, looks delicious.' He closed the magazine and tossed it to the floor.

'Edie loved hers. Although she had the veggie version.'

'To be eaten in her "workshop"?' he asked before shoving a spoonful of stew into his mouth. 'Mmm, that is good.'

'Thanks. Yeah, she's quite dedicated to her art. And also incredibly talented.' Tish figured if Edie wasn't ready to speak for herself, she might as well put in a good word.

'That she is. I'm always amazed by her designs. And her sewing skills are off the charts. We could probably wear her costumes for the next twenty years.'

'She might put herself out of a job stitching like that.'

'I guarantee she has absolute job security.'

'She must. Edie told me how Jenny wanted to do away with costumes altogether.'

'Jenny was young and eager to make a big splash. She thought doing away with costumes would make our productions less expensive and more appealing to younger audiences. I disagreed, but I remembered being that idealistic kid who thought I could run a theater group better than anyone, even though I had no experience. So, I retained Edie's costumes for the group and let Jenny be in charge of her own wardrobe. It irritated Edie no end, but it didn't hurt the group's bottom line any.' He slurped back another spoonful of stew. 'Mmpf. Is there cinnamon in here?'

'Yes, it's a blend of spices the Elizabethans used in their cooking.'

'Never would've thought of using cinnamon in stew. It's nice, though,' he praised, still chewing.

'Thanks. You know, I didn't get to see every second of today's performances, but I couldn't help but notice the chemistry between the cast members. Even Lawrence and Martina seem like they've been with the group far longer than two days. Which is remarkable on such short notice.'

'Well, they're remarkable entertainers. That's why I called them in.' He sat back in his chair, smugly chewing.

'Yes, about that. I spoke with Lawrence just a little while ago and he was rather baffled as to why you said he could help with lighting and other backstage tasks. He has absolutely no stagehand experience.'

Rolly placed his spoon back into the bread bowl and glared at Tish. 'OK, I called him in because I was planning on firing Bailey Cassels. Last week, I attended a holiday party with theater managers and directors from the Maryland, Virginia, and capital area. During that party I learned that Jenny, with Bailey's help, was auditioning for an ensemble up in Annapolis. If Jenny took the gig, Bailey was going with her.'

Tish feigned ignorance. 'And neither of them gave you notice?'

'Neither of them even raised as much as a complaint.

Looking back, Jenny was probably disappointed I didn't make her a partner, but I couldn't. There was still so much she didn't know about theater and still so much I didn't know about her. She'd only been with us eight months and yet she was so intensely disliked by certain members of the group. Surely there must have been some measure of truth behind their feelings. So, I stalled her and said we'd discuss it after she'd been with us for another season.'

'So Jenny asked to be a partner?'

'With a pay increase on top of it. She claimed she'd brought in unprecedented crowds this season and that, at age twenty-two, she could continue to do so for the next two decades. Presumably, while the rest of us rotted away,' he snickered. 'Truth is, Jenny *had* increased ticket sales – not as much as she claimed, but by a reasonable margin.'

'Then it wasn't a completely unreasonable request,' Tish assessed.

'Not completely. As I said, the timing was poor, but I don't think less of someone with ambition. I might have even negotiated a pay raise – without the partnership – for next season, had she not said what she said next.'

Tish raised a questioning eyebrow.

Rolly accommodated. 'When I tried to put Jenny off a pay increase by saying I didn't have enough cash in the budget, she suggested I get rid of Justin Dange.'

'Justin?' Tish was genuinely surprised.

'Yeah, I was surprised, too. I knew they'd broken up and all, but he was the one who got her the spot here. He also defended Jenny against Frances and anyone else who badmouthed her.'

'Did Jenny give a reason for wanting Justin gone?'

'She said he made her feel uncomfortable.'

'Because they were exes?'

'She didn't elaborate, but I got the feeling it went deeper than that.'

'Deeper?'

'Yeah, just from the way she said it. What she meant, specifically, I have no idea.'

'Do you think perhaps Jenny wanted to get back at Justin?'

'Maybe, but why? She broke up with him, not the other way around. And as far as I could see, Justin had accepted that.'

'So he wasn't at all hostile?'

'Hostile? Justin? Nah. You saw how he defended Jenny just the other night. No, never Justin. I've known him since he was a scrawny college kid. We all have. There's no way he would have done anything to harm Jenny. No way in hell. It was one of the primary reasons I hired Justin. He was a decent actor, of course, and good-looking, but what really appealed to me was his good nature and earnestness. He wanted to learn everything we could teach him about theater, and so I started him at the bottom and let him work his way up. Didn't matter what task we gave him, he never complained. He's still the same way – a true gentleman.' Rolly sighed. 'Jenny. I hired Jenny because she had the gift – that innate theatrical sense that merely needs a bit of guidance to find its true course. It was like an answer to a prayer. I was desperate to give a jolt to ticket sales and, suddenly, there she was. Someone young, talented, and beautiful. The perfect thing to breathe new life into our performances and our box office.'

'Was business slow at the time?'

'No, on the contrary, we were doing quite well. We'd built ourselves up to the point where each of us would bring home between forty and forty-five thousand dollars a year. Not a salary that will allow for cruises and vacations, but not shabby for an independent theater company.'

'Not shabby at all, considering we're in the digital age.'

'We've had to be both flexible and creative in order to navigate that one. No doubt about it, art is highly devalued in our current world. Free music streaming, YouTube, audience members filming your performance with their phones and sharing it on social media. It's difficult to earn a decent living while trying to provide families with reasonably priced live entertainment, but we've managed so far. Keeping our fees low, cutting them completely for small events and venues and, instead, taking a cut of the gate. It's been a tough climb, but we've done it. Even with that success, I wanted to do better.' Rolly went on to explain. 'I wanted to give us all a cushion; a little extra cash after paying the bills and the health insurance premiums.' He tucked into his stew and added quietly, 'I also wanted to set some money aside so I could finally marry Edie.'

'Congratulations,' Tish extended.

'Thanks, but I haven't asked her yet. I wanted enough money in the bank to give her the wedding and life of her dreams. A designer wedding gown, a honeymoon in Paris, and the assurance that she could focus her attention on her designs instead of being the group's resident dam-plugger.'

'So you know,' she asserted.

'Know what? That Edie's happiest when in front of her sketchbook and sewing machine? Yes, I've known that all along. I've always loved her for it. Her artistry, her focus, her generosity in giving her time to the group when she'd much rather be doing something else.' Rolly jolted to life. 'Have you seen the dressmaker dummies?'

Tish laughed. 'Yes. Yes, the designs are wonderful but . . .'

'But not exactly a mood-enhancing addition to a bedroom.'

'No, I wouldn't want to wake up to them at three in the morning.'

'Neither would I, but I would if I absolutely had to, just to be near Edie. Those dummies were in my plan, too. A bigger apartment back home and a larger camper so she could have her own workspace. All of those things require cash.'

'And what about Jenny?'

'What about her?'

'Not to cause trouble between you and Edie, but she just told me that she thought – and still thinks – that you were in love with Jenny.'

'I was appreciative of Jenny's talent and, yes, she was young and pretty, but my heart never once wavered from Edie. There was, I admit, a time when I enjoyed Jenny's flattery and sharing knowledge about our craft, but when I saw the divisiveness she sowed, that all faded away. Pretty soon, I began to wish that Jenny had never joined our little group. I began to wish that we'd never met her at all.'

SIXTEEN

'You look like a landlady who's come to collect the rent,' Justin Dange noted as Tish entered his trailer bearing her insulated food delivery bag.

'Hmm? Oh, it's been a long day,' she remarked as she extracted a cardboard container and a wax paper parcel from the bag and handed them to Justin. 'Jacob Marley's bean and barley, and a turkey and cheddar sandwich.'

'Thanks for letting me order from the lunch menu.' He grabbed the food containers and placed them on the foldaway kitchenette table before taking a seat. He was wrapped in a heavy fleece robe over a white T-shirt and a pair of track pants. 'I couldn't stomach a big portion of beef stew before tonight's show. But maybe afterwards?'

'I'll save you some,' she promised. 'So, how are you doing?'

'As long as I'm busy on stage, I'm fine. Waiting around here for the next curtain call is difficult. My mind automatically goes to Jenny. I'm sorry I ever brought her to Williamsburg. Sorry I suggested she join the group. If I hadn't, Jenny might still be alive, and our group wouldn't have become so divided.'

Justin's words of regret were startlingly similar to Rolly's. 'You did what you thought was right at the time.'

'Did I? Or did I do what was right for me?' he sneered. 'Did I bring Jenny back because I couldn't bear to leave her on the street? Or because I simply couldn't leave her?'

Something about the line of questioning harkened back to Opal Schaeffer's words about men wanting to possess beautiful women. Had Justin been clinging and controlling? Was that why Jenny wanted him out of the group? 'Justin, Rolly told me that Jenny tried to get you fired.'

'What? That's a lie. That's an utter and complete lie!'

'What reason would Rolly have to lie?' she challenged.

Justin fell silent.

'Jenny told Rolly that being around you made her feel uncomfortable. Why would she say that?' Tish asked.

He burst into nervous laughter. 'I was her ex. Of course things were awkward.'

'Rolly believes she meant something other than simple awkwardness.'

'He would, wouldn't he? He's always been suspicious.'

'He actually spoke out on your behalf.'

'OK,' he capitulated after a drawn-out sigh. 'Things between Jenny and me got a little heated last week. I lost my temper, which I rarely do. I wasn't thinking straight and made a scene and grabbed her by the wrist. I didn't grab her tightly, but it was wrong. Entirely wrong and I hated myself immediately for doing it, but . . . there it is.'

'You became angry because Jenny had broken up with you,' Tish surmised.

'No, not at all. I'd accepted the breakup months ago. I realized, for starters, that Jenny should have been with someone younger. I also understood Jenny had difficulties maintaining close relationships, so I did what I could to maintain a friendship. What I was angry about was Jenny leaving the group.'

'Jenny was leaving?' Tish feigned ignorance.

'Yes, she had an audition booked for over the Christmas break. I was furious. She'd only been here eight months and she was already looking to cut ties and, in her words, move on to bigger things. Bigger things,' he scoffed. 'She was finally earning a decent wage, could afford decent clothes, and had a roof of her own over her head, rather than a shelter. Most of all, she was safe here. Or so I thought.'

'Was there something in particular Jenny needed to be safe from?'

'The world. Life on the streets. Her own past. I'd intended this to be a new life for Jenny, but she treated it, me, us, as mere stepping stones.'

'How did you find out she was leaving?' Tish asked.

'She told me. Bragged about it even. Well, "brag" might not be the most accurate term. She taunted me with the fact she was leaving. That she was getting out and moving on, while I was still stuck here. As if I ever felt stuck. The group nurtured me when I was younger, and they continue to do so every day. I admit I wouldn't mind branching out now and then, spending a few weeks playing with a group that puts on less family-friendly fare, but there's a way to do so without burning bridges. Jenny wasn't even going to give Rolly notice. After all he did for her, she was just going to vanish without a word.'

'Is that when you lost your temper and grabbed her?'

'No. I was angry, but I still managed to hold myself together. It was when Jenny started trashing other members of the group. The things she said were so cruel. So vile.'

'What did she say?'

'It doesn't matter now. It's over,' he sulked.

'It's far from over. Jenny's killer is still roaming free.'

'Jenny trashed the group. Called it third-rate. Then she went on to say that she owed nothing to Rolly because he didn't want to make her a partner in the group, and probably only hired her because she was hot.' Justin looked Tish in the eye. 'I can assure you, that wasn't the case. Rolly's not that type of guy. And Jenny was genuinely talented, so she didn't need a hand-out.'

'And that infuriated you?' Tish posed.

'No, she—' Justin took a moment to compose himself. 'After calling Ted Fenton boring and Frances Fenton a busybody – fair assessments, but not her place to say anything about – she went after Lucinda. Jenny called her a has-been and a whore who'd slept her way into the group. She even went as far as to say Lucinda had a secret child some-where. Lucinda! So kind, so beautiful, so graceful. She'd never been anything less than kind to Jenny and that's how Jenny repaid her. That's when I grabbed Jenny by the wrist in a stupid attempt to snap some sense into her. I shouldn't have done it. I'm ashamed that it happened, but you have to understand that Lucinda didn't deserve that. None of it. Not a single word.'

SEVENTEEN

In the short time Tish had been gone, the sun had set and the fairgrounds had transformed into a magical fairyland of holiday lights and old-fashioned gas lanterns. As Santa arrived on stage, accompanied by the Hobson Glen Fire Department, Tish returned to the booth to find a small crowd of people huddled at the counter, ordering hot drinks, cakes, and the odd sandwich. The dinner rush was still an hour away.

'I'm back, girls,' she announced to Celestine and Mary Jo. 'Which of you would like to take a break first?'

'Break?' Mary Jo questioned.

'Yes, you should both take a breather before the dinner crowd gets here. I'll cover for you.'

Celestine laughed. 'Darlin', that ain't happenin'. You're needed elsewhere.' She jabbed an index finger toward the area just beyond the front of the booth where Jules, his elf's hat pinned securely to his head and Biscuit, in his Santa suit, tucked beneath one arm, was conducting a sound check with the Channel Ten news camera crew.

'What? Is it time for that already?'

Celestine and Mary Jo nodded in unison.

'Tish,' Jules shouted. 'Get over here. You're on in ten minutes.'

'But I can't do that now,' Tish protested to Celestine and Mary Jo. 'There's too much going on. You both need your breaks and I need to get ready for the dinner rush.'

'You can't back out. Do you know what this might mean for your business?' Mary Jo urged.

'You have to do it, sugar,' Celestine cajoled. 'You don't look a gift horse in the mouth. My uncle Clyde did once, and it kicked him in the head.'

'OK, but when I get back, you're both taking a break,' she vowed before joining Jules.

'Oh, honey. You look plumb tuckered out,' Jules lamented upon her arrival.

'It's been a hectic day.' She combed her hair with her fingers self-consciously.

'No worries. I have a solution. Destiny,' he summoned.

An impeccably made-up dark-skinned woman in her mid-twenties answered his call.

'You know what to do. Work your magic,' he instructed.

Destiny pulled a series of cosmetic palettes and brushes from a blue train case and began utilizing them on Tish's face.

Tish was caught off guard. 'You have a makeup artist on staff?'

'We do now. Just hired her last week at my prompting. I told my boss that we may be small-town, but we shouldn't be *that* small-town.'

As the cosmetologist applied a layer of ivory foundation, Tish assessed the outfit she had selected for the day. 'I wish I was slightly better dressed.'

'You look fine. The apron advertises your business and your coat and hat make you look chic, yet approachable. And if there are a couple of splotches on that apron, that's good. You've been dishing up scrummy food all day.'

'Maybe, but I would have prepared more for my first television appearance. A haircut, a new outfit, or maybe a different coat, or I might have visited that new brow bar that opened at the back of the nail salon. I hear a lot of women talking about it.'

'Brow bar? Oh, no, honey. Why would you do that? First off, you're blonde. You have no eyebrows.'

Tish wrinkled her forehead and cast her eyes heavenward to ensure her eyebrows hadn't suddenly disappeared. She couldn't see them, of course, but she was reasonably certain that they did, indeed, exist, even if in some vague form.

'Second,' Jules continued, 'their stylists' mission is to try to make your brows thicker and stand out from your face, so you have a menu of shapes to choose from, but all of them leave you looking either like a Kardashian or Ernest Borgnine. There's not much middle ground.'

Tish frowned. An eyebrow menu? The most she ever did was use a pencil to cover a few random gray hairs. Apart from that, she didn't give her brows much thought apart from their biological usefulness in protecting the eyes from sweat or dirt.

'And third, even though the word "bar" is in the title, I was horrified to learn that not a single drop of booze is available on the premises. Not a single drop. That's false advertising.'

'You mean you've been to the new brow bar?'

'Yes, I took Mrs Wilkes there the other day. She wanted to treat herself for Christmas, but I'm not sure about the results. She's happy with them, but I think they're arched too severely. Every time I look at her, I think she's asking me a question that I somehow didn't hear.' Jules looked at his phone. 'Almost show time. A little "jhooze" to her hair and I think we're good to go, Destiny.'

Destiny pulled a bottle of golden oil from her train case and rubbed a few drops between her hands. 'You have a bit of frizz,' she said as she massaged the oil through Tish's hair with her fingers. 'Don't worry. That's normal for women your age. It means your hair is drying out and turning gray.'

'Thank you,' Tish replied. In twenty years her transformation to poodle-headed crone would be complete, but it was comforting to know it was 'normal.'

'Tish,' a man's voice shouted from the crowd that had gathered around the news crew. It was Schuyler, dressed in a casual Saturday ensemble of jeans, a fleece-lined tan suede jacket, tan work boots, and burgundy scarf. 'Break a leg,' he wished as he moved to the front of the crowd and blew her a kiss.

Tish returned the kiss with one of her own and stepped on to the spot Jules had designated for their interview. Blinded by the lights, Tish listened as the camera operator counted down from ten and shouted, 'Action!'

Tish smiled and watched as Jules gave his introduction, bracing herself for her first interview question. Oh, how she hated public speaking.

'The Twentieth Annual Hobson Glen Holiday Fair is in full swing. It's been three days of fun, festivities, theater, and food, but it's not over yet! There's still one more day to go before this year's fair is one for the books.'

The pom-pom on Jules's hat bobbed to and fro as its owner spoke animatedly. 'Speaking of books,' Jules segued, 'I'm here with Tish Tarragon, owner of Cookin' the Books Café. Tish has brought her literary-inspired recipes to the fair for an extremely worthy cause: literacy.'

At the word 'literacy,' the pom-pom on Jules's green elf's hat swung into the flame of a nearby gas lantern and ignited.

Jules, however, was blissfully unaware of the fire burning at the top of his head. 'Tish, tell us about your program to promote proper nutrition and healthy reading habits.' He thrust the microphone in Tish's face.

'I–I–I,' Tish stuttered, temporarily hypnotized by the flames. 'Jules, your hat is on fire.'

Jules glanced at the camera and chuckled. 'That's just the reflection of the camera light in the gas lamp. Now, let's get back to the library initiative.'

'Your hat is on fire,' she repeated. 'Your hat is on fire!' She lunged forward, grabbing Biscuit from Jules's arm with one hand and swinging at the flaming hat with the other. It was no use. The conical cap was securely fixed to the reporter's head.

'I've got it!' Schuyler rushed forth with a blanket he'd snatched from a nearby vendor.

At the same time, Mary Jo ran out from behind the booth, carrying the fire extinguisher Tish had brought to keep in line with town fire codes.

The pair converged on Jules simultaneously, leaving him just enough time to shout, 'Cut! Cut!'

The order came too late. The last scene Channel Ten viewers saw was a shrieking Julian Jefferson Davis being tackled to the ground, smothered with a blanket, and then engulfed in white foam.

'I told the camera man to cut,' Jules lamented as he watched the resulting video on YouTube. Fortunately, the wool blanket had shielded Jules's clothes and face from the soaking foam of the fire extinguisher, meaning that after a quick rinse with soap and water, a brush to his coat and pants, and a re-styling of his hair, Jules was back to his well-groomed self. 'Why didn't he cut?'

'He was probably as stunned as I was,' Tish explained.

'It's already had five thousand views,' he cried.

'Hey, that's quicker than the Poe Museum snowplow video,' Mary Jo exclaimed. 'You got a whole lot of job perks after that went viral. I can't wait to see what the station gives you for this one.'

'I don't want perks. This weekend was to be a test of my journalism chops. I really wanted the station and my audience to take me seriously.'

'In an elf's hat?' Celestine questioned.

'Hey, I didn't wear it for the murder segment.'

'I'm just glad you're OK.' Schuyler spoke up. 'You're sure I didn't hurt you when I tackled you?'

'I'm a little sore, but otherwise I'm fine.'

'Sorry, I think I might have relived my high school football days there for a minute.'

'I'm just happy you acted so quickly.' Tish gave Schuyler a kiss of appreciation. 'You too, Mary Jo.'

'Amen,' Celestine seconded.

'I'm grateful to both of you for putting the fire out,' a humbled Jules replied. 'And to you, too, Tish. Had you not grabbed Biscuit, he might have been injured.'

'Of course. I'm always watching out for my furry little nephew,' Tish replied with a wink. 'So, riding this wave of gratitude, why don't you put away the phone? There's nothing you can do right now except to prepare for the late-evening broadcast.'

'If there *is* a broadcast. I wouldn't be surprised if I've been fired.'

'Well, did you get a call?' Celestine asked.

'No. But that doesn't mean it isn't coming,' he whined.

'When are you on again?'

'Eleven, but as there have been no new developments, they're re-running my Inkpen murder spot. And I'm giving a brief recap of the day's events at the fair with footage we shot earlier.'

'It's been an hour. If they didn't want you, you'd have heard something by now,' Schuyler reasoned. 'A warning or word that a replacement is on the way.'

'And you never will get that call. You're a publicist's dream.'

Mary Jo had worked in public relations before her children were born. 'Everyone and his brother is going to be Googling Julian Jefferson Davis and Channel Ten news, and then tuning in tonight. I wouldn't be surprised if people were streaming it around the globe just to see what you do next.'

'Yeah, but they'll be tuning in for the wrong reasons.'

'There's no such thing as a "wrong" reason. They might be tuning in for reasons you wish were different, but the fact of the matter is they're still tuning in. So show them what you can do. Give them a different reason to tune in tomorrow, and the next day, and the next.'

Jules smiled. 'You're right. At least they're watching my segments.'

'You got it. The more people who tune in, the more people to appreciate your indisputable talents.'

'I *can* be rather charming,' he asserted.

'You can be,' Celestine agreed. 'Now, if you could turn those charms toward the dinner crowd, that would be mighty handy.' She gestured toward the sudden influx of people descending upon the booth.

Jules tied an apron around his waist. 'I'm ready. Actually, serving drinks sounds like fun. It will provide a nice distraction from the broadcast. I'll chat with the customers and spread some holiday cheer.'

'Is there anything I can do?' Schuyler offered to Tish.

'If you don't mind, could you deliver orders? Augusta and Edwin did it during the lunch rush and it really helped minimize the logjam.'

'Absolutely. Then, when the crowd is gone, I'm going to meet up with a few of the town council members, if that's OK with you?'

'Sure. I thought you attended the last council meeting of the year this morning.'

'I did, but there are a few loose ends I'd like to tie up before Christmas.'

'Yeah, that's fine with me.'

'Good. I was also thinking—'

'Uh-oh,' Tish teased.

'As per our most recent conversation' – he took her hands

in his – 'maybe tomorrow night, when the fair is over, you might stay with me? The café's closed Monday and I have an early-morning meeting, but I should be back by the time you get up – leisurely – finish the coffee and pain au chocolat I leave you, shower, and dress. Then I was thinking—'

'You seem to have been doing a lot of that,' she noted.

'I was thinking that, as I have no Christmas decorations in my house, maybe we could go out and get a tree. Together. And maybe decorate it together? If you say yes, I'll need to get some lights, but I'm not sure if I should buy clear or colored, blinking or non-blinking.'

After the fair and helping to investigate Jenny's murder, Tish wanted nothing more than to crawl into her own bed and sleep for a day, but Schuyler's invitation was irresistible. Although she'd decked the café out with garlands, lights, a menorah, and an artificial tree she'd picked up at the local thrift shop, Tish's apartment was utterly, and depressingly, devoid of holiday decor. 'Non-blinking. Definitely. As for color, I lean toward clear, but colored lights can be fun, too. It's all about tradition.'

'Or new traditions,' Schuyler beamed. 'No cooking on Monday, by the way. We'll gather up all the ingredients for an indoor picnic: some cheese, smoked salmon, those olives from Provence you like so much.'

'Sounds perfect.'

'Oh, maybe a bottle of Prosecco to toast the holiday season,' he added.

'Or a nice red,' Tish suggested. 'It's perfect for a cold night.'

'Supposed to feel even colder with the wind chill factor.'

'Really? I didn't know it was supposed to be windy.'

'Do you ever watch my forecast?' Jules shouted from the drinks station. 'I said as early as Wednesday that we could be looking at rain and wind early next week.'

Tish rolled her eyes. 'I forgot, Jules. I've been kind of busy.'

Jules was about to shout a snappy comeback when he noticed a young boy approach the counter. He was approximately six years old with straight dark-brown hair and glasses. In a small, chubby hand, he held one of the red-and-white swirled peppermint candy canes Santa's elves were distributing on stage. 'Well, hello,' Jules greeted.

'Say hello to the man and tell him what you want, Hemmingway,' his henna-tattooed, ripped-jeans-and-puffer-jacket-clad mother instructed before ordering their meal from Tish.

'Cocoa,' Hemmingway demanded.

'That's the little man,' his mother encouraged without even the suggestion of adding the word 'please.' She went back to chatting with Tish about whether the vegetables in the stew were heirloom varieties grown locally and if the spices used were Fairtrade.

'Someone saw Santa,' Jules observed. 'Did you tell him what you want for Christmas?'

Hemmingway nodded. 'A remote-control fire truck.'

'Cool. If you're a good boy, I'm sure Santa will bring you one.'

Hemmingway nodded and then suddenly exclaimed, 'Hey, I know you! You're the silly man with the burning hat.'

'Pardon?' Jules feigned ignorance in the hope that the boy would believe he was mistaken.

Hemmingway, however, was undeterred. 'You're the silly man! The one in the video. Your hat went on fire and some man knocked you down and then some lady sprayed you with white stuff.' He laughed.

'I have no idea what you mean.' He poured the cup of cocoa.

'I saw the video on my mom's phone. We all laughed at how dumb you are,' Hemmingway heckled.

Jules looked to Hemmingway's mother to intervene, but she was too busy scanning the ingredient list on the bag of greens Tish used for her bitter salad. 'I can't eat arugula or chicory,' she explained. 'They're far too peppery.'

'Well, it *is* a bitter greens salad,' Tish replied as she smiled through clenched teeth.

Meanwhile, Hemmingway delighted at his discovery. 'Silly man. Silly man,' he sang. 'I'm going to tell all my friends I met you.'

'Aw, you're precious, aren't you? I hope Santa brings you that fire truck, Hemmingway.' Jules handed the child his cup of cocoa, leaned in close, and whispered, 'And that the wheels fall off as soon as you get it.'

Hemmingway's jaw dropped open and his eyes grew wide. Taking the cocoa with him, he followed close behind his mother as she moved to the end of the counter toward the till.

Satisfied with his handiwork, Jules folded his arms across his chest, sniffed, and flashed a smug grin, only to be met by Tish's cold stare. 'He's six, Jules. Six.'

'Yes, your point being?'

'Be an adult,' she instructed.

'Me?' He pointed to his chest and burst into laughter.

'Never mind.' She sighed. 'I forgot who I was talking to.'

EIGHTEEN

With the dinner crowd fed and settled in for the first of two back-to-back performances of *Twelfth Night*, Mary Jo and Celestine both took a much-needed break, leaving Jules to take Biscuit for a walk, and Tish to watch, breathlessly, as Martina took the stage in the role of the fool, Feste. Her voice was ethereal and heartfelt, her pitch and delivery perfect:

'Come away, come away, death,
And in sad cypress let me be laid;
Fly away, fly away breath;
I am slain by a fair cruel maid.
My shroud of white, stuck all with yew,
O prepare it!
My part of death, no one so true
Did share it.
Not a flower, not a flower sweet
On my black coffin let there be strown;
Not a friend, not a friend greet
My poor corpse, where my bones shall be thrown:
A thousand, thousand sighs to save,
Lay me, O, where

Sad true lover never find my grave,
To weep there!'

As the audience erupted in thunderous applause, Tish reflected upon the structure of *Twelfth Night*. It had been decades since she'd seen the play and even longer since she'd read the text, but upon seeing it again, she was struck, once more, by the beauty of Shakespeare's words but also the duality present in the storyline.

Two sets of twins: Olivia and her late, unnamed, brother, and Viola and her brother, Sebastian. Two brothers – one dead, the other presumed dead – leaving behind two grieving sisters. Two sets of disguises: Viola masquerading as Cesario and Feste disguising himself as Sir Topas. Two characters prone to melancholy: Olivia and Orsino. Two servants in the form of Maria and Malvolio, and two rogues in the form of Sir Toby and Andrew Aguecheek. The double meaning of several of Feste's lines. And, finally, the double life being lived by Viola as a result of her disguise.

Tish pondered the role of Viola. 'Conceal me what I am, and be my aid for such disguise as haply shall become the form of my intent,' she recited to herself. Like Viola, Jenny Inkpen was also leading a double life and had asked Justin to conceal it. 'What else may hap to time I will commit. Only shape thou thy silence to my wit.'

As the evening wore on, Tish thought about the duality also present in the Inkpen murder case. Everywhere she looked, there were pairs and symmetry at work. A theater group founded by two sets of couples – Rolly Rollinson and Edie Harmes, and Ted and France Fenton – and joined by another two couples, Lucinda LeComte and Justin Dange, and then Bailey Cassels and, finally, Jenny Inkpen.

Jenny herself was a study in duality. Two suitors – the sensitive and mature Justin Dange and the young, impression-able, and easy-to-lead Bailey Cassels. Two older men whom she could charm – Ted Fenton and Rolly Rollinson – and their significant others – Edie Harmes and Frances Fenton – who would like nothing more than to give Jenny's eyeballs a good clawing. Two descriptions of Jenny: one as a conniving double-talker, and the other as a wounded young runaway scared of intimacy. Jenny led two lives, had two names, a dubious past, and now, to top it all off, there were seemingly two Jennys – one alive, the other dead.

'This youth that you see here I snatch'd one half out of the jaws of death,' Tish quoted with a smile.

'Who are you talking to?' Jules asked. He, Mary Jo, and Celestine had long returned from their breaks and were preparing for the beverage-and-snack rush that would invariably follow the end of the first performance.

Tish was roused from her thoughts. 'Just myself.'

'You've figured it out, haven't you? You know who killed Jenny.' He rubbed his hands together with excitement.

'No. No, but it's all very much like *Twelfth Night*, isn't it? All about twins and pairings.'

'Wait. Twins? Twi-i-i-ns,' he sang in comprehension. 'The Jenny we've been seeing is a twin.'

'Or a sibling. A sister or even a brother.'

'Yes, between the buzz haircut and the clothes, the Jenny we've been seeing is kinda . . .'

'Androgynous?' Tish filled in the blank.

'Yeah. Wow, I'm blown away.'

'Really, Jules? You didn't believe we were actually seeing Jenny's ghost, did you?'

'No, of course not,' he sniffed. 'Well, yeah, maybe.'

Tish laughed and placed a hand on her friend's shoulder. 'Yeah, it freaked me out so much that I wondered for a little while too.'

'Thank heavens I'm not the only one. So what do you think is going on?'

'Off the record?'

'Seriously, Tish? Yes, it's off the record.'

'I've yet to sort everything out, but like I said, it's all very much like *Twelfth Night*, from Jenny's assumed identity right down to the androgyny.'

'Meaning?'

'Meaning that, if I'm not mistaken, this whole case has more to do with Jenny's past than it does with anything that might have happened on stage. Who was Jenny Inkpen? I don't just mean her identity, but who was she as a person?

We know she was talented, ambitious, and charming, but what did she believe in? Whom did she love? We need to find her mysterious sibling and ask those questions. And, while we're at it, we need to know if Jenny was aware that this sibling was here in Hobson Glen. If she was aware of this person's presence, did Jenny summon them? Were they reuniting for the purpose of achieving some mutually beneficial goal? Or was this sibling the person Jenny was trying to elude? Was this person the reason Jenny changed her name and destroyed all traces of her past?'

'If Jenny was trying to elude this person, then they might . . .' Jules's voice trailed off as he realized the implication behind Tish's words.

'Then this person might be Jenny's murderer,' she confirmed. 'It would also explain the look of surprise and fear on Jenny's face when she died.'

Tish fell silent as she recalled the murder scene.

After several seconds had elapsed, she spoke again. 'Then again, if this person is the killer, why stick around and risk being seen? Why not slip out of town before anyone knows you exist?'

'Because he or she thinks their disguise is impenetrable?' Jules ventured.

'Yeah, as impenetrable as Clark Kent's,' she scoffed.

'Hey, it worked for Superman.'

'Fortunately, people in real life have much better eyesight,' she laughed.

Jules smiled. 'You know, speaking of pairs and twins and the like, there are two times when I can count on you to be absolutely beaming. The first is when you're devising a new recipe for the café or for a catering gig menu.'

'I do enjoy that,' she conceded.

'And the second is when you're on a case.'

'Really?'

'Yes, really. Your face just glows when you're doing what you love.'

She frowned. 'I'm not sure about this one, Jules. There's something off – either with the case or with me.'

'It's not you. You're entirely in your element.'

'Thanks. I don't know. I'm probably just tired. And more than a little distracted by Reade's warning to me last night.'

'Warning?'

'Yeah, he was afraid this case was a dangerous one. Warned me from getting too involved. And yet – here I am.'

'He's probably scared you'll solve it before he does,' Jules joked.

Tish raised a skeptical eyebrow. 'Unlikely.'

'Wanna bet? He's headed this way right now. Probably to ask for help again.'

Tish looked up to see a pensive Reade traversing the fairgrounds. 'Hey,' he greeted as he neared the booth. 'Hey, Jules, I saw your TV piece. Glad you're OK.'

'You saw it, too?'

'Yeah, one of my officers played it on her phone.'

'Your officers? So the entire sheriff's department has seen it?'

'Not sure about the *entire* department, but a majority of us, yes.'

Jules groaned. 'Ugh, I may have to wear a mask to serve drinks tomorrow.'

As Jules whined to Celestine and Mary Jo, Reade addressed Tish. 'I wanted to give you an update. You have a minute?'

'Yeah, sure.' She led Reade away from the booth and out of earshot of the others. 'I owe you an update as well.'

She filled him in on the details of her dinner deliveries.

'So Justin Dange has some violent tendencies,' Reade remarked.

'And more than just a soft spot for Lucinda,' she replied. 'Lucinda Gilcrease.'

'Ah, so she is the mother of the girl in Pensacola.'

'Yep. Were you able to reach the baby's adopted family?'

'No, we called a few times and got voicemail. We left a message, but we'll try again in the morning. However, I received some news this evening that might make that communication a bit less urgent.'

'What kind of news?'

'We have a lead on that photo we distributed, courtesy of Jules. After more troll calls than I can possibly count, a woman named Bonnie Broussard – from Baton Rouge,

Louisiana – reached us. She claims the photo is of her niece, Genevieve.'

'Jenny,' Tish whispered.

'Yeah, one of the few names we didn't check,' Reade admitted.

'Well, it's not exactly common, is it? At least not in this part of the country. What did Ms Broussard have to say?'

'Her story fits. Genevieve's mother – Bonnie's sister – died when the girl was eleven years old. She was then left to be raised by her stepfather. Genevieve was theatrical, dramatic, artistic. She loved her dance classes, old movies, and acting in school plays. She was also given to telling tales. Genevieve ran away from home – not at eighteen, as Jenny told Justin, but at sixteen. That was six years ago. Ms Broussard hasn't seen her since.'

'Do you think Genevieve and Jenny are one and the same?'

'I need more proof, but, yes, I do. Same age. Same physical description. Same likes. Same temperament. Only difference is the age at which each girl hit the streets. I checked out Broussard's story and she filed a missing person's report with the police in Mobile, Alabama, for a missing sixteen-year-old.'

'Mobile? I thought she lived in Baton Rouge.'

'She did. She does. But Genevieve lived in Mobile.'

'Why didn't Genevieve's stepfather file the report?'

'That's a story for another day.'

'Hmm, so assuming Jenny is Genevieve, she lied to Justin about the age she left home.'

'Yep, seems plausible to me. Most people leave home at eighteen for college, military, one thing or another. Sixteen is another matter entirely.'

Tish agreed. 'Telling someone you left home when you were that young opens up a whole bunch of questions. Questions she obviously didn't want to answer. Did Ms Broussard mention if Genevieve had any siblings?'

'Trying to explain the recent Jenny sightings?' Reade guessed. Tish nodded.

'Ms Broussard didn't say and I didn't ask. She was in quite a state on the phone. We're putting her on a flight to Richmond tonight. She'll be here to identify the body first thing in the morning.'

Tish grimaced. 'As much as I'd like to talk to Ms Broussard, I'm glad I won't be there to witness her reaction.'

'Yeah, it promises to be a difficult morning,' Reade remarked. 'And you? What are you up to in the morning? Still delivering breakfast?'

'Yes, last delivery of the weekend. Unless the group wants me to provide them with dinner, but I think they'll have had their fill of my limited menu by then.'

'Well, I'm not going to tell you what to do.'

'Thank you.' Tish was genuinely appreciative.

'But—'

'Oh, here we go.' She gave a playful sigh.

'Can someone go with you on your deliveries? Mary Jo? Celestine?'

'No one in the group will talk to me if I'm not on my own. You know that. I'm like the friendly neighborhood bartender and hairdresser all in one. People eat my food, feel comforted, gossip, tell me things they would never, ever admit in polite conversation, and trust that I won't repeat it. Bringing someone else along would ruin that sense of privacy.'

It was Reade's turn to sigh. 'You're right. I know. I even let Ted Fenton eat your sandwich in my makeshift office in the hope it might act as a truth serum.'

Tish laughed out loud. 'Really? Did it work?'

'Somewhat, but I'm not you.' Reade sighed again. 'I'm sorry for trying to cramp your style, but something doesn't feel *right*, for lack of a better word.'

'I know. I feel it too. All the better that you're getting to the bottom of Jenny's identity.'

'Yeah. Since I'll be in town tomorrow morning, I've instructed my officers to keep an eye on you. Should anything seem strange, creepy, or suspicious to you – anything at all – just send up a flare to them.'

'I will. I'll be fine, Clemson.'

'OK, but . . .' Reade gave a long pause. 'Be careful.'

'I will,' she reassured him. 'Now, I'd best get back. The show's ended.'

Reade accompanied her to the booth and was about to

bid the Cookin' gang goodnight when a metallic clang rang through the air.

'What's that?' Tish asked in alarm.

'Sam Noble.' Reade gestured across the grassy area where the audience had been assembled. Noble was leaning over the corner guy ropes of his tent. His daughter, Lily, was nearby, waving a sparkler in the air. 'He's over there with a sledge-hammer. This might be a temporary fairground, but we're still in a residential area. He's lived here long enough to know there's a noise ordinance. If someone complains, he'll be fined.'

'Sam's just tamping down the stakes on his tent,' Jules explained. 'A northwesterly wind is whipping through the region tonight and he wanted to make sure everything's secure before he closes. Because' – his eyes darted toward Tish – 'unlike someone else I know, Sam watched and listened to my weekend forecast.'

'Is this the same forecast that said we could see unseasonably warm temperatures today?' Reade asked as he pulled the collar of his coat up around his neck.

Jules blushed crimson and fidgeted with the zipper on his jacket. 'I said "could." It *could* be warm.'

'And Sam still believes you?' The sheriff teased, 'I *could* fine him on that count alone.'

NINETEEN

I t was just past ten thirty p.m. when Tish met Schuyler at the town council tent, where, after adding a bell-ringing concert and the purchase of some candles to their holiday-themed date, she bestowed upon him a passionate goodnight kiss and drove back to the café.

Using the flashlight on her phone to illuminate the back door, she slipped her key into the lock, let herself inside, and switched on the kitchen light. Upon a brief inspection of the premises, she determined everything was in order and bolted the door behind her. Then, with Sheriff Reade's words of warning echoing in her ears, she checked the front door and windows, threw on all the café lights, including those on the Christmas tree and in the parking lot, and closed the blinds.

Unless Jenny's killer was a vampire, Tish was uncertain how the light might ward off a potential evildoer. However, given that the last case Tish worked on had led to her being assaulted in a darkened café parking lot and the windows of her car smashed with a tire iron, she saw no harm in taking the added precaution.

With the café both bright and secure, Tish contemplated her next move. Although bone-weary, she was in no mood to sleep. She was chilled and achy – byproducts of both fatigue and lack of food. Despite feeding hundreds, the only food she had consumed all day was a slice of avocado toast at six thirty in the morning and part of a peppermint candy cane given to her by one of Santa's firemen, who'd also asked, albeit unsuccessfully, for her phone number.

Retrieving a pot of leftover chili from the refrigerator, she placed it on the front burner of her industrial Vulcan range and turned on the gas. She then moved to the cupboard nearest the stove, extracted a bottle of Pinot Noir and a wine glass, and poured herself a drink.

Still dressed in her hat and coat, she plopped on to a counter stool and took a sizable sip, breathing in as the jewel-colored liquid warmed her digestive tract and then, slowly, her extremities.

Unbuttoning her coat and removing her hat, she checked on the chili and gave it a stir before lowering the heat. Allowing the chili to come to a slow simmer, Tish hung her coat by the back door and trudged upstairs to her bedroom where she changed into a red T-shirt, plaid flannel pajama pants, and fuzzy slippers. Her night-time shower would have to wait until morning.

Descending the staircase to examine the pot of chili on the stove, she was startled by what sounded like gunfire in the distance. Moving to the café window, she peered through the blinds to see red and green flashes of light in the night sky above the recreation park.

More fireworks. She closed the blind and went back to her

glass of wine. Since when had the Yuletide holidays become synonymous with Fourth-of-July-style pyrotechnics? Even little Lily Noble had been waving a sparkler outside her father's tent.

Tish took a sip of wine and wandered over to the stove. The chili was heated through and bubbly. She turned off the gas, moved the pot from the burner, and plunged into it with a spoon. The chili was warm, comforting, and richly seasoned.

Picking up the pot, she walked back to her spot at the counter, plopped the pot on to a trivet, and tucked into her late-night repast.

Fireworks, she thought to herself again. Had there not been rockets going off the night of the murder, someone might have heard the fatal gunshot and seen the killer leave Jenny's trailer. Lucky for the killer, the shot was lost in the noise of the fireworks. Or *was* it luck? Was it possible the killer had set off some of those rockets him or herself to divert attention from the one loud bang that actually mattered?

Tish put her spoon down and took a sip of wine. The stress of the day began to melt away, and her mind, frazzled from keeping a litany of suspect and catering details in check, relaxed before once again leaping into high gear.

The gunshot wasn't the only sound that needed to be disguised, she suddenly realized.

There would have been a God-awful racket when the killer broke into the equipment shed to steal the rifle. According to Reade, the chained padlock was broken off and the door ripped from its hinges. Such a clatter would most certainly have woken the residents of the campground. Indeed, the metallic clanging of Sam Noble as he hammered his tent stakes further into the ground resonated throughout the fairgrounds, garnering questioning stares from visitors hundreds of yards away. The din created when smashing a padlock and hinges into oblivion would have been deafening, unless concealed by the sound of rockets firing in succession.

Tish exhaled sharply and slurped another spoonful of chili. Her theory was absurd. The killer would have needed strength, agility, speed, and two sets of hands in order to break down the shed door, steal the rifle, shoot Jenny, *and* simultaneously light enough fireworks to conceal any audible traces of the crime.

Unless . . . she reasoned as she leaned her elbows on the counter and drank her glass of wine. *Unless he or she had an accomplice.*

Bonnie Broussard snatched a tissue from the box on Reade's desk and blew her nose noisily.

'I'm so very sorry, Ms Broussard.' Reade expressed his condolences as he presented the grieving woman with a cup of tea.

'I don't know why I should feel like cryin' so. I ain't seen Genevieve in six years. I always hoped she'd come back to us, but in my heart I always knew it might end up like this,' she said with a shiver.

In her mid-fifties, Bonnie Broussard was neatly turned-out with freshly trimmed, shoulder-length bleached blonde hair, but her cable-knit sweater, although clean, was pilled and worn, the knees of her jeans were bordering on threadbare, and her waterproof navy-blue jacket was better suited to spring than the heart of winter.

Reade took the woman's shiver as his cue to drape an emergency services blanket over the woman's shoulders.

'Thank you. Helluva lot colder here than in Baton Rouge,' she laughed through chattering teeth.

'Welcome to Virginia. Where the heat, humidity, and mosquitoes of a Deep South summer meet the damp, cold, and ice of an East Coast winter,' he quipped and sat back down at his desk. 'I need to ask you some questions about Genevieve, but before we start, did you, um, did you eat anything on the plane?'

'No, couldn't find anything that flew direct to Richmond, so I got two shorter flights without food service. I connected in Atlanta and nearly missed my flight, too. Ice and rainstorms moving up the coast.'

'Let's get you something, then.'

'Oh, no, that's mighty kind of you, but I couldn't. I'm not even sure I could eat it.'

'You've been through an ordeal. You need some food in your stomach. Do you like eggs?'

'Yeah. Yeah, I do, but you don't have to—'

Reade held up a silencing hand and called out of his office door to one of the fresh-faced desk officers on duty. 'Clayton, could you get some eggs and toast for Ms Broussard? Scrambled or fried?' he asked over his shoulder.

'Scrambled is good,' Bonnie Broussard replied.

'Scrambled eggs and toast,' Reade amended his instructions to Clayton.

'Scrambled eggs and toast, sir?'

'Yes, Ms Broussard has traveled a long way.'

'Um, OK.'

'Thank you.' Reade passed the officer a ten-dollar bill and attempted to shut the door.

'Um, sir?'

'Yes?'

'Where am I supposed to get eggs and toast? All we have in the break room is a microwave and a Keurig.'

'Where else? The café.' Reade shook his head and shut his office door.

'My eldest boy is like that. Heart of gold, but if he threw himself to the ground, he'd probably miss,' she chuckled.

'Yeah, Clayton is a good policeman. He's just slow to connect the dots at times.' Reade sat down again.

She drank her tea and smiled. 'Thank you, again, Sheriff. I wasn't looking for a hand-out, but truth be told, what with Christmas coming and having to take today off from work, my bank account's a little lean.'

'We've all been there,' he sympathized. 'So, tell me about Genevieve.'

'Genevieve was all about the drama. From the time she could walk and talk, she was repeatin' movie lines and dancin' with her hands on her hips. When her mama – my sister, Sally – passed, Genevieve got lost in her own little world. Nothing mattered to her other than play-acting. Nothing. Her grades dropped, she lost friends, and she stayed in the house when she wasn't at school or actin'.

'I did my best to keep up with Genevieve after Sally passed. I really did.' Bonnie blinked back her tears. 'But between raisin' two boys of my own, workin' two jobs, and livin' almost three hours away, it was hard. Damn hard. I couldn't afford to visit as much as I would have liked, but I called twice a week and made sure the girls spent a few weekends a year with me and their cousins.'

'The girls?' Reade asked.

'Genevieve and her little sister, Briony. Sally always did have a thing for those exotic names. She got it from her husband, the girls' father. Thomas Savernake. Talk about a name. He was a nice fella, though. Was good to my sister and the girls. Probably why God took him. He always takes the good ones.'

'What happened to Mr Savernake?'

'Brain tumor. Died before the girls were even in school. Sally was devastated, but she kept goin' for the girls' sake. They were her reason, you know? If she were alive today, she'd have been heartbroken to lose Genevieve. That's the only saving grace in all of this – that Genevieve is back with her mama.' Bonnie choked out the words before breaking into sobs.

Reade pushed the tissue box closer and waited in deferential silence until the woman could regain her composure.

'Sally,' she eventually went on, 'found someone new less than a year after Tom's death. He was attentive to Sally and adored the girls. They married just three months later. It was a private ceremony. No one else was invited to the wedding. At least, no one from Sally's family. I admit, my nose was out of joint about Sally not wantin' me there. After all, we were sisters. Blood. But I was happy things were lookin' up for her – or at least I thought they were.'

'What happened to change your mind?'

'Little things. Sally and Armand – that was her husband's name – kept themselves to themselves, which was fine. They'd just become a family, so I respected their privacy. Pretty quick, though, it became clear that things weren't quite right between my sister and her husband. If I was on the phone with Sally and Armand came home, she'd hang up. When Sally would bring the girls for a visit, she'd come alone. Armand was always busy, yet the entire time Sally was with me he would be on the phone, checkin' in. Not just once or twice a day like most men would, but five, six times a day. Sally would get upset that Armand was callin' so much and they'd argue, but then they'd make up before Sally went back home. I'd hear her cryin' and apologizin' and tellin' him how much she loved him. Happened every time.'

Bonnie clicked her tongue. 'My husband ran off on me and my boys over eighteen years ago, so I'm not one to judge marriages, but the whole thing just seemed odd to me. Still does.'

'What about the girls? Were things fine between Armand and them?' Reade asked.

'More than fine. They were happy. Briony spent her time drawin' and sketchin'. Genevieve acted in plays and made up stories and bossed my boys around. I think that's why Sally put up with Armand's strange behavior. With him around, those girls didn't want for a thing. Singin' lessons, dance classes, art camp. Then Sally got sick,' Bonnie explained. 'Ovarian cancer. She went for chemo and radiation, but six months later, she was gone.'

'I'm sorry, Ms Broussard. You've had a great deal of loss in your family.'

'Everyone does, don't they? If they live long enough.' The shiver Bonnie gave as she pulled the blanket around her shoulders belied the indifference of her words.

There was a knock on the door of Reade's office. 'Come in,' he ordered.

The same fresh-faced officer appeared in the doorway, this time bearing a circular aluminum foil container with a white cardboard lid and some cutlery from the break room. 'Your eggs and toast, sir. There's some bacon in there too.'

Reade thanked the officer and presented the food to Bonnie Broussard. 'There you go. That's from the best breakfast place in Hobson Glen. Maybe even all of Richmond.'

Bonnie removed the lid and smiled appreciatively. 'I actually am kinda hungry. I missed supper last night, too.'

'Then, please, eat up,' Reade advised. 'I'll give you a minute or two to enjoy your food and then, if you don't mind, I'd like to ask you some more questions.'

Bonnie shook her head and nibbled on a slice of buttered toast. 'If it will help find who did this, you can ask all you want.' She plunged her fork into the fluffy, pale-yellow pile of eggs and scooped some into her mouth.

'Mmm,' she moaned. 'These have cream in them. I can taste it. My mama used to put cream in hers. That was back before milk cost almost four dollars a gallon.'

Reade smiled. 'I'm glad you like them.'

'Uh-huh. Thank you again for your kindness.'

'Not a problem. You, um, mentioned earlier that you weren't surprised that Genevieve wound up like this. Why did you say that?'

'Because of her storytellin'. She always told tall tales. Always. If she ate the last piece of cake, she'd deny it and say it dropped on the floor and she landed in it face first and that's why she had chocolate on her mouth.' Bonnie laughed. 'After Sally passed, it got worse. She was still tellin' tale tales, but the tales were more serious. If Genevieve got a bad grade in a class, it was because she'd walked in on her teacher kissin' another teacher and the teacher was gettin' even. When she came home with a new dance costume, she claimed she'd borrowed it from a friend, only to have that friend's mother call home complainin' that Genevieve talked that friend into givin' it to her. And then' – Bonnie paused – 'well, then there was the granddaddy of 'em all.'

She took a sip of tea and wiped her mouth with a tissue. 'Genevieve and Briony were at my house one weekend. It was summer, just a few weeks before the kids were supposed to go back to school. I didn't have a lot of money, but I tried to make a fun weekend for them all. Burgers, hot dogs, and smores on my little hibachi grill, some time at the beach, card games, watchin' movies on TV in the dark with popcorn, campin' out in the backyard. Genevieve would bring her iPod over and she'd show us the latest dance moves. Briony would sketch our portraits. Mostly, we'd laugh.'

'Sounds like good times,' Reade remarked.

'They were. Maybe too good. At the end of the weekend, Genevieve came to me, cryin'. She didn't want to go home. I wrote it off. What kid wants summer to end? I told her she had to go home and that maybe she and Briony could come out Columbus Day weekend. That's when she went into meltdown. She could hardly talk for her cryin', but when she finally did, she told me Armand had been' – Bonnie bit her lip and lowered her voice – '*touching* her.'

'In a sexual manner,' Reade presumed.

Bonnie nodded. 'I didn't believe her. I didn't believe it was true. Genevieve had lied to get herself out of trouble and lied to get what she wanted so often that I didn't believe her. I couldn't. Armand had done so much for both the girls. He supported their dreams of bein' an actress and an artist. They loved him. They called him "Dad." He would never have hurt them.'

'So what did you do?'

'I sent them back home, but I told Armand what Genevieve told me. What if Genevieve told her drama coach or someone at school? I thought I should warn him so he could get Genevieve some help.' Her eyes turned downward, and her voice filled with grief. 'It all blew up in my face. I only wanted to help, but Armand accused me of poisonin' Genevieve against him. Me, of all people. I loved those girls. I loved them like I loved their mama.'

'What happened?' Reade prompted.

'Armand banned me from seeing them. They weren't allowed to talk to me, or visit, or write. They weren't allowed to visit, write, or talk to my boys either. We were all just written off. That weekend in the summer was the last time I ever saw Genevieve or Briony.'

'Did you contact an attorney about your rights as the girls' aunt?'

'Nah, I didn't have the money for that. Even if I got a free consultation, I'd wind up payin' somewhere down the line. I tried callin' Armand to talk some sense into him, but he wouldn't take my calls. Then, two months later, I got a call from Armand. I never will forget that night. It was the middle of October and the first cool evening we'd had in months. It was eleven o'clock and Genevieve still hadn't come home from school. Armand wanted to know if she was with me or the boys, or if she'd tried to call any of us. She hadn't done either, but Armand didn't believe me, so I called the police.'

'That's why the missing person's report was in your name.'

'Yup. Didn't take long for the police to figure out Genevieve had run away. Her clothes and iPod were gone, and she'd taken money out of a savings account Sally and Armand had set up for her. Whether or not she ran away with someone, they never did find out.'

'What do you think? Did she run away with a friend? Or maybe a boyfriend?'

'I think Genevieve was alone,' Bonnie asserted as she picked up a strip of bacon with her fingers and munched on it. 'After her mama died, she didn't much like or trust too many people. She enjoyed her own company more than she enjoyed anyone else's.'

'You still didn't explain why you thought Genevieve might end up murdered,' Reade mentioned.

'Well, not only is a young girl out on her own on the streets a target for lunatics, but it was only a matter of time before she told a tall tale about the wrong person.'

'Ms Broussard, do you happen to know the whereabouts of your younger niece?' Reade asked, much to Bonnie Broussard's surprise.

'Briony? No. After Genevieve ran away, Armand's attorney filed an order statin' that if I or my boys contacted any of them – Armand, Briony, or Genevieve – we would go to jail.'

'So you quite literally haven't seen or heard from your nieces or your brother-in-law in six years?'

'That's right. I'd call the Mobile police to check in and see if they'd found anything about Genevieve. But after a couple years, when she would have turned eighteen, it was clear they'd put it down as a runaway case and weren't pursuin' it any longer.'

'I know it's been a while, but can you think of anyone in Genevieve's past who might have wanted her dead?'

Bonnie shook her head. 'No, as I said, she didn't have many friends. And although Armand and I didn't always see eye to eye, I know he loved her with all his heart. Same with Briony. She looked up to her big sister. Everyone in the family loved Genevieve. Everyone.'

TWENTY

After scrambling some eggs for the young member of Sheriff Reade's staff, Tish gathered breakfast for the theater group. In deference to those vendors who might attend Sunday church service, the fair was scheduled to open at noon, rather than eleven, and the first theater performance was slated for one in the afternoon rather than twelve, thus pushing the group's breakfast to eight thirty.

Tish was happy for the delay, not because it gave her a chance to sleep in – her café still opened bright and early – but because it gave her an extra hour to ensure that Mary Jo and Charlotte were prepared to deal with the Sunday post-church lunch crowd. Giving the roast chickens for her Sunday lunch special a generous slathering of lemon, sage, and onion butter, Tish put the hens into a hot oven, left instructions for their further cooking, and took off for the fairgrounds.

As she pulled the Matrix out of the café parking lot, the familiar ring of her cell phone resonated through the stereo speakers of her car. Pressing the Bluetooth button on the steering wheel, she answered. 'Hello?'

'Hey, Tish. It's Reade. Got a minute?'

'Hey. Yeah. I'm just on my way to the fair.'

'OK, I'll make it quick. I got a positive ID this morning. The body in the morgue is Genevieve Savernake.'

'That makes sense. Last night, just before I went to bed, I remembered how Jules went on about Jenny's name having a double meaning, so I Googled the name "Inkpen." That village in Berkshire, England, you mentioned? It's located in the Forest of Savernake.'

'I told you lies are sometimes rooted in the truth,' Reade reminded.

'You did,' she acknowledged. 'You were absolutely correct in this case.'

'Thanks, but do me a favor? Don't tell Jules his theory was partially true. Otherwise, he'll take up residence in my office.'

Tish laughed. 'You have my solemn word. So did you learn anything else from Jenny's aunt after feeding her my sodium-pentothal-laced eggs?'

'What?'

'I heard you've opted to use some of my investigative techniques in your interviews. Namely, bribing the witness with food.'

It was Reade's turn to laugh. 'Not true in this case. Ms Broussard had traveled a long way and hadn't eaten. Besides, I learned my lesson with Ted Fenton. Apparently, I'm missing something in the combo.'

'Or maybe you have a little something extra. Like a badge?' Tish suggested. 'It's far easier to talk to a caterer than a cop.'

'True.'

'So what else did you learn from the victim's aunt?' Tish asked as she pulled the Matrix to a halt behind her food booth and cut the engine.

'Not too much that might be relevant to the case. More like details in a character study. The first big takeaway is that Genevieve had a younger sister, Briony. Ms Broussard has no idea of her current whereabouts, but she did say the two girls inherited their dark features from their late father.'

'Inherited? So Genevieve and Briony weren't adopted.'

'Nope. Bonnie said they always bore a strong resemblance to each other.'

'"Strong resemblance" is putting it mildly.'

'The second takeaway and the biggest bombshell of the conversation is that Genevieve ran away from home shortly after telling her aunt that her stepfather had sexually abused her.'

'Wow! What happened to him?'

'Nothing. Ms Broussard didn't believe her niece's story. Genevieve had a lifelong history of telling wild tales – a habit that only got worse when her mother passed – so Broussard dismissed the allegations and told her brother-in-law to get the girl some counseling. Said brother-in-law didn't take it well and banned Auntie from contacting the family. Genevieve ran away shortly afterward.'

'How sad. The girls were Ms Broussard's only link to her sister, and Ms Broussard the girls' only link to their mother. Did the girls' stepfather say why he cut communications?'

'No, Bonnie Broussard thinks he either assumed she was the one who put Genevieve up to the sex-abuse allegations or that Genevieve was using the abuse allegations to cover up the fact that she was sexually active with someone at Ms Broussard's house, such as one of Ms Broussard's sons' friends.'

'Could either be true?'

'No. Bonnie Broussard had no motive to level that kind of accusation. She praised the way her brother-in-law took care of her nieces. Likewise, she had a tough enough time taking care of her own children; she didn't need two more mouths to feed, so she definitely wasn't looking for custody. As for the boyfriend angle, Bonnie claims the girls were never out of her sight. When they visited, they slept in her bed while she slept in a nearby cot. Moreover, during cousin visits, Broussard's boys were barred from meeting friends as it was considered valued family time.'

'Hmm, sounds like a dead end in relation to the murder.'

'It does, but at least we now have a name to possibly help us fill in what happened during the six years Genevieve was on the streets. Speaking of names,' he segued, 'I heard from the parents of the adopted baby girl in Florida. Their daughter is alive, well, and home for the holidays from a graduate theater program at Florida State University. Now that we know Jenny, or Genevieve, wasn't Lucinda's daughter, however, none of that information helps much with the case.'

'No, but it might help Lucinda. I understand we can't give her the information you found—'

'That's right. The adoption records were only unsealed because the sheriff's office petitioned the court.'

'But it might provide Lucinda some solace to know her child was adopted at birth and not bounced around the system. Given how Lucinda suspected, and even hoped, that Jenny might be her child, I think she needs to hear something to put her heart and mind at ease.'

'I totally agree. And telling Lucinda her daughter is in Pensacola means that she'll know which court to petition should she wish to make contact.'

'Mmm,' Tish murmured in agreement. 'Say, Clemson, I know this might seem off-topic, but did you and your team happen to learn anything about the fireworks this weekend?'

'Fireworks?'

'Yes, the ones that were being shot off the night of Jenny's murder and then again the past two nights.'

'As a matter of fact, one of my men brought in the perpetrators right around midnight. A bunch of local high school students. They're each looking at a maximum twenty-five-hundred-dollar fine and the possibility of imprisonment, but since they're minors with no priors, I'm sure they'll get off with five hundred each and community service.'

'Did they tell your officer how they got the fireworks?'

'No, they were surprisingly silent. Kids in their position typically share what they know to appease their parents and redirect the blame on to an adult, but not these guys. Why do you ask?'

'I was wondering about the timing of those fireworks. It was awfully convenient for the killer that those rockets should be going off at the exact same time he or she was breaking down the shed door and aiming a rifle at Genevieve Savernake's chest.'

'Are you saying the fireworks were set off on purpose?'

'I am. Think about it, Clemson. No one at that campground recalled hearing the shot. Why? Because it was lost in a sea of other "shots." Same goes for the lock. You heard Noble tamping down the stakes on his tent last night. If the killer made half as much noise breaking the lock on the door, the entire group would have been outside their campers in thirty seconds.'

'Go on,' he urged.

'Well, the killer could hardly have managed to break down a door, steal the rifle, jog to Genevieve's camper, and pull the trigger, all the while simultaneously lighting rockets, so he or she had to have an accomplice.'

'You think the kids were the accomplices?'

'They might be. They're teenage kids who just attended their last day of school before two weeks of vacation. Give them fireworks and it's a safe bet they're going to set them off that night, rather than save them for a rainy day.'

'Then why were they still setting them off last night and the night before that?'

'That I can't answer. However, if they were anywhere near the murder scene, we have no idea what they may have witnessed.'

'That's a valid question I'll need to ask them.'

'Yes. It's also entirely possible that those kids weren't the ones setting off fireworks the night of the murder. They may have been "hired," for lack of a better word, to set them off the rest of the weekend so that the presence of fireworks on Thursday didn't seem unusual.'

'If the kids didn't set off the fireworks on Thursday night, then who did?'

'An actual accomplice. Someone complicit in the crime.'

'Then we'd be looking for a pair of murderers,' Reade presumed.

'Exactly. And this case is full of pairs.'

'That seems a more likely scenario than the killer giving away eight to nine hundred dollars' worth of fireworks to a bunch of kids,' he opined.

'Does it, really?'

'Well, yeah. Who would spend close to a grand on an alibi?'

Tish frowned as she considered the amount of desperation behind such a move. 'Someone with a great deal to lose.'

TWENTY-ONE

Tish disconnected from her call with Reade and set off for the campground. As had become her custom, she placed the canteen of coffee and its fixings on the central folding table and then knocked on the door of the Fentons'

Winnebago. Frances, in her pink chenille bathrobe, came to the door and waved Tish inside.

'Morning, Frances,' Tish tendered as she placed the bag of food on the table of the kitchenette. 'I have your breakfast burrito with extra peppers and oven-roasted tomato salsa. Eventually, I'll find a supplier with a greenhouse so I can get decent tomatoes in winter. Until then, oven—' She looked up to see a bleary-eyed Frances Fenton quietly crying into a tissue. She looked as if she had been weeping for hours. 'Frances, what's wrong?'

Frances shook her head. 'Where do I even start?'

'Can I get you anything?'

'Some coffee would be great.'

'Sure.' Tish headed out to the folding table. She returned several seconds later, Stevia-sweetened brew in hand, to find Frances flopped on the sofa.

'Here.' Tish presented Frances with the steaming hot cup.

Frances sat up and drank the coffee greedily. 'Thank you, Tish.'

'Not a problem. Would you like your breakfast?'

'Yes,' she answered distractedly. 'Yes, I probably should eat something. It's been a long night.'

Tish pulled the foil-wrapped burrito from the insulated bag and passed it, along with a couple of napkins, to Frances. Tish had already anticipated Frances's reply to her next question, but she pulled the container of over-easy eggs and hash browns from the bag and asked anyway. 'And Ted's breakfast?'

'Ted's not here.' Frances's face was puffy and red, but the shot of caffeine did much to restore a sense of calm to her demeanor.

'I'm sorry. I didn't mean to pry. I'll just leave you to—'

'No, please.' Frances leaned forward in her seat. 'Please stay, Tish. I feel as though I can confide in you. Our conversation yesterday helped me come to terms with what I needed to do.'

'Which was?'

'I needed to tell Ted how I felt about our relationship and how lonely and dissatisfied I've been. I also needed to tell Ted that I knew about Jenny and him, and about the things I'd done. I needed to be completely honest with him.'

'You told him about your online bullying?' Tish was stunned.

'I did. I needed to come clean about it. There was no way either of us could move forward if I didn't.'

'How did he take it?'

'Not well. I expected him to react poorly. I didn't expect him to leave.' She took a bite of egg-filled tortilla.

'I'm sure it was just a knee-jerk reaction,' Tish reassured her. 'Do you know where he went?'

'No.' She washed the eggs down with a sip of coffee and dabbed at the tears forming at the corners of her eyes. 'As much as I wanted to run after him and beg him to stay, I realized I've been chasing after him for years – not physically, perhaps, but emotionally. I've been waiting for Ted to be "present" and available and put time into our relationship. For years, I've asked him to join me for a visit to the museum or a lunch date or maybe to take some time off from his duties and hobbies to take a vacation. His answer has always been the same: he's "too busy." Too busy pursuing his interests and, more recently, a young woman, to spend time on his marriage. Meanwhile, I was pursuing him. Trying to pick the right combination of activities and words so that he might accept my invitation. Putting my own needs and desires aside while I waited for the day when he'd finally find the time.'

Tish perched on the edge of the banquette and listened. The Fentons' marriage was, as she'd told Reade, a case of two people drifting apart, but it didn't make the scenario any less heartbreaking.

Frances ate a bit more of her breakfast before speaking again. 'It hasn't been a healthy situation. I never realized until now just how damaging these few years have been. What I did to Jenny wasn't normal. It wasn't me. That's not who I really am. I'm not excusing my behavior or blaming anyone else, but when so much of your life revolves around another person, the prospect of losing them makes you do . . . desperate things.'

The tone of Frances's voice made Tish wonder, once again, if she had, indeed, confessed all her wrongdoings. Would Ted have left Frances over online bullying? True, it was an odious, cowardly, and immature way to handle the situation. It was also true that Frances had spent the couple's money on establishing some of her online aliases, but considering Ted was guilty of adultery – if only in his heart – his reaction to his wife's transgressions seemed rather harsh. Or did he, too, question whether Frances was capable of something far more sinister?

'I was in a dark place,' Frances continued as if prompted by Tish's thoughts. 'A terribly dark place, and I'll do everything within my power to ensure I never revisit it.'

Tish exited the Fentons' Winnebago and headed to Edie Harmes's trailer. All the while, Frances's words echoed in her head. Steeling herself against the cold and an ever-increasing, yet unidentifiable, sense of uneasiness, she knocked on the door and was relieved to be greeted by Edie's smiling face. The seamstress was dressed in a resplendent red kimono and matching plush slippers, and her long brunette hair was pinned into a neat bun on top of her head. The look was a far cry from the previous morning's ensemble of oversized shirt, socks, and unkempt locks.

'Good morning,' Edie greeted as she flung the door open wide.

'Morning,' Tish replied, happy to be free of the oppressive atmosphere of the Fentons' Winnebago. 'I have your *Dante's Inferno* eggs.'

'Two helpings, I hope.' Edie grinned as Tish stepped into the neon-lit living room.

'Two?'

Rolly Rollinson, clad in a luxurious velour robe, appeared from the bedroom door and rubbed Edie's shoulders. 'Yes, Edie's looking after me now.'

'Looking after?' a bewildered Tish questioned. Meanwhile, Edie flashed a beatific smile. 'You're engaged?'

'We are. Finally.'

'And you' – Tish pointed at Rolly – 'slept *here*?'

'I did. It was ridiculous, really, staying away as I did. I finally got it when Ted Fenton came knocking at my door at midnight. He's a good man, but he hasn't been as attentive to

Frances as he should have been. He's taken his good fortune for granted.' He glanced at Edie. 'As I have. Waiting for the perfect moment to get married just meant one more day that we weren't together. And that's all that really matters, isn't it?'

'Rolly texted me a little after midnight and asked if he could come by,' Edie added.

'Fortunately, she was still awake, working on one of her designs.' Rolly continued the narrative. 'So, I came over and immediately dropped on one knee and proposed.'

'And I immediately said yes.'

'We'll shop for a ring together over the Christmas holidays.'

'A modest one,' Edie inserted. 'I told Rolly I don't need flashy things. I just need him.'

'That's terrific news. Congratulations.' Tish placed her insulated bag on Edie's mid-century coffee table and retrieved the two foil containers bearing her interpretation of *Eggs in Purgatory*. 'In honor of your special news, breakfast is on the house.'

The couple accepted with a hearty round of thanks.

'Do you have a date set?' she asked as they tucked into their food.

'No, it's all been so spur-of-the-moment,' Rolly explained and scarfed down a hunk of sourdough toast dunked into a golden-red combination of egg yolk and fiery tomato sauce. 'We've only told a couple of people the news.'

Edie had a better concept of a timeline. 'Ideally, I'd love to get married early next year, but that all depends. I don't want a big wedding. A lovely gown, some flowers, a visit to a justice of the peace, and then dinner with a few close friends and family suits me fine. I would, however' – her voice dropped to a near-whisper – 'prefer for this whole mess to be over before we send out invitations.'

'Whole mess?' Tish repeated.

'Jenny's death,' Edie elucidated. 'I didn't much care for the girl, but it feels wrong to be planning a wedding when she hasn't even had a proper burial.'

Rolly voiced his opinion. 'I don't think there's anything wrong in planning. I just wouldn't get the address book out yet.'

'But it just feels . . . tacky. And insensitive. Jenny's not even cold yet and her killer is still on the loose.' She turned her eyes toward Tish. 'You live here. Do you have any idea when they might arrest someone?'

Tish shook her head. 'No. I just know Sheriff Reade and his team are doing all they can.'

'I hope they hurry things up. Until this case is closed, I'm going to have a tough time relaxing. And I'm afraid wedding planning will have to wait, Rolly. Otherwise, people will think we're celebrating Jenny's death.'

Rolly looked up from his breakfast long enough to snap back, 'Well, it's not as if they'd be completely wrong, is it?'

Tish left the newly engaged couple to their breakfasts and talk of wedding plans, and meandered over to Rolly Rollinson's trailer, where Ted Fenton had, by Rolly's account, stayed the night. On her way, she spied Justin Dange and Lucinda LeComte walking, side by side, back to camp.

'Morning,' they greeted in unison.

'Morning,' Tish volleyed. 'You two are out and about rather early.'

'Yeah, I woke up and couldn't go back to sleep,' Justin explained. 'Then I looked over and saw a light on in Lucinda's trailer, so I called her up and asked if maybe we could *not* sleep together.'

As Tish suppressed a grin, Lucinda gave a heavy groan.

'That sounded a lot funnier in my head,' Justin admitted.

'Well, next time, keep it there,' Lucinda joked. 'Shall we go inside and have some breakfast?'

'Normally I'd love to, but I promised to call my mother this morning,' Justin pardoned himself. 'She's beside herself with this whole murder thing and I didn't have a chance to call her yesterday to put her mind at ease. Rain check?'

'Absolutely,' Lucinda agreed. 'Thanks for the walk.'

'Thank *you*. It really helped to clear my head.'

'Good. I'll see you on the boards later.'

Justin took his breakfast sandwich and returned to his Travato as Tish followed Lucinda into the vintage Airstream.

'Tea?' Lucinda invited as she removed her emerald-green wool coat and rushed to the kitchenette to put the kettle on.

'Sure. But just a quick one; I still have to deliver Ted's breakfast and then I have a lot to do to get my booth ready for the day. It was in a bit of a shambles when I left last night.' Tish reached into her bag and pulled out Lucinda's customary egg-white sandwich.

'So, did you hear?' Lucinda asked. 'There's a wedding in the works.'

'Yes, Rolly and Edie told me this morning.'

'Edie texted me last night, right after it happened.'

'Are you OK?'

'Oh, yeah. It's about time Rolly "put a ring on it." Edie's good for him. I'm happy for them both.'

'And your lack of sleep this morning?'

'Hormones,' she dismissed and smoothed her ivory cable-knit tunic sweater over her hips.

Tish folded her arms across her chest and raised a skeptical eyebrow.

'Oh, all right,' Lucinda sighed. 'It's the holidays. The end of another year. I don't know about you, but my mind tends to wander. I don't mind being alone at Christmas. I enjoy going back to my quiet apartment after a busy season. It overlooks the James River and I catch up on my reading on a bench in the front living-room window. I pull out the silver table tree my mother used to put up when I was a kid and nosh on my favorite chocolates. Christmas Eve, I participate in a show at the local YMCA, and then on Christmas Day I meet up with some of my single friends for Prosecco and lobster. It's a great time, but every now and then I see families lining up to see Santa and I grow a little misty.'

'Memories of Christmas past?' Tish asked. 'Or ghosts of Christmases that might have been?'

'Both.' The teakettle began to whistle. Lucinda removed it from the heat, poured the contents into two mugs, and joined Tish at the dinette set. 'I remember those carefree years when all we worried about was whether we were good enough for Santa to arrive and all we had to cry about was Christmas dinner being served before we could finish playing with all our new toys.'

'And then falling asleep beneath the glow of the tree,' Tish added, 'our bellies full and our hearts content at the prospect of a week of unlimited playtime and sweet treats before us.'

'Yes, every year I remember those things and pray that my child has known such simple pleasures.'

'That she's had a chance to revel in the innocence of youth,' Tish paraphrased.

'Exactly. And, every year, I assure myself that she has. That I made the right decision. This year, however, after meeting Jenny, I wonder.'

'I have some news for you, Lucinda. Jenny wasn't your daughter.'

'She wasn't?' Lucinda seemed surprised, relieved, and disappointed all at once.

'No, Jenny's aunt came up from Baton Rouge to identify the body this morning.'

'And was it . . .?'

'Yes, Jenny was her niece. A niece who had, in her aunt's words, "inherited her father's dark good looks," so she clearly wasn't adopted.'

Lucinda drew a long draft of tea. 'Good God. Poor woman. How is she?'

'I don't know. Sheriff Reade is with her, so she's in good hands, but still, it's quite a blow.'

Lucinda bit into her sandwich while Tish sipped her tea, both in silence.

After several moments had elapsed, Lucinda sighed. 'Jenny always struck me as being so tortured, so much in pain. I never knew why, but I started to think that perhaps, if she were Rolly's and mine, she might have been angry that we . . .'

'Gave her up for adoption? No, I have no idea why Jenny was the way she was, but that wasn't it.'

'But the birth certificate, the one that bore my name . . .'

'The birth certificate was for a baby girl adopted by a family in Pensacola, Florida,' Tish revealed.

'Pensacola? Is she doing well? Is she healthy? Happy?' Lucinda nearly leaped over the table.

'I couldn't say. I've never met her. Nor have the police.'

'No, of course. I understand.' Lucinda lowered her head and ate her sandwich.

Tish was aware that Lucinda had to personally petition the court in order to obtain further details, such as the girl's name, family name, and address, but she saw no harm in sharing the few details she had. 'Look, all I know is that your daughter is home on break from a master's program at Florida State University. But if you let on to anyone that I told you—'

'Master's program? She's a–a genius?' Lucinda's face brightened as she rose from her seat at the dinette and twirled about the camper.

'Possibly.' Tish laughed. 'Now, you have to promise you won't tell a soul I told you that.'

Lucinda sat back down and grasped Tish's hands in hers. 'You have my word.'

'For any other information, you need to petition the courts to open the adoption records. The police and I can't help you.'

'I do understand. And I promise I won't tell anyone what you've told me.' She removed one hand to make the sign of a cross over her heart. 'I swear.'

'Good.' Tish gave Lucinda's hand a squeeze and went back to sipping her tea.

'My mind and heart are more at ease than they've been for weeks, and it's all thanks to you.'

'Oh, I'm not sure it was *all* me.' Tish gazed out of the window at the black Travato parked next door.

'What? Justin? Oh' – she waved her hand in the air – 'I told you, we're just good friends.'

'Sounds like the perfect foundation for a romantic relationship, if you ask me. You help him through his grief, and he helps you confront your past. That is, if you choose to confront it.'

Lucinda swallowed a bite of sandwich. 'You mean, do I plan to contact the daughter I gave up?'

'You seemed awfully curious.'

'I am,' she confessed. 'But I'm not sure if I should. She has her life and is obviously successful. She doesn't need the upheaval.'

'She also may have felt the same way about you,' Tish reasoned. 'She may have wanted to find out who you were but didn't want to dredge up the past. Especially if you'd moved on with another partner.'

'Which is yet another reason not to get romantically involved with Justin. I'd feel as though I'd have to tell him about the baby.' She frowned. 'No, it simply wouldn't work.'

'I think you're not giving Justin enough credit. If he was understanding enough to overlook Jenny's flaws, he'd certainly be accepting of what occurred in your past.'

'But he knows Rolly,' Lucinda argued. 'It's different. And then, if I did tell Justin, would I have to tell Rolly? And what about Edie? They're finally getting married. I'm not going to do anything to interfere with that.'

'You have a lot to think about, and I'm not going to tell you what to do; just know that if you need to talk, I'm here,' Tish offered.

'Thanks, Tish. If I need to, I'll definitely take you up on that. I'm not sure how much longer we'll be staying now that the fair is ending. Although your sheriff seems determined to keep us here.'

'Protocol,' Tish explained.

'Yes, I know. I'm just eager to get back to my apartment and my books and my silver tree.' She gazed out of the window at the black Travato. 'But I guess a few more days here wouldn't be so bad.'

'Ted? Breakfast,' she called following a tap on the door of Rolly's camper. Whether Ted would be in the mood for either breakfast or company remained to be seen.

Standing back in case the door suddenly swung outward, Tish tucked her chin beneath the collar of her coat and patiently waited for a reply. Despite Jules's predictions of a snow-free, mild weekend, the day promised to be even colder than the previous one.

A scuffling noise came from inside the trailer and the door swung open. Ted Fenton, dressed in jeans and a wrinkled, untucked plaid cotton shirt he'd quite obviously slept in, welcomed Tish inside. 'You must have seen Rolly.'

'I did. I have your eggs and hash browns,' Tish said softly.

He ran a hand through his thinning, unkempt hair and sighed. 'Not sure I'm very hungry.'

'You should at least try,' she urged. 'It's a cold one today. You'll need some fuel to keep you warm out there on stage.'

Ted capitulated with a nod of the head and sat down in Rolly's velour recliner. Tish passed him his container of food, a napkin, and a fork.

Ted left everything in his lap. 'I, um, I suppose Frances told you what happened.'

'About your argument? Yes, she told me.'

'Then I assume she told you what she did to Jenny.'

'She did,' Tish admitted.

'I just don't understand. Frances has never been one to behave in that manner. She gets angry and lets loose, and then we talk it out and things are better. She's never been one to brood and skulk, and she's most definitely never been the type to torment someone.'

'Is that why you left?'

'I didn't want to leave Frances, I really didn't, but I couldn't stand to look at her – not because of what she'd done, but because of what I did to push her there. Looking at Frances reminded me of the woman I married and was now gone. The hopeful, feisty, strong young actress I'd fallen in love with was now a desperate, bitter person begging for my attention and lashing out at a young woman she thought had stolen my heart. And Jenny *had* stolen it, in a way,' Ted went on to concede. 'Until . . . well, until I finally realized that she didn't care for me at all. She was playing me the same way she'd played the rest of them.'

As Ted threw his hands over his eyes, Tish ventured into the kitchenette and put on a kettle of water. For reasons unknown, she had stashed a bunch of tea bags in her coat pockets that had now proven to come in handy.

Ted sank deeper into the recliner. 'I was such a fool. Such a fool. I love Frances. I've always loved Frances. We just fell into a rut. A rut I propagated with my personal obsessions with guns and historic battles and the group's marketing. Marketing,' he scoffed. 'Whatever that means.'

The kettle, bearing just one mug's worth of water, quickly came to a boil. Tish poured its contents into the first clean vessel she could find – a circa-1980s' Walt Disney World mug with a handle shaped like Mickey Mouse's ears – plopped in a tea bag, and presented it to Ted.

'The past is past, Ted. What matters is the future,' Tish advised as she leaned against the wall near the recliner and folded her arms across her chest.

'What future? I doubt Frances ever wants to see me again.'

'I don't think that's true. It's all too fresh for decisions like that. Now, drink some tea and eat something,' she insisted.

A pouting Ted capitulated and, setting the mug of tea on a nearby table, opened the lid of his breakfast and helped himself to a bite of hash browns. 'Mmm, these are really good. Frances always tries to make them, but she adds too much onion for my liking. Not that I've told her. I've always been afraid of hurting her feelings.'

'Well, I certainly wouldn't tell her now,' Tish noted, eliciting a vague smile from Ted.

'No, I suppose not,' he chuckled.

'When do you plan on talking to Frances?'

'I don't know. I thought maybe I should wait until she talks to me. I don't want to upset her any more than I've already done.'

Tish shook her head in disapproval. 'It's your decision, of course, but I think you should make the first move. You said yourself you've been absent from your relationship.'

'And neglectful,' Ted added.

'That's why you need to talk to her as soon as possible. Apologize for the past. Let her know you recognize what you've done. Then talk about the future and what you plan to do to ensure her happiness.'

'Do you think it will work? Do you think I can make it up to her?'

'I honestly don't know. I don't have a say in this. It's completely between the two of you. However, I will say that with the end of the fair in sight, and the group breaking for the holidays, it might be a good time to work on resolutions for the New Year.'

'You're right, and we're stuck here for a little while longer, according to your sheriff,' Ted stated as he munched pensively on his breakfast. 'A few extra days in our Winnebago, with no shows to perform, would give us plenty of time to try to hash things out.'

Tish was uncertain that a few days spent camping out at the Hobson Glen Recreation Park was sufficient time to address years' worth of marital issues, but she said nothing. Ted was hopeful and determined to save his and Frances's marriage and that, in itself, was enough.

TWENTY-TWO

Tish walked back to her booth only to find Schuyler, zipped into his suede jacket and jeans, seated on the hood of her car. In his right hand, he held a cup of coffee. In his left, he clutched a wax paper bag.

'Hey, you,' she greeted.

'Hey, yourself.'

Tish threw her arms around his neck and kissed him.

'Was that for me or the coffee I brought you?' he asked.

'Both.' She grinned as she took the insulated cup off his hands and drew a sip.

'Just wait until you see what else I have for you,' he teased.

'I already know what you have,' she smirked before kissing him again.

'Oh, yeah, well there *is* that, but there's also this.' He opened the bag to reveal a heap of golden scrambled eggs and sliced avocado wedged between two slices of multigrain sourdough bread.

'Ooh! With wholegrain mustard?' she asked excitedly.

'Enough to make your eyes water. Just the way you like it.' He passed the bag to her and they stepped into the booth. Tish switched on the electric generator that powered Jules's tiny space heater and set her sandwich down on the counter.

'What a nice surprise. How did you know I hadn't eaten breakfast?'

'I looked for you at the café. MJ told me you'd already left and that you hadn't eaten anything. She made me promise I'd bring that to you.'

'I'm grateful. For the sandwich *and* the messenger.' She sunk her teeth into her breakfast. 'Mmm. Was there a reason you stopped by the café?'

'Missed you, that's all. I wish you could have stayed with me last night, but I also understand how much work you have on your hands right now.'

'I wish I could have stayed with you, too.' Tish embraced him and buried her head in his shoulder.

'Everything OK?' he asked.

'Yeah, I just got a little unnerved last night and turned on every single light in the building.' She laughed at herself and wandered back to her sandwich.

'Did something happen?'

'No, I'm just overtired. Sheriff Reade had cautioned me against investigating the Inkpen case a few days ago, and I let my imagination build on it.' She took another bite of sandwich.

'He may be right, you know. His job is to protect the public. He wouldn't say something like that to scare you.'

'I know,' Tish acknowledged. 'It's all been fine, though. And, as of right now, I'm officially done with the case. Breakfast has been delivered and, with the exception of serving members of the group some afternoon and evening refreshments right here at the booth, I'll have little to no contact with any of them.'

'And tonight you're home with me,' he added as he wrapped his arms around her waist and pulled her closer.

'I can't wait.' She placed her hands on the back of his shoulders. 'Oh, I do have to come back for a bit tomorrow to empty this place and bring my gear back to the shop.'

'I'll come with you to help. After we drop everything off at the café, we'll go hunting for that Christmas tree. I did some Googling and there's a farm a few miles outside of town where you can cut down your own.'

'I would love that.'

'Good. I'll bring my saw. I was also thinking about that indoor picnic we talked about. You'll be tired and hungry after the fair, so why don't we move it to tonight? Then, tomorrow, I can cook you up that salmon and couscous dish you like so much.'

'How could I resist an invitation like that?'

'Well, you could, but I'm glad you didn't.'

'Never. I'm looking at tonight and tomorrow as a romantic getaway, even though we're not really getting away.'

'Hey, I'm totally down with a stay-cation, especially when that stay-cation is spent preparing for our first Christmas together.'

'First Christmas,' Tish repeated. 'After my divorce, I never dreamed I'd spend a "first Christmas" with anyone ever again. The crazy part is, I was fine with that. I enjoyed the decorating and the baking for friends and coworkers, but the day itself had always felt a bit anticlimactic, so I didn't mind spending it on my own. Not that I always was alone, mind you. One year, Mary Jo's parents flew in from California, so I was invited to Christmas dinner. And another year, I accompanied Jules to his mother's house in West Virginia. That was a trip!'

'Is Jules like his mother?'

'A complete chip off the block. Sassy, energetic, sweet, and an utter hoot.'

'Sounds like you had some fun holidays.'

'I did.' She smiled as she stared off into the distance. 'But I'm excited about our holiday. Spending some quiet cozy time with you before Christmas, decorating the tree, enjoying the glow of the lights, taking stock of all the good things that happened to me this year. And I'm actually excited for Christmas itself. I feel badly about Mary Jo and the kids being without Glen this year, but I'm glad to have my makeshift family around me. I'm going to spoil the kids while they're still technically kids, revel in every swear word Jules utters while losing at charades, guide Mary Jo into her new life, and take every opportunity to kiss you under the mistletoe.'

'There's mistletoe hanging at the café?'

'Not yet, but there will be.' She bit into her sandwich.

'Let's make that our first stop after clearing out the booth tomorrow,' Schuyler directed.

'Sure.' Tish laughed. 'I'm even excited about bringing Enid Kemper a turkey dinner.'

'She still won't join us?'

'Nope. Mary Jo's asking her again today, but so far she hasn't wavered. Not much else I can do except pretend we have too much food and bring her a plate.'

Tish and Schuyler were interrupted by the arrival of Jules's Mini Cooper. Bringing the vehicle to a stop alongside Tish's Matrix, Jules turned off the motor and emerged from the driver's door. Although he was dressed in his customary parka, a pair of oversized sunglasses obscured his face, and his hair – Jules's pride and glory – was uncharacteristically tucked under a Fair Isle knit stocking hat and topped with the parka hood. He grabbed Biscuit in his ugly Christmas sweater and stepped into the booth.

'Morning, Jules,' Schuyler greeted.

'That's an interesting look,' Tish noted. 'Did you dress yourself according to your conflicting weather reports?'

'Cute,' he deadpanned. 'I have more to worry about than a few weather-reporting gaffes. I've gone viral.'

'Do you need a ride to Henrico Doctors' Hospital?' Schuyler offered. 'I'm headed that way to do some shopping.'

'Y'all are *too* funny,' Jules complained. 'Listen, this is a legitimate crisis. That YouTube video of my hat catching on fire has over fifty thousand views. It's on Facebook and Twitter and even Snapchat. Actually, I don't do Snapchat, so I'm not sure about that one, but I'm willing to bet it's there.'

'But that's good news, isn't it?' Tish asked. 'That means publicity for you and the station.'

'Too much publicity. I never thought I'd say such a thing, but it's true. I've gotten so many calls and texts from news agencies requesting comment that I've had to shut off my phone.'

'And wear a disguise?'

'Yes. I'm here to serve drinks, not talk to curiosity-seekers. The only way to do that is to obscure my natural good looks.'

Tish was going to make a snide remark, but she thought

she'd given Jules enough teasing. 'Well, if you need to answer some of those calls, I don't mind you taking some time off.'

'Thanks, but I really don't have the energy to wade through all those messages. Besides, I called my boss and they're assigning someone to handle media requests on my behalf.'

'That should help ease some pressure,' Schuyler stated.

'It already has,' Jules explained. 'But I still need to keep a low profile. Otherwise, this booth will be overrun with locals wanting my autograph.'

'Do people collect autographs of internet celebrities?' Tish challenged. 'Wouldn't they just take a selfie with them?'

'Selfies, autographs – does it really matter?' Jules waved his left hand wildly. In his right he still cradled Biscuit. 'Now, my crew will be here again tonight at five.'

'Oh, Jules, I really don't think that's such a good idea. As much as I appreciate you trying to help my business, between your coverage of the murder and now your viral video, I think you have enough going on without doing a segment on me and the café.'

'You? Oh, no, honey. The crew isn't here to cover you. Your story got bumped so that they can cover me.'

'You? But you already work for Channel Ten. What's there for them to cover?'

'My meteoric rise in YouTube fame, of course. Since Channel Ten is my home, they have the exclusive.'

Even though Tish hadn't actually wanted to be on camera, the thought that her story had been bumped still nettled. 'I've been bumped?'

'Don't worry,' Jules reassured her. 'Stories get bumped all the time. It all depends upon what our station manager thinks people will find most interesting.'

'We live in a town of ten thousand people. How many interesting stories can there be?'

Jules shrugged.

'Oh, come on now, Jules,' Schuyler jumped into the fray. 'You're not really going to serve customers in that get-up, are you?'

'Schuyler has a point,' Tish agreed. 'You look like some sort of Yuletide Uni-bomber.'

'You're just jealous,' Jules replied cattily.

'I'm not jealous,' she insisted, even though a tiny part of her was. 'You just look a bit . . . creepy.'

'I admit, the look is a bit off-putting, but I have no choice. It would be bedlam otherwise.'

'Are people really that dazzled by internet stars?' Tish questioned.

Before Jules could answer, a familiar voice called across the fairground lawn. 'Mornin', everybody. Mornin', Jules,' Celestine Rufus greeted as she wheeled a hand-truck bearing the day's fresh cakes toward the booth. 'You, sir, are in serious demand. All my grandbabies are askin' for your autograph. And they want to stop by later to have their photos taken with you, if that's OK.'

'It would be my pleasure,' Jules announced as he grabbed a pen and a pad of paper from Celestine and passed Biscuit to Tish in order to free up his writing hand.

Tish clutched the dog close to her chest and stroked his silky white hair. 'Don't worry, Biscuit,' she cooed into his ear. 'You're not the first child to be pushed aside by a celebrity parent. In a few years, when you're older, we'll write a tell-all book together and entitle it *Doggy Daddy Dearest*.'

Jules was about to retaliate when the sound of a bicycle bell rang through the frosty air. Opal Schaeffer peddled toward the booth, coming to a stop beside Celestine. 'Happy Sunday, everyone. Oh, that's a perfect shot!'

Hopping off the seat and leaning the bicycle against the side of the booth, Opal pulled her phone from her coat pocket and began snapping photos of Jules. 'Absolutely perfect!' she exclaimed. 'I can picture the story now. Hot new celebrity hunk is seduced by the dark side of Hollywood until a bold, brave, gorgeous young woman comes along to tame the bad boy and help him to find his true self.'

Jules wrinkled his nose. 'Woman?'

'That works even better. A bold, brave, handsome young man comes along to tame the bad boy and help him to find his true self.'

'This handsome young man – is he also Italian and rich?'

'I was thinking more in terms of a conflicted Scotsman.'

'Does he wear a kilt?'

'He might,' Opal allowed.

Jules looked up from his autographs. 'Deal.'

'Groovy,' she declared and snapped away. Upon capturing the desired shot, Opal replaced her phone in her pocket and retrieved a heavy canvas bag from the front basket of her bicycle. 'Tish, I have that produce I told you about.'

'You needn't have rushed,' Tish said.

'Oh, but I did. These were ready to harvest, and I needed to bring them in before last night's freeze. Fewer plants to cover that way,' Opal explained. 'Besides, I know how you like to tinker with recipes on your day off.'

Opal loved when her produce was used in Tish's recipe experiments, not least because those experiments were quite often vegetarian and she was typically one of the first taste-testers.

'Come on back,' Tish invited her inside the booth, prompting Schuyler to make his leave.

'Do you need my help with anything?' he asked.

'No, there's a fair amount to do before opening, but with Jules and Celestine here, I should be fine.'

'I don't mind pitching in, either,' Opal offered as she scooted past Schuyler and warmed her hands over the space heater.

'Thanks, Opal,' Tish stated appreciatively.

'Since it appears that you're in good hands, this elf is heading into Richmond to pick up some treats for the next two days. Does anyone need anything while I'm there?'

'Nope, all my shopping's done, dusted, and wrapped, and my pocketbook's empty,' Celestine answered.

'I made all my gifts this year,' Opal announced.

Tish winced slightly. She hoped she would not be receiving one of Opal's homemade aphrodisiac bath bombs, dubbed "sex bombs" by the author, in her stocking this year.

Jules beckoned to Schuyler. 'There's a cute little cosmetics shop on Huguenot Street that sells Kiehl's products. Would you mind picking me up some of their ultra facial cream? This winter air is so harsh and drying, and I need to look good on camera.'

'Sure,' Schuyler agreed.

'You're a peach. I'll give you my credit card for the cream and some cash for gas.' He reached into the inside of his jacket for his wallet.

'Um, I'm an attorney, Jules,' he reminded. 'I'm not signing your name for a credit card purchase. And I filled my car up only just yesterday, so how about we settle up later?'

'That would be ideal. I'm simply up to my eyeballs at the moment.'

'Yes, I understand. Well, bye, everyone. Have a good day.' Schuyler turned to Tish, his eyes wide and unblinking.

Tish nestled Biscuit into his heated dog bed and, linking her arm in Schuyler's, escorted him to his BMW. 'I'm sorry Jules treated you as a member of staff.'

'That's OK. How much longer do you think he'll be like this?'

'Hard to say,' Tish said honestly. 'When we were at UVA, he once won the title of "Best Hair on Campus." That was in January 1997. It took May's heat, humidity, and subsequent frizz before he was remotely humble again.'

'So maybe by Easter?'

'Worst-case scenario. I suspect that when the internet finds a new darling – and it will – Jules will return to his senses.'

'Is that what happened with the snowplow incident?'

'No, that wasn't quite as popular as this video, of course, but Jules lapped up the attention just the same – until he actually watched the video and realized how silly he looked. Then he wouldn't talk about it for months.'

'Should we ask him to watch this video?' Schuyler suggested.

'Nah, let him have some fun. He'll get around to it eventually.'

'Do you think that will happen before we spend Christmas with him?'

'Maybe. It *is* the season of miracles, after all. And, if need be, interventions.'

He laughed. 'Good to know you have a back-up plan.'

'Always.'

He gave her a kiss goodbye. 'See you tonight.'

'Can't wait.' Tish waved to Schuyler as he drove off and then returned to the booth.

'Romance at Christmastime. Nothing warms my heart more,' Opal stated as she rubbed her hands together in front of the space heater. 'Now, if it would only warm the rest of me.'

'You need some fuel in that body of yours, girl,' Celestine advised. 'Did you eat breakfast this morning?'

'I can't remember. When I sit down at my desk to write, I lose all sense of time and space. I can tell you I had coffee, though, and a cigarette. Or was it two?'

Having witnessed Opal's chain-smoking first-hand, Tish was doubtful the writer had limited herself to just two.

'No wonder you're cold. Here, try this.' Celestine pushed a paper-wrapped slice of golden fruitcake across the counter.

Opal shook her head. 'As good as your cakes look and smell, I can't partake. I simply can't do gluten.'

'What I gave you is gluten-free.'

'No!' Opal protested. 'It can't be.'

'It is. I used almond meal instead of flour. The rest is dried pears, dried apricots, golden raisins, and crystalized ginger.'

Opal took a bite of the fruit-laden cake. 'That is absolutely fabulous. I would never have believed that was gluten-free.'

'I'll fix you an awesome soy latte to accompany that cake once I finish signing these autographs,' Jules proposed.

Celestine glanced over at Jules. 'Just how many pages are you plannin' to sign?'

'All of them.'

'You're signing the whole pad?'

'Yes. I thought you wanted me to.'

'No, I only wanted eight. How many grandkids do you think I have?'

Jules avoided the question. 'I was trying to be generous.'

'That's all well and good, but that's the pad I use for my weekly grocery list.'

'You can still use the backs of the pages. Or you can sell the extra autographs to your friends.'

'Do I look like the kind of woman who would hawk autographs to her friends?'

'Well, I, er . . .' he stammered.

Tish left Jules and Celestine to work out their issues. 'Opal, what goodies have you brought me?'

The writer took another bite of cake and, still chewing, unloaded a collection of beautiful winter vegetables from the canvas bags: three verdant leeks, a head each of curly and flat-leafed kale, a half dozen late carrots, and a dozen or so red potatoes. 'No cabbages just yet, but next week looks sunny and mild, so they should have all they need to plump up before January.'

'No worries. This will work quite well until then. I'll add some beans, tomato puree I froze from the summer, and some pasta for a hearty minestrone.'

'Yum, sounds delish.'

'As usual, you'll get the first batch.'

'You know how I look forward to that.' Opal glanced over her shoulder at Jules and Celestine, who were still bickering. 'Are they OK?'

'Oh, yeah. They go back and forth sometimes – usually when Jules's head has gotten too big.' She pulled Opal closer. 'Speaking of which, you're not really using Jules's photo for a book, are you?'

'I probably will, actually. I've been wanting to branch out into other sub-genres, and this is an excellent opportunity. But don't worry, it will be some time before the book is released, so Jules's head will have had some time to shrink by then.'

'Thank goodness.'

Opal removed her phone from her pocket and pulled open the photo gallery. 'When I finally coaxed him to remove the sunglasses, hat, and hood, the photos turned out quite well.'

She scrolled through several photos of Jules hunched earnestly over Celestine's notepad, pen in hand. Always the ham, in each photo he tried a different facial expression.

'Goofball,' Tish chuckled.

Opal laughed along and then stopped at the best of the lot. 'This is the one I want to use.'

'You're right. Given the context of the story you described, it's quite good.'

'Yes, I think so too.' Opal went back to scrolling, but none of the remaining photos compared with the one she and Tish had both approved. Suddenly, the image of Jules mid-autograph switched to a black-and-white close-up of a young person with a buzz cut, delicate features, and expressive doe eyes. Like Jules's current disguise, the person was cloaked in a dark hood. 'Sorry, scrolled too far.'

'No, wait.' Tish grabbed Opal's hand just as she was about to scroll backward.

'Yes, it is a striking photo, isn't it? You can feel great sorrow coming from that face.'

'When and where did you take this?'

'Yesterday. Over there, by the games.' Opal pointed across the green, toward the row of white tents assembled behind Sam Noble's and the other food vendors. 'She, or he – it is difficult to tell, isn't it? – was running the shooting gallery. You know that game where you shoot at ducks with an air rifle? I watched this person help some children with their aim. Whoever they are, they're a crack shot!'

TWENTY-THREE

After all three of her calls to Reade were sent directly to voicemail, Tish walked over to the department's mobile headquarters, only to be told by a uniformed officer that the sheriff was out following a lead. Return time, unknown.

With the fair drawing to a close in the evening and attendance anticipated to be lower than it had been the previous three days, Tish was fearful that Briony – or the person she suspected was Briony – might leave town early if her services were no longer needed. Leaving instructions for Celestine and Jules with the promise that she'd return shortly, Tish headed across the food court area and toward the fairground midway.

The selection of family games present on the midway required very little in the way of set-up to be crowd-ready, so it was still a bit too early to expect the tent in question to be open, but Tish thought she'd take the chance.

The chance paid off.

A short, plump, balding man in a green jacket had pulled

up by the front of the tent and was working on rolling up the sides. He was in his late sixties, with the leathery complexion of one who had spent his lifetime working outdoors.

Tish approached. 'Good morning.'

The man turned around, startled by the interruption. 'It is a good mornin'. Been a successful weekend and now we're gettin' outta here before the snow starts fallin'.'

Tish reflected upon Jules's forecast. 'Snow? I don't think anyone predicted that.'

'They didn't. I feel it in my bones. It's this awful rheumatism. Hurts like hell, but I'm a fine barometer.'

'Well, I don't suffer from rheumatism, but I'm inclined to agree with you. There is a whiff of snow in the air.'

The man nodded and picked up an insulated coffee mug from its spot on the ground. 'I recognize you,' he announced after taking a sip from the thermos. 'You're from that booth across the green. I remember that library lady pointin' you out the other day while I was standing in line for a burger.'

'Yes, that's me. I'm Tish Tarragon.'

'Hello, Trish. Bob Woodford.'

Tish was tempted to correct Bob Woodford's pronunciation of her name but decided to let it pass.

'I'm not much into books,' he went on, 'but I tell my grandkids to keep up with their readin'. Sounds like it's a good thing you're doin' for the people of this town.'

'Are you from the area?' Tish asked.

'No, ma'am. Georgia born and bred. Live in a town called Thunderbolt, just outside Savannah. Lived there my whole life. Much as I like visiting this area, these northern climes disagree with me.'

Tish nearly jumped out of her skin. *Another connection to Savannah.* 'It does get much colder here, doesn't it? You know, I have a soup-and-sandwich special you might like for lunch as well as plenty of hot beverages to refill that canteen of yours. And since you're a fair vendor, your meal is on the house.'

'Free?' Bob was skeptical. 'Ain't nothing free in this world.'

'You're right. This isn't entirely free. I need to speak with your employee, Briony.' Tish extracted a café business card from the back pocket of her dark-blue jeans and wrote 'Free lunch as per TT' on the back, just in case Bob visited the booth when she wasn't there.

Bob did a double take. 'That's all? That's the only catch?'

'That's it.'

'That's mighty kind of you, Trish, but I don't feel right taking that lunch. You didn't need my permission. I don't keep tabs on my workers,' he insisted. Then asked, 'So why do you want to talk to Brian?'

Brian? The name gave momentary pause, but Tish assumed she'd either misheard or Bob had misspoke. 'A friend of mine is looking to sign her grandchildren up for shooting lessons. She was here yesterday taking photos of Briony's technique and was greatly impressed.'

'Ain't surprised. Brian's the best employee I've ever had. Conscientious, polite to the customers, good with the little ones, and don't mind putting up with my old, cranky ass. Don't make a half bad cup of coffee either.' He raised his mug.

Again, Bob had called his employee Brian. He must have spotted the question flash across Tish's face, for he immediately added, 'I know he don't look much like a Brian, but that's his name. Don't bother me none. You work with carnies, you see all sorts of things. They're good folk, though, and, as I said, Brian's the best of the bunch.'

Tish nodded. 'I understand. So may I speak with Brian?'

'Tent behind this one. He'll be drinkin' coffee. He ain't a mornin' person.'

Following Bob's instructions, Tish entered the tent to find Brian seated on an old camp stool, drinking coffee in front of an electric heater.

Brian looked up, wild-eyed and startled. 'Who are you?'

'I'm Tish Tarragon, owner of Cookin' the Books Café. I'm running a food booth over by the stage.'

'And?'

'I'd like to speak with you, if I may.'

'You already are.'

Tish fell silent. So intent had she been on finding Jenny's doppelgänger that she hadn't given a single thought to what she might say once she found them. She decided to be completely open. 'I need to ask you about your sister.'

'I have no sister,' was Brian's immediate reaction.

'No, you don't any longer, do you? Not now that she's dead.'

'Dead?' Brian laughed uncomfortably. 'Look, I don't know who you are and what you're doing here, but I have absolutely no idea what you're talking about.'

Tish wondered for a moment if she had made a mistake. Was it possible this person wasn't Jenny's sister? No, talking to Brian was like talking to Jenny's ghost. The face, the expressions, the mannerisms were all the same. 'Your sister was Jenny Inkpen.'

'Inkpen? Who the . . . oh, that actress who was murdered. OK, now I know you're insane.' Brian rose from the campstool and shook his head.

'Jenny Inkpen wasn't her real name. It was Genevieve. Genevieve Savernake.'

At the name 'Savernake,' Brian's face blanched.

Tish went on, 'Genevieve had a sister, Briony Savernake. Briony bore a striking resemblance to her older sister. Just as you do, even with your buzz cut and shiny new nametag.'

'What do you want from me?' Brian demanded.

'To help me and the police find your sister's killer.'

'I'm not talking to any cops.'

'You don't need to. You can talk to me.'

'Why should I do that? Look, I don't care who murdered my sister. My sister ran away and left me behind just so she could become some famous actress. I figure she got what was coming to her.'

'You're angry,' Tish noted.

'Damn right, I'm angry. You'd be angry too if—'

'If what?'

'Nice try, but I'm not answering your questions. All I want is to survive the day and then get the hell out of this goddamn town.'

'Survive? Are you in some kind of danger?'

'Yes, of losing my temper. Now, would you leave me alone? I already told you my sister can rot in hell for all I care.'

'And what about your Aunt Bonnie?'

'What about her?'

'She's here in town to identify Genevieve's body.'

Brian was silent for several seconds. 'She can rot in hell, too.'

'I thought you and your sister were close to your aunt.'

'We were until she bailed on us. Never called, wrote, or texted. She just disappeared off the face of the planet.'

'Your aunt didn't bail on you and Genevieve. Your stepfather barred her from contacting the family,' Tish explained.

'Is that what she told you?'

'That's what she told the sheriff.'

'Well, she still could have tried.'

'She did, Brian. Your stepfather took out a court order prohibiting her and her sons from visiting, calling, or contacting you in any way. She wanted to fight the court order, but she didn't have the money to hire an attorney. That's why you didn't hear from your cousins either.'

Brian sat back down on the campstool, looking completely devastated.

'Are you OK?'

'Just go,' Brian pleaded.

'I will, but if you decide to talk, here's my number.' She took out a business card. 'And my booth is just on the other side of the green.'

As Tish turned around to exit the tent, she heard Brian's voice call her back. 'Tish?'

She turned around.

'You did say that was your name, right?' Brian clarified.

'Yes.'

'Then you might as well know mine. My name *is* Briony. Not Brian. I'm not transgender, bi, gay . . . I'm not anything actually. I shaved my head, put on boys' clothes, and took the "y" off my name so that men would stop looking at me and touching me and making their disgusting comments. So they'd leave me alone.'

Tish stood in the tent opening for several seconds while she thought about what to say. 'I'm sorry you felt the need to do that.'

Briony wiped away a tear. 'I am, too,' she whispered. 'I am, too.'

*   *   *

Tish left the tent and the shooting gallery behind and, after giving Sheriff Reade another call, marched straight to Justin Dange's Travato.

Within moments, the actor, in full makeup as the younger Scrooge, opened the door. 'Tish, what brings you here?'

She didn't mince words. 'You once said that Jenny was broken and damaged. I need to know why you called her that and I need to know it now.'

TWENTY-FOUR

It was late afternoon and at the tail end of the group's final performance of *Twelfth Night* when an anxious Reade appeared at Tish's booth. 'There's less than two hours until the fair closes. Are you still certain Briony will contact you?'

'One hundred per cent certain? No. That's why you have a member of your team posted in the tent across from the shooting gallery. So if she and Bob pull up stakes, he can stop them. However, I don't think it will come to that.'

'I wish I shared your optimism.'

'I'm nervous, too, Clemson,' she confessed. 'I don't want to let Briony go, but I also think she'd be more likely to open up to me.'

'Yeah, that's why I went along with your plan. It's the waiting that's killing me.'

'Me, too, but your guy on the scene said it's been a busy afternoon. Briony is an excellent employee. She wouldn't leave Bob alone to face the crowds while she talked to me. She knows far too well what it feels like to be abandoned to do it to someone else.'

As if summoned by magic, the phone in Tish's back jeans pocket chimed. 'Oh,' she exclaimed as she retrieved the device. 'It's a text message. It's from Briony. She wants me to meet her in the tent where I met her this morning.'

Reade pulled his phone out of his pocket and began to dial. 'What are you doing?' she asked.

'Putting an extra body on the shooting gallery surveillance.'

'You obviously believe Briony's the killer.'

'And you obviously believe she isn't.'

'I think it's possible, but I'm not entirely convinced.'

'You yourself said Briony was angry.'

'Yes, I did. I'm just not sure she was angry enough to kill her sister.'

'According to Bonnie Broussard and now Justin Dange, Jenny claimed to have been sexually abused as a child. If true, when Jenny ran away, she left her sister with an abuser. If that's not motive for murder, I'm not sure what is. When you factor in Briony's shooting skills and that she got some traveling carnival gig based in Savannah, the story becomes even clearer. She followed her sister here and took revenge.'

'I'm not refuting what you're saying, but if Briony did murder her sister, then why has she been sitting in a tent behind a shooting gallery the past few days? Why not leave town instead of risk being seen? If Jules, Opal, and I hadn't seen her, no one, including you, would have known she was even here.'

'I can't explain it. Criminals do odd things. They also do stupid things.'

'And what about the fireworks?'

'What about them?'

'Briony works at a shooting gallery. Where would she have gotten the money to pay for that many rockets? Bob Woodford certainly doesn't have it.'

'Genevieve and Briony's stepfather must have been doing OK financially if he was able to afford acting, dance, and shooting lessons.'

'So Briony uses abusive stepdad's cash to bump off her sister for leaving her with abusive stepdad?' Tish challenged.

'Maybe we're reading too much into the timing of the fireworks,' Reade suggested.

'Just because it doesn't fit with your theory doesn't mean you get to write it off as coincidence.'

'You're right. You sound like me, but you're right. Can you come up with anything better, though?'

'At the moment, no. Have you learned anything more about Briony's past?'

Reade shook his head. 'It's a Sunday, and the last one before Christmas. Everyone's working with a skeleton crew.'

'Well, I'll see what I can find out,' Tish announced as she turned to leave for the shooting gallery.

'Um, Tish,' Reade called her back. 'Bonnie Broussard is on her way over. She's staying in town for the night, but no restaurants are open, so I suggested she come here.'

'Sure. We'll fix her up with whatever she wants.'

'Thanks, but that's not why I mentioned it.'

Tish's thoughts went to Briony. 'I'll see how things go before I say anything.'

Reade nodded. 'My phone's on if you need me. Be careful.'

'I always am,' she reassured him before setting off across the green and toward the midway.

She arrived at the shooting gallery, where Bob waved her toward the back tent. There, she found Briony seated in the same spot she'd been that morning; however, now the young woman's expression was more of weariness than apprehension. 'I know you're talking to the police, so I want to say right off the bat that when I arrived here at the fair, I had absolutely no idea Genevieve was here.'

'How can that be? Didn't you see her on the stage?' Tish questioned. 'Or on the theater group advertising?'

'I can't see the stage from here,' Briony explained. 'And I didn't see the advertisements. I never bothered to look. One fair looks pretty much like another after a while. This is also the last festival of the season, so I was busy thinking about what I was going to do for work over the winter.'

'When did you finally realize Genevieve was here?'

'After she was dead,' she answered with tears in her eyes. 'The morning her murder broke on the news, some customers came by the shooting gallery talking about it. They showed me the theater group website on their phones and pointed to her photo. She was older and had a different name, but it was definitely her. I just about screamed, but, naturally, I couldn't.'

'And you hadn't seen Genevieve at all prior to the day the news broke?'

'I hadn't seen her since the morning of the day she ran away. She walked me to school – I was in junior high, she was in high school – gave me a hug, and waved goodbye.'

Tish heaved a loud sigh.

Briony reacted to the sound. 'You don't believe me.'

'I do believe you, and yet I find it strange that your employer is based out of Savannah, Georgia.'

'So?'

'So, your sister was in Savannah busking in the parks before she moved to Williamsburg to join the theater group.'

The expression on Briony's face was one of genuine surprise. 'I had absolutely no idea. I swear!'

'What were you doing in Savannah?'

'I'd gone there to attend SCAD on a full scholarship. You know, the Savannah College of Art and Design. I'd been there just a year when I started having nightmares and panic attacks. The college health center put me on meds, but they didn't help much. I made it through both semesters, but I'd reached the point where I couldn't face being cooped up in a classroom, so I spoke with my advisors. They let me take this year as a gap year, so I could rest and recuperate.'

'So what are you doing working in a shooting gallery?'

'The fresh air and mindless work helps me,' she stated.

'And what about seeing a medical professional outside the college health center?'

'Hard to do that when you don't have insurance.'

'But you're only – what? – nineteen. You're a student. Aren't you on your stepfather's insurance plan?'

'No. He kicked me off years ago.'

Tish was horrified. 'Why would he do such a thing?'

'He was ready to move on to a new life, I guess. Things were, um, *different* after Genevieve left.'

'They must have been extremely difficult for you. It sounds as though you and your sister had been close,' Tish noted.

'I thought we were, but then she left without a word. She left me alone with . . .' Briony took a few moments to compose herself. 'I'm sorry, I haven't told anyone other than the SCAD counselors about this.'

'Take your time.' Tish grabbed a second camp stool and sat across from the young woman.

'After Genevieve left, my stepfather began . . . "visiting" my room at night. He worked weird hours, so he often came home late. I'd lie in bed and listen for the sound of his car in the driveway and shiver. Many times I wished I could run away like my sister had, but my stepfather had me on lock-down. He hired some housekeeper/nanny-type person to take me to and from school and stay with me. I'd hear him come home and say hello to her. Then he'd come upstairs and knock on my door. Like I had any other choice but to let him in.'

'Did you ever tell anyone what was going on?'

'What, that my stepfather was having sex with his thirteen-year-old stepdaughter? No one would have believed me. Everyone loved my stepfather. "Poor Armand, look how brave he is. Raising two girls who aren't even his." Had I told anyone, I'd have been labeled a problem child, just like my sister.'

'I'm so sorry, Briony.'

'Yeah, well, I was one of the lucky ones. I only had to endure two years of it. When I turned fifteen, Armand sent me away to boarding school. Guess I was too old for him and no longer his type. He came to visit me maybe twice after I arrived at school, then that was it. He never called or visited again.'

'Not even for graduation?'

'No, I stayed with a friend's family that summer and then I was off to SCAD. You know, I never even told my friend what happened, because, deep down, I've always wondered what I'd done to make my stepfather do what he did. Did I say or do something to make him think that I – that he . . .?' She drew a hand to her face and began to sob.

Tish placed a consoling hand on the girl's shoulder. 'You didn't do anything wrong, Briony. You're the victim here. Not him.'

When Briony's tears subsided, Tish said, 'Briony, I need to tell you something. Just before your sister ran away, she accused Armand of inappropriately touching her.'

Briony's face was a mixture of horror, confusion, and disappointment. 'No, I–I can't – why didn't she tell me? I was her sister. I was her sister!'

'I don't know why she didn't tell you. We'll never know, but perhaps she felt the same way you did. Perhaps she felt that she'd done something to deserve what was happening to her. And maybe she was trying to protect you, too. You still loved your stepfather at that point, didn't you?'

The young woman nodded. 'Genevieve was very protective of me.'

'There you go.'

'How do you know Genevieve accused Armand of touching her? Who did Genevieve tell?'

'Your Aunt Bonnie. Your Aunt Bonnie, in turn, told your stepfather.'

'Is that why my aunt was barred from seeing us?'

'That's when it started, yes.'

'Do you think that's why Genevieve ran away? Because of what my stepfather did to her?'

'Only your sister knew the answer to that question, but I'm sure it must have been a factor.'

'God,' Briony beseeched as she threw her head back and looked heavenward, 'how I hate him! The things that man has taken from me. I wish—'

'What?' Tish prompted.

'I wish I knew what I know now when I saw him the other day.'

'You saw your stepfather? I thought you were no longer in contact with him.'

'I wasn't,' Briony answered matter-of-factly. 'I'm not. I saw Armand while we were setting up on Thursday afternoon. I went out by the vendor parking area for a quick smoke and a pickup truck drove past me. The driver didn't see me, but I saw him, clear as day. He was older and his face was a bit heavier, but it was definitely my stepfather. It was, without a doubt, Armand Grenable.'

Tish couldn't believe her ears. 'Your stepfather is here, at the fair?'

'He was. I don't know if he still is.'

'Is that why you've been disguising yourself with sunglasses and a hood?'

'I didn't want him to recognize me. I damn near panicked

yesterday. I ran after a kid who left his mittens behind at the gallery and the glare from the sun was so bad that I had to remove my sunglasses in order to pick him out of the crowd. Not a fun moment.'

'That's when I saw you,' Tish told Briony. 'That's when I saw you for the first time.'

'I'm happy it was you and no one else.'

'I am, too. Look, you need to talk to Sheriff Reade about your stepfather. Not only did he break the law years ago but his being here puts a whole different slant on your sister's murder.'

'I really don't want to get involved with the police.' Briony squirmed in her seat.

'I know you don't, but this is important.'

'You don't understand. I, um, I don't want to get into trouble.'

'Trouble? I already told you: you were the victim, Briony,' Tish insisted.

'It's not that,' the young woman explained. 'When I saw Armand, I waited and watched as he got out of the truck and came to the fairgrounds. I was so angry for what he did to me – the abuse and then boarding school and preventing me from seeing a doctor, I just wanted to make him pay, so I . . .'

'What did you do?'

'I left an anonymous note on his windshield, telling him I knew about his past and what he'd done to his stepdaughter. I told him if he left ten thousand dollars in cash beneath the bleachers by the football field, I would forget what I knew.'

'You tried to blackmail him,' Tish paraphrased.

'Yes.' Briony began to cry again.

'What happened?'

'Nothing. I snuck down here and watched the bleachers all night, but no one showed up with the money.'

'Did you happen to get the license plate number of your stepfather's truck?'

'No, why?'

'It could help us track him down.'

'Do you think I'll be in trouble?'

'I'm no legal expert, but if you didn't receive any money

as a result of that note, then I doubt the police can do anything to you. Your stepfather would have to file charges against you. As he's not exactly in a position to do that, then I think you're safe. Now, I'm going to call Sheriff Reade, fill him in on what you've told me, and tell him to come by and get your statement.'

'Oh, no!' Briony leaped from her seat. 'I don't want him here. Bob will be full of questions I really don't want to answer. I also don't want him to think I've done something wrong. I like working for him.'

'OK,' Tish capitulated. 'I'll call Reade and tell him we're coming to meet him.'

TWENTY-FIVE

Tish escorted a hooded Briony out of the shooting gallery and down the midway, Reade's officer close at their heels. The performance of *Twelfth Night* had just ended, sending a wave of audience members spilling on to the fairgrounds and, with the fair soon to close, the adjacent parking areas.

As the trio drew closer to the food concession area, Briony stopped in her tracks and let out a tiny yelp.

'What is it?' Tish urged.

The young woman squeezed her arm with one hand and pointed with the other. 'It's him! It's Armand.'

Tish's eyes followed the length of Briony's arm, hand, and index finger, finally coming to rest upon the figure of Sam Noble, standing at the till, counting out the day's earnings.

Suddenly, everything clicked into place.

The officer looked at Tish, his face a question. 'Ma'am?'

'Get Sheriff Reade here.'

The officer was about to dial his phone when the sheriff, who had been watching the trio from Tish's booth, appeared on the scene. 'What's going on?'

'That's my stepfather,' Briony informed Reade while

frantically gesticulating at Sam Noble and trying to obscure her face. 'I don't want him to see me. You need to get me out of here.'

A confused Reade glanced between Briony and Tish. 'Slow down, Ms Savernake. You're saying Sam Noble is Armand Grenable?'

'If the man at that cash register is Sam Noble, then yes. He abused my sister and me. I want you to arrest him. I want you him to make him pay.'

Tish wrapped a comforting arm around Briony as the young woman burst into tears. 'That might not be the only reason to arrest him, Clemson.'

'What?' a shocked Reade questioned. 'What do you—?'

Before the sheriff could finish his question, he was interrupted by the arrival of Bonnie Broussard. 'Thanks, Sheriff, for that supper. And thanks to Tish, too.'

Sheriff Reade gestured to the caterer. 'This is Tish.'

'Nice to meet you, Tish. That was the best stew I've ever had.' The woman's smile faded away as her gaze settled on the figure nestled in the crook of Tish's arm. 'Oh, I'm sorry. I didn't know y'all were here on official police . . .'

Briony blinked back her tears and looked up at the blonde woman. 'Aunt Bonnie?'

Bonnie Broussard drew her hands to her open mouth. 'Briony? Is that you?'

Briony nodded.

'I can't believe you're here in front of me. I thought you were gone from me forever.'

'Not gone. Just a little lost.'

As Bonnie's body convulsed into sobs, the two women embraced.

'I want you to know I never abandoned you,' Bonnie wept into Briony's shoulder. 'Not a day's gone by that I haven't prayed to God to let me see you again. I even spoke to your mama and asked her to help guide you girls back to me. I just wish it had been sooner.'

'Me, too.' Briony sniffed.

Bonnie stood back, took Briony's hands in hers, and examined her niece. 'Oh, my stars! You've grown into such a beautiful young woman. Your mama would be proud. Heaven knows my heart's nearly burstin'. I just hope you can find it in *your* heart to forgive me.'

'There's nothing to forgive. I know about the court order. Your hands were tied.'

'No, don't you see? This is all my fault. All of it. If only I'd believed Genevieve when she came to me and told me your stepdaddy had been touching her. If only I'd listened and done somethin', there never would have been a court order.' Bonnie's eyes grew wide. 'Briony, your stepdaddy never did anything to hurt you, did he?'

The young woman remained silent and stared down at the ground.

At the response, Bonnie released a guttural cry. 'Lord, no. What have I done?'

'Ms Broussard, you have no reason to feel guilty. You're as much a victim here as your nieces. Abusers isolate their victims from family and friends and do their best to discredit them so that people won't believe their accusations. That's exactly what Grenable did to you. I'm willing to wager that most of those tall tales Genevieve told, you only learned about when speaking to her stepfather.'

Bonnie's eyes narrowed as if searching her memory. 'Come to think of it, you're right. I did get those stories second-hand.'

'Armand's not going to manipulate and hurt us any longer,' Briony declared. 'Sheriff Reade is going to bring him to justice.'

'No, I'm going to bring him in for questioning,' Reade clarified. 'That's after I get your statement and after you decide to press charges. But first, I need to get you to the mobile headquarters.'

Reade gestured to his officer to escort Briony to the police trailer parked on the campgrounds, but the young woman wouldn't move. 'No, I want to see you take him in. I want to see him squirm.'

Bonnie Broussard jumped into the fray. 'Briony, are you sayin' Armand is here in this town?'

'More than that. He's right here at the fair.' She pointed toward Sam Noble's food tent.

Bonnie charged toward the tent like an avenging fury. 'You pervert! You pedophile! You piece of scum! You raped my nieces! You're gonna burn in hell!'

Reade and his officer corralled the woman before she could get too close to the Hobson Glen Bar and Grill proprietor, but her screams had garnered his attention.

'Clem,' Sam addressed the sheriff as he approached. 'Is there some problem here?'

'You bet there's a problem,' Bonnie shouted as the officer restrained her.

'You mean you don't recognize this woman?' Tish challenged.

'Course not. Why would I?'

'Nor do you recognize this young woman?' Tish motioned toward Briony, who had partially hidden herself behind Reade.

At the sight of Briony, Sam's face blanched. Still he denied knowing her. 'No, never seen either of them before in my life.'

'I say you're lying.'

'Yeah, you lying, worthless, little—' Bonnie started.

Tish held her hand aloft in a bid for silence. 'These two women positively identified you as Armand Grenable.'

Sam's eyes narrowed. 'Who?'

'Armand Grenable, brother-in-law and stepfather of these women.'

'What?'

'Yes, I was rather shocked, too,' Tish admitted. 'Then it all began to click. Sam's a popular nickname in the South, isn't it? Even if your name isn't Samuel. And Noble, well, that's just an Americanization of Grenable.'

Sam laughed. 'You know, Tish, people in this town already think you're a bit eccentric, but it sounds like you've completely gone off the rails this time.'

'Ah, yes. Gaslighting. Another of those techniques abusers use, right, Clemson?' she asked of the sheriff.

'Yep. A common one, too.' He folded his arms across his chest.

Meanwhile, Sam's wife, Heather, had stopped cleaning tables beneath their food tent and took her spot beside her husband.

'Abuser? I'm not an abuser,' Sam maintained.

'Oh, but you are,' Tish insisted. 'Briony here recounted to me what happened when you would come home from work late at night – a restaurant owner even then, I presume.'

'He ran a burger bar on the outskirts of the city,' Briony inserted.

'You'd come home late from the burger bar and creep upstairs under the pretense of saying goodnight to Briony. You'd knock on the door, she'd tell you to come in, and then you would rape her. You did the same with her older sister, Genevieve – better known as Jenny Inkpen. Do you know how I know you did the same thing to Jenny? Because when I went to deliver her breakfast the other morning, I was advised not to knock on the door without calling her name first. Hearing a knock on the door out of the blue was too startling and upsetting to Jenny. No doubt a holdover from her days being traumatized by you.'

As Bonnie sobbed, it was now Sam's turn to shout. 'That's not true!'

'My husband is a kind and gentle man,' Heather rejoined.

'Is that why you married him, Mrs Noble?' Tish asked.

'One of the reasons, yes. I thought he'd be a good father to my daughter, Lily.'

'Yes, *your* daughter, Lily. So Lily is Sam's stepdaughter. I admit Lily's presence threw me for a minute, since Sam's only been gone from Alabama for three years. And Lily is nine years old.'

'We prefer not to use the term stepdaughter, Ms Tarragon. Sam is just as much a parent to Lily as I am.'

Bonnie spoke up. 'My sister thought your husband was a great dad when she was married to him, too.'

Heather bit her lip. 'I'm sorry about your sister and your nieces, but my husband was not responsible.'

'Then why change his name?' Reade challenged.

'He didn't. You have the wrong man. My husband is a wonderful husband and father.' She turned her attention to the dark-haired girl who had wandered out from her parents' tent. 'Isn't he, Lily? Daddy would never dream of hurting you, would he?'

Lily didn't answer. She turned on one heel and ran away, choking on her own sobs.

Heather, her face a sudden shade of gray, stared wide-eyed and open-mouthed at her husband before giving chase. 'Lily! Lily!'

'That's it. I won't have you upsetting my family any longer,' Sam threatened.

'Family? Which one?' Reade cracked.

'Clem, I swear to you, man to man, I've never seen this girl before in my life' – Sam pointed to Briony – 'and I never once met Jenny Inkpen.'

'Again, you're lying,' Tish accused. 'Everyone here saw your face turn white at the sight of Briony. Is that because you were surprised to see her or because you wondered if you'd murdered the wrong sister? Spoiler alert: you did murder the "wrong" sister.'

'Murder?' Reade repeated.

'You mean he wanted to murder Briony?' Bonnie slipped from the officer's grasp and rushed forth to envelop her niece in a protective embrace.

'Sam wasn't sure whom he wanted – or shall I say *needed* – to kill. All he knew is that someone left an anonymous letter on the windshield of his truck on Thursday morning. That letter threatened to reveal that Sam had sexually abused his stepdaughter unless he coughed up ten thousand dollars in cash and left it under the football field bleachers later that night. You were dumbfounded, weren't you, Sam?' Tish asked. 'At first you probably weren't even sure if the note was real or just a prank. Then, at some point during the day, you looked up and saw Genevieve Savernake on the stage during the dress rehearsal. She didn't see you – no, as Justin Dange informed me a few days ago, Genevieve threw herself into her roles to the point where she was oblivious to what was going on in the audience. But you – you have a great view of the stage from this angle. And saw her quite clearly. Indeed, Jules remarked the other morning that these food court booths are so close that he could see the edges of Scrooge's prosthetic nose.

'When you saw Genevieve, you naturally assumed the letter

was from her. The letter itself even pointed in her direction, for it made reference to your abuse of your stepdaughter. Singular. Of course, Genevieve had left home before you targeted Briony, and she'd have had no knowledge that you'd abused her as well.

'The sight of Genevieve caused you to panic. You couldn't let Heather see the note. Nor could you go to the police, lest they discover your secret. However, you also couldn't pay Genevieve. Not only did you have absolutely no guarantee that she wouldn't ask for more money at a later date, but how would you explain an expenditure of that magnitude to your wife, if you even had the money at all?

'So you decided then and there to murder her, but you had to do it soon, because if you didn't pay her that night, she might expose you for who you really were. Given that you're a vendor here at the fair, it was easy to follow Genevieve backstage and figure out which trailer was hers. Armed with that knowledge, you then had to figure out how to kill her. You'd seen the re-enactors open the fair with their parade, and since business was slow for you Thursday evening, you'd probably wandered over to watch their rifle-loading and firing demonstrations. Likewise, given your access to the entire fairgrounds, it was easy for you to figure out where the rifles and the gunpowder were stored.

'And so you went to the equipment shed that night, armed with a hammer. The same hammer we saw you use to drive the stakes of your tent further into the ground. The hammer Reade's officers will no doubt find in the bed of your truck.'

'That's why we didn't find it on the grounds or in the woods,' Reade commented.

Tish nodded. 'But there was still a certain matter to which Sam/Armand needed to attend. Noise. Hammering on a padlock and shooting an antique rifle would have woken the entire campground, so he needed to drown out the sound. As the owner of the local night-time hangout, he knew where to buy illegal fireworks and also which kids in town wouldn't mind taking the risk of celebrating the school holiday by shooting them off.'

'You have no proof of any of this,' Sam argued.

'You forget,' Reade said, 'that I also know who sells fire-works in this town. It should be pretty easy to track down who sold you a few hundred dollars' worth of fireworks in December.'

'A few hundred dollars' worth of fireworks and a packet or two of sparklers. Remember, we saw Lily playing with them last night?' she asked of Reade.

'Yes, I do,' Reade corroborated.

Tish thought back to when she had witnessed her own father with their housekeeper so many years ago. In the few months after being caught, her father would 'gift' Tish money. A twenty-dollar bill here, a fifty-dollar bill there, an extra present on her birthday. He claimed it was for being a 'good daughter,' but even at her young age, Tish inherently understood what was implied in being 'good.'

Tish swallowed hard and looked Sam straight in the eye. 'You bought the sparklers because even while murdering your eldest stepdaughter, you still sought every opportunity to purchase your youngest stepdaughter's silence, because silence is what men like you rely upon in order to perpetuate your wretched deeds.'

'Silence? Get out of here! Silence for what?' Sam challenged.

'You're telling me your stepdaughter ran off in sobs just now for no good reason, Sam? Men like you don't change,' Reade volleyed. 'They never do.'

Sam remained silent, but it was clear from his steely gaze that he knew he'd been caught.

Tish went on, 'You ensured Genevieve's silence was perma-nent. Only you'd silenced the wrong sister. It was Briony who'd seen you drive into the vendor parking area that morning. It was Briony who'd written the letter and left it on your windshield. She asked for the money, not only to make you pay but so that she might finally be able to afford the mental health care she needed. The mental health care you denied her when you kicked her off your insurance plan, even though you were the reason she needed that care in the first place.'

Bonnie Broussard pulled Briony close to her and the pair wept.

'But, of course, you wouldn't have noticed Briony. She was working on the midway, just a short distance behind your tent, but was well disguised with her buzz cut, hood, and sunglasses. Like the siblings in Shakespeare's *Twelfth Night*, Genevieve and Briony had each established a new identity – Genevieve through her acting and Briony through a change in appearance. Yet, despite their new identities, they couldn't shed the past or their invisible bond with each other. After nearly crossing paths several months ago in Savannah, fate finally drew them – unbeknownst to each other – here to the fair and, consequently, to you. Briony hadn't the faintest idea her sister was up on that stage when she wrote that letter to blackmail you, but when you didn't show up with the money she requested, she took extra care not to wander too far from the shooting gallery where she worked. Fortunately, you never spotted her, for I have no doubt if you had, she'd be dead, too.'

Reade stepped forward. 'Looks like your time is up, Grenable. We're taking you in.'

Before Reade could even place him in handcuffs, Sam reached beneath his greasy apron and whipped out a .38 that had been concealed in the waistband of his jeans. 'You couldn't leave well enough alone, could you?' He pointed the barrel of the gun at Tish. 'Always having to prove how smart you are. How much better you are than anyone. It wasn't enough you took the library sponsorship away from me. You had to go messing around in my business.'

'Put the gun down,' Reade's officer shouted as he trained his own gun upon Grenable.

Sam turned the weapon on Briony and Bonnie. 'And you two bitches. All you had to do was keep your goddamn mouths shut! I loved you, Briony. You and your sister. All I did was show you that love. It might not have been the love you expected, but it was pure and true.'

'You're a monster,' Briony shouted. 'A monster!'

Briony's outburst was the distraction Reade needed. As Grenable's jaw dropped, Tish lunged forward to push Bonnie and Briony out of the line of fire. Meanwhile, the sheriff tackled Grenable from behind, grabbing him around the waist and knocking him, face first, to the ground, but not before

Grenable could squeeze the trigger, discharging a single shot in the direction of the three women. Knocking the still-smoking gun from Grenable's hand, Reade pinned the man's arms behind his back while his officer cuffed him.

Before Reade could issue Grenable his rights, Briony screamed. After being thrown to the ground, she and her aunt had risen to their feet.

Tish, however, had not.

In the soft glow of the festival lights, Reade watched as a dark spot on the back of Tish's wool coat slowly grew in size. In anger, he raised the hand bearing Grenable's gun and raised it over the back of his prisoner's head.

'Sir! No!' The officer grabbed Reade by the wrist.

Relinquishing the firearm to his officer, Reade rushed to Tish's side. 'Tish! Tish!'

She did not respond.

'Call for an ambulance,' he directed.

Meanwhile, officers from Reade's department arrived from the campground, answering the sound of shots fired. Quickly, they cordoned off the scene of the shooting and kept onlookers at a safe distance.

Fighting for admittance, Celestine could be heard shouting to one of Reade's well-intentioned officers, 'We're not onlookers. We're family!'

Reade waved to the officer in question to allow Celestine and Jules into the taped-off area.

'Oh my God,' Jules exclaimed at the sight of his friend.

'Is she gonna be all right, Clem?' Celestine asked.

'I don't know.' He removed the scarf from his neck and the all-in-one tool fastened to his holster. Using the knife function, he cut a slit in the back of Tish's coat and then cut his wool scarf in half and packed it into the wound.

'Shouldn't we be waiting for an ambulance?' Jules asked.

'There's an ambulance here at the fair, but it's going to take some time to navigate through the crowds to get here. In the meantime, you two can give me a hand. Jules, I need your belt.'

Jules placed Biscuit on the ground and hastily removed the brown leather belt from around his waist and handed it to the sheriff.

Reade took the belt and slid it beneath Tish's abdomen and then fastened it just tightly enough to prevent the scarf bandage from moving. 'OK, I need you two to help me log-roll her on to her back.'

Celestine and Jules knelt beside Reade. 'You sure about this?' Celestine asked.

'Only choice we have. I need to make sure her airways are clear and then administer CPR. Now, on three,' he instructed. 'One . . . two . . . three.'

The trio gently rolled Tish from her stomach on to her back, taking great care not to twist her torso. Her face was ashen, and her lips were tinged at the edges with blue. 'She's cyanotic,' Reade said as he tilted her head back, opened her mouth, and checked her airways for blockages.

'Oh, I can't watch!' Jules exclaimed, picking up Biscuit and clutching him to his chest. 'What else can I do?'

'Blankets. Anything to keep her warm.' Reade removed his wool peacoat and draped it over Tish's legs.

'On it!' Jules headed off into the crowd.

'There's some at mobile HQ,' Reade shouted after him. 'Celestine, remove her boots.'

Celestine did as she was told. 'Should I raise her legs?'

'No. Just massage her feet. Try to keep her warm and her blood circulating.'

Reade unbuttoned Tish's coat and began to administer CPR. 'Come on, Tish!' he begged after the first two rescue breaths. 'Come on.'

Celestine massaged Tish's feet and watched in horror as the blue tinge spread further across her lips.

'Tish, don't go. Please don't go. Don't leave me,' Reade pleaded as he applied rhythmic chest compressions.

There was still no response.

'Tish, listen to me. You can't die on us. Too many people need you.'

Having completed the cycle of thirty chest compressions, Reade leaned in and delivered two more rescue breaths before starting another cycle of compressions. 'Tish, please. Please don't go. I don't know what I'd do without you.'

As light snow began to fall, Tish sputtered and coughed.

The sound moved Celestine to tears. 'Oh, thank you, Jesus.'

Jules returned with Biscuit tucked under one arm and a wool blanket and a pile of billowy white fabric in the other. 'Lucinda, Frances, and Edie gave me a blanket from the stage and their petticoats too. How is she?'

Tish's face was still ashen, but color had been partially restored to her lips.

'Oh my God, is she breathing?' Jules dumped his finds by Reade, who proceeded to arrange them over Tish.

'She is,' the sheriff replied, 'but she's not out of the woods yet.'

The ambulance arrived, sirens muted, blue lights flashing. A team of paramedics emerged from the back door and swooped in on Tish. One of them approached Reade for a quick debriefing.

'Victim was shot once in the back with a thirty-eight. I packed the wound, followed protocol for moving a patient with possible spinal cord trauma, and then administered CPR. Victim responded and resumed breathing shortly before your arrival,' Reade reported in an emotionless voice.

He then stepped back and out of the way of the emergency workers, wandering over to where Celestine and Jules stood huddled together. The three of them silently observed as the paramedics connected the unconscious Tish to an assortment of tubes and wires, hoisted her on to a gurney, and loaded her into the back of the waiting ambulance.

All the while, the snow kept falling.

Standing in his shirtsleeves in the cold and damp, Reade became cognizant of a warm, comforting hand on his shoulder.

'You did good, Clem.' A tearful Celestine moved her hand from his shoulder and down his arm. 'I'm gonna get my car so Jules and I can follow the ambulance to the hospital. I know you have your own sources, but I'll call you to let you know how she's doing.'

Reade bowed his head, reached for Celestine's hand, and clutched it in his. No other words were exchanged. No other words were needed.

Celestine and Jules departed, and the paramedics slammed

closed the doors of the ambulance. Left alone amid the chaos of the crime scene, Reade watched the blue flashing lights of the ambulance as they pulled away from the fairgrounds and faded into the distance.

TWENTY-SIX

After undergoing emergency surgery to remove the bullet and treatment for a punctured lung, broken ribs, muscle damage, and moderate blood loss, Tish was discharged from the hospital on Christmas Eve – just five days after the shooting. It was, her doctor clarified, an accommodation for the holiday more than an 'official' discharge, but she also felt strongly that being home among friends and loved ones at Christmas would probably be more beneficial to Tish than lying in a bed, critiquing the hospital's sad attempt at roast turkey.

That said, Tish *was* on strict orders to rest, avoid any strenuous activities, and to use a wheelchair until she could return to the hospital after the New Year for a thorough evaluation.

Tish lamented her inability to dive back into work at the café, but as she was so grateful to be alive and out of the hospital, she wasn't about to complain. Tish was therefore quite surprised when Schuyler, upon picking her up from the hospital, drove directly to the café instead of his condo on the edge of town.

'What are we doing here? The café should be closed by now, but the lights are still on. My electric bill is going to be sky high!' She suddenly took note of the number of cars in the parking lot. 'OK, what's up?'

Schuyler parked his BMW in front of the ramp leading to the front door. 'I know you're under strict orders not to be at the café, but the doctor never said anything about attending a welcome-home party here, did she?'

'A party? You mean all the lights and all the people . . . are for me?' Tish leaned back in the passenger seat and drew a hand to her mouth.

'They are,' Schuyler confirmed as he leaned in close and planted a kiss on her lips. 'Merry Christmas.'

'Merry Christmas.' Tish wept tears of joy and gratitude as she threw her arms around Schuyler's neck. 'Did you do all of this?'

'Um, no. When I learned that you were coming home today, I called Mary Jo, Jules, and Celestine and asked if they could join us for a small gathering, as we'd originally planned. After that, it was entirely out of my control. Mary Jo spoke with Augusta May, Celestine spoke with Opal, and Jules, well, Jules—'

'Spoke with everyone,' Tish sounded in unison.

'Yeah, so now we have a welcome-home-slash-Christmas-slash-town-pot-luck party.'

Slightly self-conscious about the number of guests she was about to receive, Tish took her makeup bag from her handbag, pulled down the visor, and applied a fresh layer of mascara. 'Potluck?'

'Yes, everyone thought you would like it if they cooked for you for a change.'

'I love it!' Tish smiled broadly, tears still in her eyes. 'Well, let's get started, then.'

As Tish added a quick swipe of lipstick, Schuyler, looking cozy in a cream-colored cable-knit sweater, jeans, and suede jacket, got the wheelchair from the trunk of his car and pushed it to the passenger side door where Tish stood waiting. 'You're supposed to be resting,' he reminded her.

'I'm standing, not jogging.' She sighed. 'Even in the hospital I got some steps in every day.'

It was Schuyler's turn to sigh. 'OK, OK, I just don't want you to overdo it.'

'I won't,' she promised and sat in the chair. Sunday's surprise snow had dumped six inches of the white stuff in central Virginia, but all that remained was a thin layer of slush. 'Unless the term "overdo" is in reference to Celestine's chocolate-and-peppermint-candy-cane brownies.'

'Given you've lived solely on hospital food for five days,

I think you're more than entitled,' Schuyler allowed as he pushed her up the ramp to the front porch and swung open the door.

The scene inside the café was magical. Tish had done a good job of decking the halls earlier in the season, but someone (most likely Jules) had truly gilded the lily, adding a layer of fine tinsel and glass icicles to the tree and wrapping the pine garland that ran along the perimeter of the space with strand after strand of clear, star-shaped lights. The counter, which during business hours would have provided space for patrons to eat, was laden with just about every Southern cold-weather potluck staple: chicken and dumplings, squash casserole, creamy shrimp and wild rice, sweet potato souffle, cheesy baked grits, green beans simmered with a salty ham hock, and, of course, biscuits.

And then there were the sweets. Silver platters piled high with divinity, praline fudge, pecan sandies, Linzer tarts, snickerdoodles, jam thumbprints, frosted sugar cookies, rum balls, gingerbread people, and, of course, peppermint-candy-cane brownies.

But by far the most beautiful sight of all was that of the friends and neighbors gathered within the café's walls. 'Welcome home,' they shouted as Tish was pushed through the doorway.

Tish had no chance to reply. She was instantly ambushed by Jules and Mary Jo, who both knelt down and embraced her until her bullet wound ached – in a good way.

Mary Jo, looking lovely in a black velvet tunic, matching leggings, and flats cried, 'Oh, how I prayed you'd be back home for Christmas.'

'I just prayed you'd come back home,' Jules added, a magnificent caricature of himself in a red suit jacket, jeans, white dress shirt, and light-up Christmas tree tie. 'Honey, if you ever feel badly about not being the most interesting person in town again, let's talk. You don't have to be shot at by some scumbag to make the top story. Oh, when I think about what happened . . . I *told* you there was something wrong with that man and his menu.'

'And you were right, Jules,' Tish agreed. Jules, indeed, had an aesthetic sixth sense, but she was not in the mood to discuss it, as they'd already expounded upon the subject at length while she was confined to a hospital bed. 'By the way, this place looks absolutely fabulous.'

'Thanks! I wanted you to feel like Jimmy Stewart in the finale of *It's a Wonderful Life*, minus the quiet desperation and the five o'clock shadow.'

'And the table loaded with cash,' Mary Jo added.

'Yeah, we don't have that either.'

Tish laughed. 'I'm more than fine with that counter of food and good company. Speaking of which, I can't believe how many people are here.'

'Oh, that's mostly the Rufuses,' Jules explained.

'Guilty,' Celestine, dressed in an emerald-green blouse, jeans, and her Yuletide jewelry, stepped forward and gave Tish one of her usual bear hugs. 'Glad to have you home and healthy, sugar.'

'Glad to *be* home and healthy.'

'I hope you don't mind me bringing the whole tribe,' Celestine said as her younger grandchildren took Biscuit, a leash connected to his battery-operated light-up Christmas collar, outside to play in the café's side garden.

'Of course not – you know you're family to me.'

'Likewise, darlin'.' Celestine clasped her hand. 'That's why we're all takin' your place at the interfaith center tonight.'

'You're what?' Tish was incredulous. 'But your family Christmas Eve tradition—'

'Traditions are good, but sometimes you need to shake things up. My kids and Mr Rufus know how much this place and y'all mean to me. Every day when I get home, I tell them how we laugh and cook and poke fun and cry together. That's why they helped me make all those cookies and fudge. That's also why they're here this evening. Knowin' Schuyler, Jules, and MJ would be needed here tonight, I talked to my kids about what you'd promised to do down at the interfaith center and we decided to represent the café as a family. My daughters and daughters-in-law all agree that it's high time the younger ones learn about givin' back to others. And so, after we fuel up, Team Rufus will be dishin' up dinners for the less fortunate.'

Tish was overwhelmed by the Rufuses' generosity. 'I don't know what to say.'

'Don't say anything yet. Knowin' my bunch, you might regret this,' she cackled.

'From what I've seen tonight, I sincerely doubt that.'

'Well, maybe not. I only gave Cookin' the Books aprons to the well-behaved members of the bunch,' Celestine said with a wink. 'By the way, y'all are invited to join us for dinner tomorrow. We have two giant hams and all the sides. And we'd love to have you.'

'That's kind of you, Celestine, but we're actually sticking to our original plan, except we're doing it at Schuyler's as I'll be living there now.'

'That's fine . . . but who's cookin' the turkey?' Celestine glanced nervously at those standing near her.

Schuyler raised his hand. 'Me, technically. Tish will be directing me in the kitchen.'

'Well, um, good luck with that, Schuyler.'

'Thanks, I'll need it.'

Opal Schaeffer, decked out in a green Peruvian-style printed boiled wool jacket, red broomstick skirt, hobnail boots, and a newspaper boy's cap, came forth from the crowd, planted a kiss on Tish's cheek, and placed a clear mesh bag of dried green leaves in her hand. 'Welcome back, Tish! As much as I adore everyone at the café, this place isn't the same without you.'

'Hear, hear,' Jules seconded.

'Aw, thanks, Opal.' Tish examined the bag the writer had given her. 'What's this?'

'My special healing herbal tea, made from yarrow, gold-enrod, and calendula. I had some dried flowers in my cellar, so I made a batch just for you. I also brought the squash casserole. It's made with non-dairy cheese and butter. I'm eager for you to try it.'

'Is that what that is?' Celestine looked over at the counter. 'Mr Rufus just put a big helping of it on to his plate. He's such a picky so-and-so about vegan stuff, I'm gonna have to take a photo of him eatin' it!'

She dashed off toward the buffet.

'Since y'all mentioned tea, can I get anyone something to drink?' Jules offered. 'I have a pitcher of pomegranate martinis, a batch of warm cranberry-and-apple cider, and hot chocolate, as well as the usual suspects.'

'It's Christmas Eve. Martini for me, good sir,' Opal ordered.

'Yes, ma'am,' Jules jokingly saluted.

'White wine for me,' Mary Jo requested.

'Cider for me,' Tish added. 'They gave me a pain pill this morning. But tomorrow, I will definitely indulge in a cocktail.'

'If Schuyler's cooking, we might *all* need to indulge in a cocktail,' Jules quipped as he made his way to the drinks table.

'Hey, now,' Schuyler shouted after him as he followed along to assist.

As Tish, Opal, and Mary Jo were joined by Augusta May and Edwin Wilson, Enid Kemper wandered through the doorway and stood in front of Tish without as much as an 'excuse me.' 'Hmph. You don't look like someone who's been shot,' she assessed.

'Thanks,' Tish replied.

'I was worried there for a time. Langhorne and I come here for lunch after church each Sunday. It's the only place that gets Langhorne's order right. Everyone else overcooks his spaghetti. You serve it al dente.'

'I know how particular Langhorne is about his pasta. Ms Kemper, since you've walked all this way, why don't you fix yourself something to eat?'

'Oh, I couldn't impose. Did you cook it all?'

'No, I'm not quite up to that just yet, but I'm sure you'll find everything is quite tasty.'

'Nah, I should get back to Langhorne. He's covered and tucked in for the night, but one never knows when he might have one of his squawking spells.'

'I understand. I was just hoping you'd help us eat some of this food. We have a ton and I wouldn't want it to go to waste.

There's even a bowl of salad greens somewhere in there. You could take some home to Langhorne, since it will probably be wilted before the café reopens on Sunday.'

'You say I'd be helping you out?'

'Definitely.'

'Well, in that case . . .' She unbuttoned her ragged coat and undid her scarf.

'Thank you, Ms Kemper,' Tish smiled. 'And Merry Christmas.'

Enid Kemper paused for a moment, as if uncertain how to react. A faint smile spread across her lips. 'Merry Christmas, Tish, and keep out of the line of fire. You should make that your New Year's resolution.'

'I probably should, Ms Kemper. Now if you go over to the counter, Jules can help you wrap up what you're taking back to Langhorne.'

'Jules? Is he wearing his elf hat?' The elderly woman chuckled and shuffled off toward the buffet.

'She must have seen the news broadcast,' Mary Jo presumed with a laugh.

'I'm pretty certain Enid sees everything,' Tish remarked.

'Hears everything, too,' Augusta May commiserated.

The withered form of Enid Kemper was soon replaced with a quartet of familiar faces.

'Hello.' Lucinda LeComte stood before Tish, looking glamorous in a white faux-fur jacket and matching hat. She leaned in and planted a kiss on the caterer's cheek.

'Lucinda,' Tish greeted before looking up to see the rest of the group. 'Justin, Ted, Frances! I didn't realize you were all still in town.'

'We're not,' Frances clarified as she also leaned in for a smooch. Dressed in a hot-pink wool coat with a black velvet collar and buttons, a black knit cap, and black leather gloves, she was more relaxed than Tish had ever seen her. 'We're all back home, but Williamsburg is just a forty-five-minute drive from here and we felt we needed to be here after all you've done for us.'

'Well, I'm not sure what I did to deserve a visit on Christmas Eve, but I'm glad to see everyone. Where are Rolly and Edie?'

'New York City,' Justin Dange replied, looking equally relaxed in a black puffer jacket and striped scarf. 'They eloped, but not before Rolly officially closed the theater group down for the entire winter.'

'The entire winter? How does that impact you guys and the venues that were already booked?'

'There were only a handful of venues,' Ted explained. 'Rolly just pushed them closer to spring.'

'And as for us, we're ecstatic,' Frances added.

Justin spoke out, 'We haven't had a block of time off since—'

'Ever,' Ted completed the sentence with a chuckle. He too seemed far happier than he had the previous weekend. 'We've never, in the history of the group, had more than two weeks off at a time.'

'I think this whole thing with Jenny and now getting married has made Rolly realize how focused we've been on the group to the exclusion of all else,' Lucinda described. 'It hasn't been healthy. For any of us.'

Frances and Ted registered their agreement.

'So how are you all going to utilize the time?' Tish asked.

'Well, Edie's enrolled in some design courses in New York. Meanwhile, Rolly is establishing a student-mentoring program for the group. We all loved the concept of having fresh faces around – they just need to be the right faces – so he's going to line up some college students for us to audition for the summer season.'

'Lucinda and I are going to finally branch out into other styles of theater,' Justin said. 'We have some auditions lined up in New York, so we can visit the newlyweds while we're there.'

Tish wished them luck. 'So you're traveling together?'

'We are,' Lucinda confirmed as she reached for Justin's hand. 'We've been dancing around the prospect of a relationship for so long that we decided to finally take the plunge.'

'Congratulations.' She turned her eyes toward Ted and Frances.

'I've signed up for some sketching and painting classes,' Frances announced. 'I've always wanted to try my hand, but I was too intimidated.'

'And while Frances is busy creating art, I've committed to taking care of the cleaning and dinner preparations,' Ted inserted.

'And we have a getaway weekend planned for February in Washington, DC. We'll take in both art and history museums. And then we'll try to find some things that we enjoy together. It will be our first vacation in—'

'Ever,' Ted once again completed the sentence. 'During our marriage, we've only ever traveled with the group.'

'So things are good with you two?' Tish asked.

'We're taking it one day at a time,' Frances replied.

'But we both agreed that we had too much history together to just throw it all away,' Ted expounded. 'And we have you to thank for that.'

'I think we both also agree that Tish doesn't need us chewing her ear off any longer. Let's go get some chow, Ted.'

Tish laughed. 'Not at all! It's been great catching up, but please do get some food. There's tons of it. Just promise you won't leave without saying goodbye.'

'Course not. I want to get your cell number so we can keep in touch,' Frances announced and led Ted to the buffet.

Tish turned to Justin and Lucinda. 'I can't tell you how happy I am to see you together.'

'We're happy, too,' Justin confirmed. 'It's nice to be in a caring, mature relationship for a change.'

'And one built upon a strong friendship,' Lucinda added as she clasped his forearm with a gloved hand.

'I'm still terribly sorry about what happened to Jenny,' Justin admitted. 'But Lucinda has helped me to see the light. I know I once questioned whether or not Jenny had used me to get into the group and, you know, I don't think she did. Having learned about her background, I think that acting was her only escape from the past. When I offered her a slot in the group, she saw it as a step forward, but she just couldn't handle the human relationship aspect of it.'

'I'm no psychologist and I never knew Jenny,' Tish prefaced, 'but I've spoken with her aunt and sister and I tend to agree with you. After losing her parents and living with sexual abuse, I think she lost herself in the world of theater and cut herself off from anyone who might hurt her. Her craft became the only thing that mattered.'

'Poor kid.' Justin hung his head.

Lucinda rubbed his back and gazed at him sympathetically. 'Speaking of kids,' she added after several seconds had elapsed, 'I told Justin about my "little secret."'

'And?' Tish urged. 'Have you decided to approach the courts?'

Lucinda shook her head. 'Not yet. I'm leaning that way, but I need to think it through completely. This break is just the thing for that.'

Justin draped an arm around her shoulders. 'And whatever Lucinda decides, I'll be here at her side through all of it. Just as she's been here for me.'

'That's good to hear. Have you told Rolly?' Tish asked.

'Yes,' she answered. 'It seemed an odd time to tell him, what with his engagement, but I felt he should know. He was sorry I hadn't told him sooner and even sorrier that I went through it all on my own, but he understood why I did what I did. He acknowledged that he was a different person back then and that he would have freaked out over the news.'

'And Edie?'

'Edie was absolutely amazing. She harbors no grudges for what happened before she and Rolly were together, and is fully supportive of me contacting our daughter, if that's what I want. She's also fully supportive of Rolly having a relation-ship with his daughter if he chooses. She said if she ever meets our daughter, she'd treat her like family, because that's what she would be.'

'Can't ask for more than that, can you?'

'No, I can't. I'm truly blessed.'

'Yeah, I'm feeling a bit like that myself.' She smiled as Schuyler returned with her glass of warm cider. 'I should have mentioned it while Frances was here, but I want to thank you ladies for your emergency blankets.'

Lucinda beamed. 'The crinolines? Yeah, Edie's idea – she just shimmied hers off and the rest of us followed. That makes you one of the sisterhood, you know.'

'I'm honored.' Tish bowed her head.

As Lucinda and Justin joined Frances and Ted at the buffet,

Schuyler excused himself. 'I need to get ready for something. I'll be just a minute.'

'Sure,' Tish allowed, wondering what needed to be done at five thirty in the evening on Christmas Eve.

Mary Jo, glass of white wine in hand, returned to Tish's side. 'I can't tell you how relieved I am to know you're going to be OK.'

'That makes two of us. I've been given, quite literally, a new lease of life. I'm grateful to be here and deliriously happy to be out of the hospital. Although part of me is sorry that I won't be living above the café any longer.'

'Well, if you were still living here, your days of peace and quiet would be numbered. We're trying to get moved in before the New Year.'

'Yes, and I'm sorry I won't be here for it. I was looking forward to being your roomie again. It would have been like college.'

'Yeah, it would have been fun. Aside from the part where we'd be sharing our place with my two crazy kids.' She laughed.

'Hey, don't disparage those crazy kids. I love 'em. Besides, you, Jules, and I weren't much older than Gregory when we first met and became friends.'

'That's true. Where does the time go?'

'I have no idea. I thought I had another forty years ahead of me before I considered ownership of a single-floor dwelling a desirable feature in a man. Yet here I am moving in with Schuyler ahead of schedule because I can't do stairs.'

'Aw, it will be good, though,' Mary Jo stated. 'He's awfully eager to get you settled and make this holiday a special one.'

'Yeah, I know. He's been a rock through all of this. Just another reason to be thankful.' Tish's mind traveled to Sheriff Reade and all he did to save her life. 'Hey, since I've been in the hospital, have you seen Reade?'

'No, it's like he vaporized. He always used to get his coffee and breakfast first thing in the morning, but not this week. I thought maybe he changed shifts, but he didn't stop by in the afternoons either. Maybe he took some time off to regroup or to visit family.'

'Maybe,' Tish allowed. 'It's still strange, though, because

he gave my number to Briony Savernake and Bonnie Broussard yesterday. They FaceTimed me at the hospital.'

'Really? How are they?'

'Better than I expected. Briony's moved in with Bonnie down in Louisiana and she's looking forward to spending Christmas with her aunt and cousins again. As fate would have it, one of Bonnie's jobs – she has two – is as receptionist for a mental health clinic. When the doctors there heard what happened to Bonnie's nieces, they offered free counseling to both Briony and Bonnie. So the plan is for Briony to get a job, get herself healthy, save up a bit of cash, and then return to SCAD in the fall.'

'That's awesome. I'm sure there will be some tough moments, but it's good to hear they're trying to piece their lives together again and that people are willing to help them. It gives me hope – for the world and for my kids.'

'Kayla and Gregory are going to be fine,' Tish asserted. 'They'll come through this stronger than ever. And do you know why? Because they have you as a mother.'

'Now you're making me cry again. Oh, hey' – Mary Jo wiped at her lashes and gestured to the area in front of the Christmas tree where Schuyler stood clinking a spoon against his glass of cider – 'it looks like your single-floor dweller is about to give a speech.'

As Schuyler took his spot in front of the Christmas tree, Celestine walked out to the café's side garden to relieve one of her sons from supervisory duty while her grandchildren played. 'Go on in and fix yourself a plate,' she directed. 'I've got 'em.'

'You sure, Ma?'

'Positive. Your daddy and I already ate, and we have to leave for the interfaith center in less than an hour.'

'OK.' The bearded man in his mid-thirties gave Celestine a kiss on the cheek.

'What's that for?'

'For Christmas. And for being a good mama.'

'You nut!' A smiling Celestine removed his baseball cap and tousled his hair as if he were a little boy again. 'Now, get in there and eat. Oh, and make sure you have some of Augusta

May's chicken and dumplings. They're so good they'd bring tears to a glass eye.'

'I will.' Her son trudged through the slush back toward the café.

'Jackson,' Celestine reprimanded her eleven-year-old grandson, 'if you don't stop pullin' your sister's hair, you're gettin' coal in your stockin'!'

As Jackson went into the corner of the garden to sulk, a silver SUV pulled into the café parking lot and stopped, engine still running, behind the row of parked cars. Clemson Reade, wearing a pair of jeans, black boots, black jacket, plaid scarf, and a few days' worth of stubble, exited the driver's seat and approached the front porch of the café. A festive bouquet of stargazer lilies and red roses was tucked beneath his left arm.

'Hey, Clem,' Celestine called.

The sheriff seemed reluctant to get caught up in conversation, but he approached the garden nonetheless. 'Hi, Miss Celly.'

'Merry Christmas.'

'Merry Christmas to you as well.'

'Here to join in on the fun?'

'No, I just stopped by to deliver these.' He gestured toward the flowers. 'Thought Tish would like them for her holiday table.'

'Pretty. She does like the color red,' Celestine noted. 'It's good to see you. You haven't been around much these past few days.'

'Yeah, I've been busy. I've had reports to file and packing to do.'

'Oh? You going away for the holidays after all?'

'No. I'm leaving town. I tendered my resignation as sheriff of Hobson Glen and asked to be transferred elsewhere in the county.'

'Resignation?' Celestine was flabbergasted. 'You can't do that, Clem. This town needs you.'

'What this town needs is a sheriff who doesn't try to pistol-whip a man in his custody. That's what I nearly did to Sam Noble.'

'You had good reason to want to do that. What that man

did to those girls – what he did to Tish. It was an emotional situation.'

'Exactly. I'm an officer of the law; I can't afford to lose my head. Not only did I practically assault Noble, but I also put a civilian's life in grave danger.'

'You also saved that civilian's life,' Celestine argued. 'Tish wouldn't be alive if it hadn't been for you.'

'I shouldn't have needed to save her life. I had a feeling this case was different from the others. I should have barred her from investigating, but the truth is I so enjoyed working with her, being with her, that I let her get involved.'

'"Let her"?' Honey, you and I both know Tish. You didn't "let her" do anything. You could have banned her, but it wouldn't have mattered. Tish does what she wants to do. You know that. I'm sure it's one of the reasons you're in love with her.'

It was Reade's turn to be shocked.

'I have eyes in my head, don't I?' Celestine asked rhetoric-ally. 'It's in your eyes when you look at her. It was in your voice when you begged her to breathe last Sunday night. You meant it when you said you didn't know what you'd do without her. Now it seems you're willing to find out.'

'I think that decision has already been made for me.' Reade's gaze shifted to the café window, where Schuyler Thompson could be seen leading the crowd in a toast.

Celestine watched the scene and fell silent.

Reade handed her the bouquet. 'Give these to Tish for me?'

She nodded. 'What about your house? You own that cute little brick cape, don't you?'

'Putting it up for rent.'

'Rent? So you still might come back to us?'

'Miss Celly,' he chided with a gentle grin.

'Well, it *is* the season of hope, ain't it?'

He shook his head and gave her a quick embrace. 'You take care of yourself, Celly.'

'You too, Clem. And even though you won't be livin' here, you'll still be hearin' from me.'

'I'm sure I will.' With a wave, he strode off across the parking lot and back to his car.

*   *   *

While Reade and Celestine met outside the café garden, Schuyler was busy addressing the crowd gathered inside the café itself. 'I wanted to take a few moments to thank you all for being here tonight. I know the holiday season can be hectic, so it means a lot to me – to us' – he gestured toward Tish – 'that you took time out of your busy lives to welcome home and celebrate a woman who's done so much not just for her friends, not just for me, but for this entire town. If you'd kindly raise your glasses to Tish.'

'To Tish,' the crowd echoed as they raised their glasses aloft.

'I've always been civic and community-minded,' Schuyler went on, 'but having Tish in my life has truly been an inspiration—'

Mary Jo turned to Tish, her face a question.

Tish shrugged. She had absolutely no idea where Schuyler was going with his speech, but as he spoke about his relationship with Tish being 'inspirational,' 'life-changing,' and 'beneficial,' she began to panic. *Oh, please don't let this be a marriage proposal*, she thought to herself. *I can't say yes, but I don't want to say no in front of all these people. Oh, please . . .*

It was, therefore, with great relief and surprise that Tish heard Schuyler's final words. 'And so I've decided to run for Mayor of Hobson Glen in the forthcoming election.'

Election. Suddenly, the motives behind Schuyler's diligent attendance at town council meetings became crystal clear. Schuyler had been entertaining, even while the fair was going on, a possible mayoral run. Tish's relief at the lack of a marriage proposal soon turned to annoyance. She would have thought that such a change in career direction might have warranted a conversation between the two of them.

Tish had little opportunity to allow her irritation to fester, for outside the café window she noticed Sheriff Reade walking away from the café and toward an idling silver SUV. As Schuyler shook hands and accepted friends' good wishes for his campaign, Tish wheeled herself out of the door and on to the front porch of the café.

'What are you doing out here without a coat?' Celestine

scolded as she approached from the garden. 'You'll catch your death.'

'I'm fine,' Tish shushed. 'I thought I saw Clemson.'

'You did. He brought you these.' Celestine handed Tish the bouquet.

'Oh, they're beautiful! But where is he going?'

'Out of town.'

'For the holidays?'

'For good. He's resigned as sheriff and is transferring to another town.'

Tish waved her arms and shouted to get Reade's attention, but he didn't stop. Instead, he drove out of the parking lot and turned on to the main road and away from Hobson Glen. As she watched the red taillights of the SUV disappear into the distance, a gentle, soaking rain began to fall, mixing with the remaining snow and slush on the ground to create a dense fog.

'Merry Christmas, Clemson,' Tish whispered as tears formed in her eyes. 'Merry Christmas.'

Y032572

The item should be returned or renewed by the last date stamped below.

Dylid dychwelyd neu adnewyddu'r eitem erbyn y dyddiad olaf sydd wedi'i stampio isod

Newport
CITY COUNCIL
CYNGOR DINAS
Casnewydd

Newport Library and
Information Service

To renew visit / Adnewyddwch ar
www.newport.gov.uk/libraries